PRAISE FOR *TEMPLE DANCER*

"I read this book in one day because I could not stop. It's one of those books, so clear the decks before you start. And then be prepared to be haunted and changed by the wisdom, sensuality, beauty, and fascinating history. Read this if you want to be transported and possibly changed forever."

— Jennifer Louden, author of *The Woman's Comfort Book* and *Why Bother?*

"Instantly captivating! The mystical tellings from a forgotten red diary propel us into the clandestine world of the devadasi and the lost art of Sacred Indian Temple Dancing. Following two extraordinary women's journeys, we find ourselves transported to India enticed by her fragrances, colors and the people that define her. These ingredients make for a sumptuous novel that not only entertains but interweaves the intricate teachings of mystical wisdom and spirituality with love, both romantic and transcendental. If you are interested in divine connection or just a really great read, make *Temple Dancer* your next favorite book!"

— Nischala Joy Devi, author of *The Healing Path of Yoga* and *The Namaste Effect*

"Amy Weintraub's *Temple Dancer* is a book of wisdom earned through great suffering, deep contemplation, and real compassion."

—Madison Smartt Bell, author of *Behind the Moon* and National Book Award Finalist *All Souls' Rising: A Novel of Haiti*

"Amy Weintraub's astonishing new novel, evokes the power of a lost spiritual tradition... *Temple Dancer* is gorgeous and ambitious...an unforgettable novel about a woman's search for peace and another's desire for justice."

—Foreword Reviews

"Amy Weintraub's *Temple Dancer* lifted my spirit and carried me off to other times and places. The vivid characters, drawn with love and compassion, follow unique paths, yet their quests for wholeness are timeless, connected, and universal. The contemporary scenes carry deep resonance, and respectful insights into a lost culture are a gift. I hear heartbeats on every page."

— Bonnie Marson, author of *Sleeping with Schubert*

"*Temple Dancer* is riveting. It is an amazing journey between past and present, artfully weaving the philosophy of India's ancient mythology into our world of today. The way the author paints pictures with words breathes life into people, places and experiences. It is a poetic and devotional adventure in consciousness that cannot help but awaken the heart and soul of the reader."

—Rama Jyoti Vernon, author of *Yoga: The Practice of Myth & Sacred Geometry*; co-founder, *Yoga Journal*

"I could not put this book down. Through parallel lives, one historic, one contemporary, *Temple Dancer* is a superbly written novel that takes the reader on a journey from naiveté through disgrace to redemption. Amy Weintraub is a master storyteller!"

—Stephen Cope, author of *The Great Work of Your Life* and *Yoga and the Quest for the True Self*

"*Temple Dancer* is a fascinating tale that weaves through time and memory ultimately taking the reader on an unforgettable journey of the heart and spirit. There are rich revelations and twists and turns that make it difficult to put down. It's a close cousin of *Eat, Pray, Love*!"

—Katharine Merlin, author of *The Private Lives of the Sun Signs* and *Character and Fate: The Psychology of the Birth Chart*; columnist, *Town & Country Magazine*

"This is a fascinating novel, but it is much more than that. Through her wonderful storytelling, Amy Weintraub is teaching us about ourselves. As we identify with both characters, we find parts of ourselves that need redemption and to find their strength. And we learn about Indian history and philosophy to boot!"

— Richard Schwartz, PhD, developer of the Internal Family Systems (IFS) model of psychotherapy

"This book is amazing and once I began reading it, I could not stop. Such a beautiful vignette of two lives with remarkable connections. I particularly like how real it is. Like any great spiritual story, *Temple Dancer* leaves one with a good dose of reality yet inspires hope and faith. The suffering and the joys of life are experienced in contrast; it is when we see the whole that a kind of deeper wisdom and understanding emerges for us. *Temple Dancer* does this."

—Michael Lee, author of *Phoenix Rising Yoga Therapy—A Bridge from Body to Soul* and *Turn Stress Into Bliss*; founder of Phoenix Rising Yoga Therapy

"In *Temple Dancer*, the lives of two women, apparently different yet strangely alike, are intertwined in an engrossing story that brings out the common joys, needs and frailties of people everywhere. Wendy from present-day America meets Saraswati, an Indian woman who is committed in childhood to be a dancer in a temple. This tradition (called *devadasis*) has degenerated through the years, yet Saraswati manages to convey her sense of pride in her art to Wendy in a way which uplifts and strengthens both women, worlds apart in terms of age, experiences and time, yet both with an inner strength that shines through. A compulsive, authentic read!"

—Shirley Telles, MBBS, PhD, co-author of *The Principles and Practice of Yoga in Health Care* and *Evidence-based Perspectives on the Psychophysiology of Yoga and Its Applications*

"With its thoughtful exploration of the lives of two seemingly disparate women—one a disgraced temple dancer from 1930s India, one a contemporary artist in Massachusetts—*Temple Dancer* welcomes readers with a warm embrace."

—Elizabeth Evans, author of *As Good as Dead* and *Carter Clay*

"I thoroughly enjoyed Amy Weintraub's *Temple Dancer*. It beautifully captures the emotions of the Temple Dancer 'Saraswati' through the eyes of Wendy, a true devadasi herself in search of her soul. The story of Wendy is equally beautiful. While Saraswati was taught and raised to be a Devadasi, Wendy transformed into one through her experiences learning from her mistakes and taking accountability for her feelings and actions."

—Suba Parmar, Bharatanatyam dancer; Artistic Director, Shubanjali School of Performing Arts

TEMPLE DANCER

ALSO BY AMY WEINTRAUB

Yoga for Depression: A Compassionate Guide to Relieve Suffering Through Yoga

Yoga Skills for Therapists: Effective Practices for Mood Management

TEMPLE DANCER

a novel

AMY WEINTRAUB

Published by

tumamocpress@gmail.com

ISBN: 978-0-9747380-6-2
eISBN: 978-0-9747380-7-9

Book Design by Liz Payne Merideth
Cover Artwork by Rosanna Marmont

To the music makers and dancers in my life,
Miriam Leah, Shoshana, Maayan, and Connie.

You make my heart sing.

ACKNOWLEDGMENTS

I SPENT THE WINTER of 1994 with my parents, Mickey and Mary Weintraub, in Longboat Key, Florida. Every evening, I rose from the bridge table in the lanai to share with my father the portion of Saraswati's story that I had written. I am grateful for my parents' support and encouragement so that I could be used as Saraswati's conduit, listening with awe as she told me her story.

I would like to thank Wesleyan University World Music Library and the access I received to books and dissertations on devadasi rituals and culture. In particular, I am indebted to the work of scholars of the tradition, including the work of Jogan Shankar. His *Devadasi Cult: A Sociological Analysis* was invaluable to my understanding. I also learned about the daily life and rituals performed by devadasis in *Wives of the God King: The Rituals of the Devadasis of Puri* by Frederique Apffel Marflin. I credit *Nityasumangali: Devadasis of South India* and an earlier essay, "Devasdasis and Artistic Integrity" by the scholar and Indian Classical Dancer and teacher Saskia Kersenboom-Story in helping me understand the rights of passage for a devadasi and other essential elements of their mode of living, forms of devotion, the sacred lineage of the dances themselves and the women who performed them.

Long before the therapist Jalaja Bonheim published her outstanding books on women's sexuality and spirituality, she studied, performed, taught and wrote about the discipline of Indian Classical Dance and its relationship to yoga. Her 1995 article in *Yoga Journal*, "Path of the Temple Dancer," written just after I wrote the Saraswati portions of this novel (or it wrote me), affirmed my passion to tell, through fiction, the story of the rise and fall of the devadasis. When I read the first chapter of Bonheim's seminal work, *Aphrodite's Daughter: Women's Sexual Stories and the Journey of the Soul* in 1997, I felt such a resonance with her story that I was inspired to carry on, developing a Western frame for Saraswati's voice that would in some ways mirror and carry forward the deeply entwined themes of women's sexuality and spirituality.

Abundant gratitude and pranams to Kay Poursine, a prominent performer of Bharatanatyam and the student of the renowned Indian devadasi T. Balasaraswati. Kay answered my many questions, allowed me to watch her dance in performance, and showed me the historic videos of her teacher's dance.

I am grateful to the fiction writer, feminist, and academic C. S. Lakshmi, whose fiction is published under the name of Ambai. It was in her office in Mumbai that I first encountered the face of six-year-old beedi roller Rohini, who was to be dedicated to the Goddess Yellamma. As described in the Author's Note, her picture evoked tears. I count Rohini's face as the seed that opened my heart and mind to listen, when I returned from India, to the story of a young beedi roller in 1938 named Saraswati.

Pranams of gratitude to my teacher and friend, the author Madison Smartt Bell for his insight early in the refinement of this novel and for his ongoing support through the publication process.

I am indebted to many readers who read various versions of this novel, plural, because a number of contemporary narratives were written to surround Saraswati's story and tossed aside in the twenty-six years since her voice came through me. These include Judith Porter, Andrea Diehl (1953-2017), Bonnie Marson, Shirley Telles, Naveeen KV, Nischala Joy Devi, Victoria Williams, Kate Merlin, Maria Mendola Shamas, Cate Bradley, Rama Jyoti Vernon, Elizabeth Spring, Ginny Beal, Elizabeth Evans, Rita Rogers, Suba Parmar, Stephen Cope, Jen Louden, Dick Schwartz, Rama Jyoti Vernon, and Arliss Ryan.

There are those who tolerated my reading of small portions of the manuscript in progress, some of whom are named above and also Jami Macarty, Rubin Naiman, Su L. Washington, Sheila Wilensky, Penelope Starr, and my willing friends at Tucson salons.

A portion of Wendy's story was written while I was enrolled as an MFA student in the Bennington Writing Seminars. I offer thanks for the guidance of my teachers, Rick Moody, Jill McCorkle, Lynn Freed, and my esteemed second reader Lucy Grealy. I am grateful to dear Connie Brannock for listening as I read the most recent version of the manuscript aloud. Her discerning musician's ear and clear mind helped enormously. I want to thank my brothers, William Weintraub and Andrew Weintraub, who read and commented on the contemporary sections. I am grateful to my daughter, Miriam Leah Gamliel, for her insightful comments that lent a Jewish Gen X's perspective on the events during the Raj.

For the many lessons I received at the feet of my spiritual teachers, I am eternally grateful. Early on, I received my Transcendental Meditation mantra from a TM teacher in Pittsburgh, and then gratefully, with my guide Michael Klatman, sat at the feet of Maharishi Mahesh Yogi in Amherst for the month-long Science of Creative Intelligence training at the University of Massachusetts. I am grateful for the lessons learned at the Kripalu Center, where I became a disciple of Amrit Desai, and to my sister spiritual traveler MJ Bindu Delekta (1950-2013), and former Kripalu residents, many of whom I still count as friends.

I'm grateful to the Kripalu Center, which has been a shelter for me and so many others, nourishing and supporting transformation. I honor the memory of Nitya Chaitanya Yati (1924-1999), the scholar, author, and psychologist who became my teacher and introduced me to Advaita Vedanta at the Narayana Gurukula in Ooty, India. I hope I have been a good enough student of his nondual commentaries that I have been able to convey some semblance of their understanding to you through the character of Prince Vyasa. I treasure the time spent and the lessons learned at ashrams and spiritual centers where I've studied, meditated, chanted, and taught, including Kripalu Center, Yogaville-Satchidanada Ashram, Sivananda Ashram, Art of Living, Esalen, Omega, and many yoga studios in the United States, Canada, Great Britain, Australia, and India. I offer thanks to psychologist, author, and yogi Richard Miller, founder of iRest, for his caring support to me as a mentor and friend. As a modern interpreter of the nondual path, informed by Kashmiri Shaivism, his wisdom consciously and unconsciously has been a source of my own understanding.

I am deeply indebted to the community at Satchidananda Ashram Yogaville who welcome me to what has become my spiritual home. I thank the many devoted householders and swamis, and especially the author and scholar Swami Karunananda, who offered me mantra initiation and love. I want to thank Sri Swami Satchidananda, whom I never met in person, but whose inspiration and loving presence carries me forward.

I am grateful to my production team, Liz Payne Merideth (anthill design) and Robert Merideth (wordecology.com). Together, they are so much more than line editors, but layout artists, graphic artists, and designers. Liz designed the chapter headings and the cover, based on the vibrant painting on copper by artist Rosanna Marmont (rosannamarmont.com). Thank you, Robert, for asking just the right questions to fine tune continuity. Your many slow meticulous readings have made this a better book.

There are people who, technophobe that I am, I cannot live without. Fortunately, they not only know what they are doing but are great communicators and friends. I count among them the aforementioned Liz and Robert, but also the web wizard Hillary Summerton to whom I am indebted for web design and support (onnawebdesign.com). As we neared publication we reached out and received a helping hand in all things technical from Bethany Brown (thecadencegrp.com).

Thank you to Michela DellaMonica, Andrea Kiliany Thatcher and Kellie Rendina for shepherding me and this novel through the labyrinth of publicity and promotion when so much of the publishing industry, along with the rest of our lives, was stalled by Covid-19.

Thank you to my agent Deirdre Mullane who found a home with a small press for a previous iteration of *Temple Dancer* before

I withdrew that version from consideration. Thank you, Kristine Puopolo, my editor for *Yoga for Depression* at Broadway Books, who has never stopped believing in me.

Thank you to all who have been waiting for the publication of *Temple Dancer*. Your questions and enthusiasm have spurred me on.

TEMPLE DANCER

PROLOGUE

I am running. It is dark in this place, and I do not know my way. I climb up through the brush. Suddenly the prickly scrub where the path ends catches my sari. A cow path only. I push and pull, and it will not let go. Where am I? Is this a dream? I struggle to free the charred remains, the hem once gold, now blackened and crumbling. My sari is caught like the breath in my throat. I rip and tear; the shredding sound tells me I am free. A tangle of fabric stays in the bush. I am running through the cool night. The heat is in me still. Varanima, can you forgive me? I run from you and all we have known. On this mountainside little fires below and above spit into the night. Is that my cart flaming below? I reach for her bangles and they are gone. Around my neck, the pouch, the key, the gold—all are gone! Only the gold of the flames. I burn. I run. Lord Shiva, let me awaken from this dream. There is a flash of silver like starlight on water. Trees throw their branches, screaming, and in my heart is the cry of Varanima up the stairs, singing her love chant. I am running toward the river. There is no more breath. May I wake up in my Amma's arms.

CHAPTER *One*

1997

AT 7:00 AM ON the first day of the year, Wendy Rabin boarded a train in Coimbatore, India, traveling east from the lush Nilgiri foothills to Chennai, along an ever-more-arid route toward the Bay of Bengal. She hadn't purchased her ticket in advance, so after a harrowing bus ride 7000 feet down the ribbon of single-lane highway from Ooty, she arrived at the station to find that only fourth-class seats remained. It would be a long journey, the ladies' car was full, and she was directed to a car crowded with men pressed together on worn wooden seats. For the first time in her life, she felt gawky and tall as she walked to the only seat left beside a woman, a wedge of bench by a window. The familiar view, she reminded herself, would be no different from this fourth-class window than the one from the luxury coach she had booked last time. She murmured a low apology to the elderly woman in the aisle seat, who appeared to be sleeping, and took her place, stowing her backpack beneath the seat and placing her water bottle and notebook in the small space between them.

The old woman's dark face was etched around the eyes and the corners of her mouth. There were swaths of white and pink in the teak of her complexion, but the skin on her cheeks and forehead was taut and youthful. Even in this heat, beneath her saffron *sari*, the woman wore sleeves the color of her skin—a kind of undergarment that covered her neck—and her hands were covered in flesh-colored gloves. It was clear that she had been a beauty. There was a noble radiance in her face. The rest of her small frame seemed as insubstantial as cobwebs. Yet Wendy had distinctly felt the woman's boney knee as she'd climbed over the curve of her to claim the seat. The woman's only jewelry was a small gold stud in her left nostril. Smeared across her brow was *vibhuti* ash from a recent purification ritual.

Wendy's attention shifted to the aisle. A young, bare-chested man was coming down the aisle with a tray of snacks. His white muslin *dhoti* draped between his legs and hung from his hips. Another man, older and slighter, followed him, selling coconuts punctured by straws. She bought a wax paper sack filled with *idlis*, grainy white patties that reminded her of the taste of her Oklahoma grandmother's grits. As she reached across to receive her change, the woman's mottled eyelids raised, and for a moment, before she closed them again, Wendy glimpsed her eyes.

It was hard to describe the quality of her look, although she could name the effect it had on her. Satisfaction. Or something deeper. Not quite fulfillment, but a soothing at her core. It was curious at the time, but she wouldn't understand it until later. It wasn't a personal look, not an "I love you," but rather, "I see you, and know you are lovable." Like the look her beloved neighbor Norma had given her when Wendy sat retelling her school day at Norma's kitchen table. It was the direct look that, despite the thousands of miles she had traveled, Guru Nityananda had denied her.

In that moment on the train, Wendy felt tears brimming on the edges of her lower lids, and then they escaped, and her body heaved silently. She wasn't thinking of the pummeling loss she felt now that this last miserable year of divorce proceedings was over, or the unfairness of resigning from the job she loved or what her life would look like when she returned to Boston. Nor, in that moment, was she grieving the damaged relationship with Guru Nityananda or any of her damaged relationships—her husband Aaron, her daughter Becky, Cal. It was simply the fragile play of opposites in the woman's face—beauty and its temporality—that had drawn tears. In the instant the old woman's eyes met hers, Wendy had known that there was not a thing she could keep from leaving—not her lover, nor her child, nor her aging parents, nor her body's good health and its new-found power to twist into yoga *asanas* requiring strength and flexibility.

A week after her divorce decree was entered into the public record in the State of Massachusetts and ten-year-old Becky was out of the tsunami of her grief, safely (Wendy thought) with her best friend Linny Stein at ski camp in the Berkshires, Wendy received an email from a fellow *gurukula* student. Guru Nityananda had suffered a second heart attack.

Guruji. Nitya. Nityananda. Ananda means bliss. Nitya means eternal. How she felt when she first met him—that "Yes!" a palpitation in her heart. Here is my teacher. *Finally.* But "No," had come next. Now, when she considered his name, there was a clutch at her heart, and then a breath, an opening. Memory was like that—remembered moments when the heart flooded, unbidden, like morning light. And then the terrible slam of the heart when the pounding against the door of the beloved was ignored. On her second trip to India, when she was 21, Nitya did not respond.

Nityananda, her Guruji, had ignored her, shunned her, and sent her home.

And now at forty, she had come back to sit with her dying ex-Guru, the Sanskrit scholar with whom she had studied in the late seventies, when he was in residence at Boston University. On that first trip, she had followed him back to India and had spent her junior year at the gurukula, getting academic credit for rapture.

She had returned to India this time with the hope that whatever she had done or not done on successive visits to the gurukula as a twenty, then twenty-one, then twenty-two-year-old, Guru Nityananda had forgiven her, and she could say goodbye. But this last visit had been no different. When she arrived at the mountain gurukula, the school where Nityananda had spent most of the last 40 years of his life teaching and translating and writing commentary on the Upanishads, he refused to see her. She had struggled with the why of that refusal for so many years, but this time she could let it go.

Outside the open window, the hands of children dressed in rags stretched toward her. She reached out with the *rupees* the idli seller had given her and let them fall into their hands.

She felt content to sit on the hard, wooden seat, her sleeping blanket folded beneath her. As the train left the platform, she looked at the other passengers. Most of the men were thin and small and wore a uniform of brown trousers and short-sleeved white shirts. There was a great din of high-pitched talk among them, but they respectfully kept their distance. She knew what traveling alone in a car full of men could mean for a young Indian woman, and for once she was glad for her well-covered Western-looking body and her age. She and the lady beside her were not likely to become a statistic in the rising rate of rape and murder. In that moment, the stories she'd heard of stoning and of the sexual abuse of a girl or a woman for the crime of walking unaccompanied or for trying to escape the path laid out for her by her elders, made her tremble with memory. She did not want to think about her own humiliation, but there it was, too recent to call it a flashback. It was the final straw, the turning point, when she knew she would leave. Horrible to think about now, but there was no way to not think about it. She began chanting her *mantra*, visualizing her daughter Becky, happy in the winter sun, skiing down a category blue slope for the first time, then jumping into the hot tub with her friends. And then the memory of the tub was back. She was submerged in it, hardly able to breathe. She was drowning.

She and Aaron were on that last desperate romantic getaway to heal their marriage. Aaron didn't know about Cal. There was nothing to know. Cal was merely the thought she tried not to think, the quickened pulse, the rapid heartbeat. All that, but nothing more. She had been faithful. That night at the inn in Stockbridge, she lay in the claw-footed tub, letting the cooled bath water slide out.

Aaron knocked then entered. He had something in his hand as he knelt on the floor, and he leaned over the tub. "Honey, spread your legs." His voice was gentle, and she thought he was about to overcome his inhibitions and bring her pleasure. Was this the harbinger of something other than missionary position?

But it was her hand mirror, the one he'd given her as a gift with the teak frame and the magnification that he shoved between her legs.

"Look at that. See how ugly you are?" His face was contorted.

She looked at her genitals enlarged in the mirror—the place that disgusted him. She tried to push the hand holding the mirror away, but he held it firm.

"You think a man really wants this?"

When he saw her tears, he drew back. "Cry, damn it! *Finally*. Feel something!" He flung the mirror against the wall, and she gasped as it crashed and shattered. The shards that littered the floor reflected pieces of him standing over her.

She drew her knees to her chest and wrapped her arms around them.

He stood there, rocking forward and back, shaking his head. "Oh, god damn. God damn!" He reached to stroke her hair. "Jesus, I'm sorry." He sat on the tub ledge. "I didn't mean it. I don't know why ... it's just ... I'm desperate to break through. ... No, Wendy ... you're lovely. Every part of you."

She pushed his hand away and stood, letting the water drizzle from her body. "Not to you." She took a deep breath. "Not to myself." She reached for the towel, feeling the truth and the terrible ache in her chest. Her body went hot, then cold. "I revolt you." Every word in her almost inaudible voice, a knife in her heart. And his.

She was thousands of miles away from that tub, and yet she still carried it inside her. She had needed the Guru for something—to absolve her? To love her no matter what? To forgive her? He gave her nothing. But the woman on the train sitting beside her had given her something. She didn't know what it was, but with that single look, something had shifted. Thinking about those eyes now, Wendy was no longer drowning in memory. She was looking out the window again. A group of girls were walking arm in arm, their dark braids glistening, their navy pleated skirts swinging just beneath their knees. They were laughing as though they could be friends forever, as though they could marry for love, as though none of them would be raped or burned. She hoped that would be so.

Here she was, again coming down from the mountain top, closer to sea level. She had seen her old friends. Ashvin, whom she'd met on her first college visit at the bus stop on the dusty dirt road that ran through the village of mud huts and shanties, still took her to town in his auto-rickshaw. Sudhir, Ashvin's best friend, a college student back then, living in a hovel with his one-legged father, had long ago quit school. Now he had a wife and two teenaged boys, the oldest of whom was already studying at the gurukula.

Her dearest friend, Jyothi, had been a beautiful girl, not yet twenty on her first visit. When the disciples called her "Auntie," the name seemed unfit for the vibrant life force that lit up her every movement. In flight from an arranged marriage, Jyothi had gone into service, caring for her beloved Guruji and running the gurukula; feeding and housing, with little help, the thirty or so students who lived there; going by bus to the market in town to shop for the food, and tending and watering the garden. Twenty years later, age had made a home on her face. Even the thick, black, once-shining hair had lost its luster. Wendy tried to be "Auntie" to Jyothi, then and now, giving her back rubs, taking her to town in Ashvin's auto-rickshaw to buy what she needed for the gurukula, as well as the personal items she had long denied herself—Ayurvedic facial oils, vitamins, stockings, and even a little chocolate. Was it this that had turned Guru against her?

Nityananda was a mountain of a man, tall even by Western standards. His white beard and grey hair flowed down his saffron robes. Beneath his bristly mustache, he was quick to smile, and on that first visit, he teased her about her need to practice postures and her desire to see more of India, to travel to sacred sites and *ashrams*. She loved that his library and that his talk about the ancient texts was laced with references from T.S. Eliot, Einstein, and Freud. That first year, he often invited her along on his cold morning walks, staff in hand, parka zipped over his robes, his head covered in an orange knitted cap. He was old, but his gait was brisk and strong. He told her tales she later learned were common teaching stories—the three blind men whose descriptions of the elephant didn't match, each touching the mammal from different positions; the man who thought the rope was a snake. She thought they were brilliant metaphors for the spiritual mana he was feeding her. She was special, singled out, beloved. The other disciples walked behind.

On Wendy's second visit, Nityananda was enraged. He neither spoke nor looked her way. There were no invitations for morning strolls, and he snarled when she dared to cross his path. It was as though the river of love flowing through the universe had been dammed at its source. She made up stories to explain his rejection. It was the kindness she offered when she and Jyothi were both young and possibility, at least for Wendy, had seemed endless. But if that were true, would it mean that the Guru was jealous? Fearful? How could that be?

One morning, she did yoga breathing and used imagery to give her courage and then waylaid him on his walk. "What have I done? Please tell me. Please forgive me." He had glared at her and without a word had used his staff to push her aside. At the time

Jyothi said, "Guru does this sometimes. There is a lesson in it." Since her studies with him in college and that first visit to India had left an imprint of love that continued through letters and dreams until her second visit, if there was a lesson, she wasn't smart enough to get it. She returned from India in deep depression, her body wracked with joint pain.

Almost as though there had been no change in her or in India, the train chugged slowly through a village, and she could see the girls—the shimmer of their well-oiled hair, braided and ribboned—in their uniform skirts and ironed blouses. They walked along the dusty road to school with books pressed to their chests. Bright-eyed boys, friends holding hands, as though they were lovers, but she knew better. Twenty years ago, the affection between friends had confused her. She'd felt that kind of affection for Jyothi, a kind of sisterly love that made her want to take care of her, protect her, ease the burden of her service to the Guru.

In the last twenty years, she had done some serious thinking about gurus, as one after another spiritual master stood accused. Charismatic and brilliant, those radiant beings, most but not all of them men, may have transcended body and mind to achieve *Samadhi*, but many hadn't done their psychological homework. She had come to understand that a great master might have a mind like a still pond, reflecting the divine consciousness of the universe, but the pool of his emotions was murky. As a result, most ashrams and gurukulas were not immune to petty jealousies, politics, and scandals.

Though Wendy left the gurukula without an audience with Nityananda and knew she would never see him again, she was leaving without the rash of symptoms that had plagued her last time. Nityananda had loved her once, and, briefly, like a child, she had flourished beneath his gaze. It had seemed like enough. No, it had seemed like *everything*. Since then, she had experienced the birth of her daughter and loving her only child with a fierceness she had yearned for all her life. She'd succumbed to a life-changing love affair, and then spent several years in therapy talking about it. Through it all, with her daily practice she had grown a resilience, leaving her with a feeling of deep and intimate connection to something vaster and more generous than the Guru's gaze, Cal's promises, the client's story. She marveled at how, despite Nityananda's rejection and the four-hour bus ride to sea level, her morning mantras had put her in a peaceful mood when she boarded the train. Soon, those mantras would be enough to drown out the memories. Soon, she would sleep again without the terrible dreams.

Wendy turned slightly to study the sleeping woman next to her. She might be 50. She might be 80. In that brief instant when she'd opened her eyes, the light in them had seemed ageless. She wore no customary bangles or earrings, and her *chappals* were worn and dusty. The color of her sari suggested a monastic life as a *sannyasin*, but the stud in her nose did not.

Wendy turned back to the window where the road that meandered near the tracks was clogged with traffic. Ox carts and lorries decorated to honor deities were stopped in all directions as bicycles and mopeds threaded through. Once the train moved beyond the city limits, the road veered away from the tracks, but now and then she caught sight of people—a woman in a bright colored sari sweeping the dirt around her hovel, a young boy playing by the tracks, another in a deep squat, taking care of his hygiene. As the landscape began to flatten, she could see great fissures in the dry earth, cracks that looked as old as the continent. Where she remembered a lush landscape twenty years before, the land was thorny and overgrown with weeds. The people seemed poorer, dustier. Was she seeing the effect of drought and the ongoing battle between neighboring states for water? Farmers on both sides had been fighting for nourishment and livelihood for centuries.

The woman beside her let out a low chant. "Om A-im." Wendy recognized the Saraswati seed mantra. It was unsettling, because in secret, when Wendy was nineteen, it had been given to her in a ceremony in Cambridge, Massachusetts, by a local meditation teacher. Saraswati was the Goddess of wisdom, music, dance, and the arts. Wendy looked more closely at the woman's serene face, the erect spine, the chin tilted nearly to her chest. Her hands, folded in her lap, were in *Dhyana*, the meditation mudra. Wendy hadn't noticed that before. The strange moment drew her into her own meditation, and she closed her eyes, holding her mantra at her brow point.

Wendy was floating in a spacious state of mind when she heard the bright voice of the woman beside her asking her name. Wendy had thought her a poor villager, but her English was perfect, and she spoke with a grace that indicated a keen mind. The woman introduced herself as Saraswati and explained that her mother had wanted her to be educated, and so had named her after the Goddess of wisdom. Wendy offered Saraswati her own Sanskrit name.

"Ahhh," the woman said. "Divyajyothi means Divine Light. It is an honorable name."

"I love it, but when it was given to me, years ago, by an Indian guru visiting the U.S., I felt undeserving."

"You've grown into it, I think. You are an artist, Divyajyothi?"

Rattled, Wendy felt herself redden. Saraswati could not possibly know her history—the time spent in an MFA program, the failure to get a gallery, the depressive moods, back to school for a master's in clinical social work, painting part time, and then the decision when Becky was six never to paint again. For the last four years, her drawing had been confined to a loose-leaf notebook, pages she could tear out, crumple up. And no color—only a black marker or one of Becky's number two school pencils. She wouldn't allow herself the shellac-based inks she loved or the fine hand-ground paints, not even pastels or *conté* crayons. She hadn't held a sable brush in her hand since that day.

"I see it in your eyes," the old woman said. It was as though they spoke in a dream. Wendy rubbed her arm against the rough metal beneath the window of the railcar, just to feel the physicality of being awake, of not being in a trance. "I'm a social worker now," she said.

Saraswati shook her head slowly, her eyes offering something between solace and sorrow. "We do what we must," she paused, sighed, "when we can no longer do what we love."

Wendy felt embraced and chastised at the same time. Objections spooled out in her mind—how she'd loved her clients, how she was grateful to feel those moments of wordless, intimate connection that sometimes enveloped them, how lost she would feel if she couldn't practice therapy anymore.

Saraswati continued as though she had read Wendy's mind. "You will serve with true devotion, only if you follow your *dharma*."

"But I'm not sure ..."

Saraswati interrupted. "Who is it that says 'no' to art?" She took a deep breath and turned away. "In the time of terror when everything was lost to us, even though it was forbidden, I knew I would dance again. I am an old woman, Divyajyothi, and still I dance my morning prayers." She pivoted toward Wendy. "You must paint yours."

Wendy closed her eyes. Her heart was beating too fast. She felt exposed and suddenly longed to be off the train, anywhere but here. When she opened her eyes again, the woman seemed to be in meditation.

Each time Saraswati opened her eyes after a period of silence, the story of her life continued. Wendy relaxed. Listened, awestruck. The woman spoke of *maharajas* and temple priests and women, auspicious women. "We were the bearers of ancient wisdom," she said. "Our dance was sacred, performed in the temple, surrounded by deities and gaze of only the most faithful."

After thousands of years of devotional dance, of leading the processions at festival time, of the sacred duty of caring for the temple deities, the *devadasi* were banned from dancing in the temples. "In one of the first acts of independence, the Madras Legislative Council enacted the Devadasi Act, and our tradition was decimated," she said.

"That must have been shattering. I would have thought that the British would have devised restrictions, not Indians themselves."

"We devadasi were too powerful. We were educated to dance and to please, and our patrons made us rich. No man had a claim on us." She was unmarried as a devadasi, she said, and like most, remained so after the ban. "In the days when we danced in the temple, our marital freedom was the source of our strength, but after we were outlawed, it was the source of our shame."

Wendy nodded as though she understood, but, how could she? "You must have been emotionally devastated."

Saraswati shook her head "We were struggling to survive," she said. "We did not have time for emotion."

"I'm sorry. What did you do?"

Saraswati narrated her life, moving back and forth in time—before the ban; after the ban. Before the ban they were honored, respected, and well-trained students of sacred dance and song. When a devadasi reached womanhood, she was dedicated to God and ritually deflowered by the temple priest or the maharajah of the kingdom. "So, when the monsoon of shame swept through in 1947, we were not marriageable. A few of my sisters moved to the city." One devadasi she knew had become internationally known before the temple ban, so she continued to dance but only for show. "It broke her heart that she could perform in cities around the world, but not in the temple." A few managed to eke out a living as teachers to wealthy European and American students, but not to the middle-class Indian daughters who now studied the "high art" of Bharatanatyam.

Schools were established; most often staffed by the male dance masters, who taught a cleansed Bharatanatyam. "The proper schools drained every milligram of sensuality, what is called the *sringara,* the erotic portion, from the dance. Once we were vital to temple ritual, and then we starved." Forced from their temple housing, with no means of support, many had become prostitutes. Others died an early death, rolling beedis on the street or in wretched factories and working in the tobacco fields where Saraswati herself had grown up.

"How did you survive this fate?"

Saraswati looked at her with eyes of fire that Wendy sensed had seen the burning of worlds. "I did not." She turned away and seemed to be considering. When she turned back, she grasped

Wendy's hand. "I think we have met for a special reason." Wendy looked down. The fingers that held her were long, bony, and surprisingly rough. When she let go, Wendy's hand felt cold, as though she'd touched metal in the frigid Northeast. The woman pulled a small red book out of a cloth sack she had strapped to her chest and paused again, then placed it in Wendy's hands. "Please, take it back to America. It is up to you, Divyajyothi, to let the world know how the devadasi were once valued, honored in our villages and cities. You must show the world how we danced with God!"

She looked down at the book in her hands, opened it to words in a small, cramped handwriting she could not understand. "But … I don't know anything about translations or publishing. I mean, I'd like to help you, but …"

Saraswati covered Wendy's hand with hers. "If you paint us, you will not fail. There will be no more shame." When Saraswati closed her eyes, Wendy did as well. Through the cold vessel of her hand, the heat of the word pulsed so that she had to swipe at the strands straggling out of her bun to wipe the sweat at the back of her neck. Even before her mind sought a story, her body understood shame. It had been her intimate companion since she was a teenager. Shame had put a stop to making art.

She sensed that shame had been born in her long before she had the word to name it. Shame was very young and also very old. *A limbic response without cortical understanding*, would be how she might sum up a client's response in case notes. A shiver in her belly, heat rising through her chest and the back of her neck, a catch in her breath. She wasn't breathing now. But there were no coherent memories, only flashes—a boy's hand where it shouldn't have been, a teacher asking a question she couldn't answer, an email she had to delete—like the images that surface and dissolve just before sleep.

For a long time, Wendy felt the chill of Saraswati's hand and then she did not. When she opened her eyes, the train was pulling into the station in Chennai, and the seat beside her was empty. The small red volume was in her lap.

CHAPTER
Two

2016

BUT SHE *HAD* FAILED. Even if she unrolled her canvas, bought new paints or watercolors, how could she paint what she couldn't read? After her return from India in 1997, it had taken her two years to find a willing translator. At seventy-two, N. M. Krishna, professor emeritus of Indian music at Wesleyan University and a *tabla* instructor, born in Karnataka, not only spoke fluent Kannada, but grew up in a time when the devadasi still danced in the temple. His father and, for perhaps thousands of years, his ancestors, had played tabla, accompanying the sacred ritual dances of the devadasi. For that reason, he had offered his services without compensation. "Seva" he called it, selfless service. An act of devotion in honor of his ancestors, he said. He would not take payment.

However, Professor Krishna died before he sent Wendy the completed translation. For years after his death, Wendy had tried desperately to find the small red book and the manuscript that she knew he'd finished. She had emailed his colleagues. She had written to his family. She had even contacted the Wesleyan music library to see if the diary might be among the professor's archived papers. All without success. By the time the PDF file had shown up in her inbox two weeks ago, along with an email from Professor Krishna's son, Ramesh, she had come to believe she had failed Saraswati and failed herself. There was no book. There were no paintings. Only lately had images of flames and eyes and abstractions of mudras become so vivid that she was thinking about buying a sketch pad.

The message from Ramesh had come like a lightning bolt, setting fire to the dry brush that had grown around her intentions. It was the controlled burn she needed to fulfill her promise. In the email message, Ramesh told her that he and his thirteen-year-old daughter had been going through boxes stored in the attic, looking through his father's music books and instrument collection, and found a package with Wendy's name on it. Ramesh asked his graduate student assistant at MIT to scan the manuscript and to research the name on the envelope. It didn't take much of a Google search to find Wendy listed as a therapist in North Kingston, RI, on the *Psychology Today* website.

Now she has the translation in her hands. It's been nearly twenty years since the small red book, hand-written in a language she could neither read nor speak, was left in her lap on a train in South India. After Professor Krishna died, she'd given up hope of seeing the translation or of finding the original again. But here is the manuscript, a miracle. She could read most of it on the late morning flight from Providence to D.C., but instead, she decides to create a personal retreat of reading, of fall color, of yoga and meditation, and of discovering why this devadasi's story is hers.

She will cap off her retreat with a business expense—a weekend at the ashram of yoga with CEUs for mental health professionals.

In the rental car lot at Dulles Airport, she loads all but her water bottle, phone, charger, tablet with audio book ready, and a credit card into the trunk. A nondescript car. As she buckles in, she can't remember the color. Gray? She thinks it's a Hyundai logo on the steering wheel.

She finds a way to charge both her phone and audio book before she pulls out of the lot. Last night, she downloaded the new Anne Patchet novel. As she drives and listens to the barks of the GPS competing with the narrator's voice, she realizes she's too distracted to follow the scenes, to get to know the characters—so many family members, two blended families. Her mind is stuck on that long-ago train ride with Saraswati and all the rationalizations for abandoning the search and failing to paint the story.

In the nineteen years since, both her parents had died—her mother from the wretched Alzheimer's disease, and her father, with his sense of humor intact until the end, from the slow ravages of age. In what felt like a torpedo slicing through the eighty percent of her that was saltwater, she had been off the grid in India in 1997 when Becky needed her most. She is still navigating that ocean of regret. And, despite the sacrifice she'd made of leaving the job she loved, Cal had kept his. Those are losses marked on a calendar, stark moments of grief and betrayal. But Wendy is becoming familiar with another kind of absence, one that is slower, without markers on the map of leave-taking. When had she lost the capacity to touch the back of her head with her toes in her yoga practice? When had it become necessary to write lists, to have a specific place for keys and glasses and phone? As she pulls into the Wegmans lot to buy lunch and almond milk and ginger kombucha for the refrigerator in her room at the ashram, she reminds herself to notice where she parks and for that matter, *what* she is parking.

It's nearly 3:00 when she climbs back in the car, with more than two hours of driving ahead. At a red light, she pulls the visor down to block the sun and sees in the attached mirror that her long, lank, brown hair threaded with silver has unaccustomed body, even a bit of curl. The humidity, no doubt. Maybe it's time to cover that silver, turn it to gold. At 59, she could afford to invest in her appearance. Filler to stretch out those lines edging her mouth? She is pulling her left cheek towards her ear, making her chin look pointy, when the light turns green. Her face is narrow as it is. She presses the gas pedal nearly to the floor to get the little car going. No Botox in her third eye. At least not until she's in her 60s. She has a wavering commitment to be a role model for self-acceptance as she ages.

After arriving at the ashram and checking into her room, Professor Krishna's translation is the first thing she unpacks. She sets it on the nightstand with her reading glasses, ready to spend a week without coffee or wine or decent cell phone service and internet access. She is on time for evening meditation.

CHAPTER Three

BACK IN HER ROOM for the evening, Wendy lifts the manuscript from the nightstand, settles on the bed, and begins to read.

Translator's Note:
I have done nothing to embellish this story, which, as I worked to translate it into English, brought back memories of an India that no longer exists. I am grateful to Ms. Rabin for the opportunity to relive a part of my past. On occasion, my tears fell to the page, obfuscating words. The story is Saraswati's. The errors are my own. Where there are variations from traditional spellings, such as substituting the name of the god "Siva" with "Shiva," I have used a spelling that will help English readers with pronunciation.

—N. M. Krishna, Professor Emeritus, World Music Department, Wesleyan University, June 3, 1999

Wendy turns the page. There's a brief passage, undated. She reads it without understanding what it is or where it belongs in the diary. Someone, a woman or a girl, is running, calling to her mother. There is fire. On the next page, the story begins, or so it seems.

1938, Kingdom of Mysore, India

Today I am eight years old, and I rolled many *chapattis* for older sister Lakshmi's wedding. I have always loved to roll out flatbread. The chapatti stand we use was our mother's favorite possession, painted with many colors all around like a mandala. I think it is the loveliest chapatti stand in the village. Amma's brother brought it from the city in honor of the marriage of our parents, so it is just one year older than Lakshmi. It has little feet like a stool. When I roll chapattis on it, I am reminded of Amma. I close my eyes and hear the low Kali Durga chant she hummed, Om Mata Kali, Om Mata Durga, Om Mata Kali, Om Mata Durga. I pretend Amma is squatting beside me as I work. Is it possible I can remember myself a baby in the hammock, where my younger brother Ganesha is now? I have a memory of watching Amma through the netting as she worked rolling breakfast chapattis each morning before Appa rose from his mat. I can almost hear the soft sound her mouth made early in the morning, so she would not wake him with her singing. It came deep from her chest, when she wasn't coughing. She almost never coughed when she sang to God.

The *aarti* lamp has never looked so fine as it does today. The brass shines like a lotus in the sun. It sits on Amma's altar. It was she who offered *puja* each morning. Appa said that the Gods could hear her prayers, even though she was a woman, because the beauty of her soul was neither male nor female. He said Amma's prayers were for our entire family, so the rest of us could go about the business of life. As soon as I was big enough, I helped Amma prepare, and then I knelt beside her. I sang the name of God until only my body remained beside my mother, and Amma had to shake me and make me drink strong tea, so that I could go to school.

Now, I am alone before the altar each morning, and it is Lakshmi who shakes me. Who will shake me when she goes to live with her husband's mother? Will Lord Shiva help me roll *beedis*, so that I will have enough *rupees* to marry? The women of our family have always rolled beedis. A girl without a dowry brings shame to her father. Poor Appa—two daughters to marry off and an infant son, years too young to help. Appa sits by the *maharaja's* gate waiting, just as his father, and his father's father and all the fathers in our family have done in days' past. But last year was the long drought and now there is little work. Dear Appa does not say it, but I feel his worry in the sorrowful way he looks at me and baby Ganesha.

How Amma would love the aarti lamp now. After aarti she chanted Hari Krishna Hari Rama. The low sweet sound of her voice would rock me to sleep, and her sharp cough would slice me out of my dreams. No one troubled about her cough. Every village woman has one. Their throats are sore from the dust of the tobacco and cloves they roll into beedis. Amma stopped rolling beedis just before Ganesha was born, but Appa did not stop smoking them. After Ganesha was born her cough grew worse, until she could only lie on her mat all day. Lakshmi and I swept and made the chapattis and cooked the dhal and took care of Younger Brother. The sister of my mother came to take care of Amma, and Lakshmi and I stopped going to school so we could do the chores. There will soon be no one but me to cook Appa's meals and roll the beedis.

Amma wanted me to go to school. That's why she named me Saraswati, the Goddess of knowledge. Amma used to say when she prayed to Saraswati, she was praying for my education. Appa laughed at her for this. "Better you should pray for a dowry for her marriage."

"That is my prayer to Lakshmi, the Goddess of fortune, for Elder Daughter Lakshmi," she would say. It made Amma so happy when I learned to read and write and could read stories to her about Radha and Krishna and all his beautiful Gopi consorts or the tale of Lord Krishna as Arjuna's charioteer, teaching him his warrior duty on the battlefield.

. . .

WENDY TAKES OFF her reading glasses and sets them on the nightstand. Her eyes are tired, and she wants to sleep, yet there are so many questions. The manuscript itself is lyrical and vivid but puzzling. If it's a diary, how can she be rolling chapatis and also writing in the present tense? Maybe it's the translation itself. N. M. Krishna wanting to improve it or make it more ... accessible to the Western reader? Kannada verbs have both past and present. She knows this from her time in India.

Saraswati sounds innocent in a sweet way yet old beyond her years. Village life in India, especially for the poor beedi rollers, was hard. With her mother gone, Saraswati would have had to grow up fast but with the emotions of a child. It's already after 9:00 pm, and the first meditation is at 5:00 am tomorrow morning. But Wendy can't resist. She puts on her glasses again.

1938

We have rolled enough beedis for my sister's dowry. I feel sad that Amma is not here to celebrate Lakshmi's fourteen-year-old birthday and to see her in her beautiful red wedding sari with roses woven in her hair.

This is the day we have been planning for so long. I am awake early to offer a special puja to Krishna and Radha. I shall ask for their love to surround Lakshmi and her new husband Shankar and to bless their marriage with many sons. Her husband is very handsome. We saw him when he came with his parents to inspect. Lakshmi was much pleased with his appearance, but now she is afraid of what will happen when she goes to live in his mother's house. It is not the work, I think, that frightens her, for she is a hard worker like me. She is afraid that a mother-in-law will make her long for our Amma all the more. That is what I would fear if I were facing the wedding ceremony today. Here, at least, are Amma's pots and *saris* and bangles. Here, I can remember her as I boil the rice in her pot or pray before her altar.

The rose petals I gathered are fragrant, and I have saved a few grains of the wedding rice we will boil later this morning. As I pray to Radha and Krishna, I offer a prayer of my own. I ask for this boon—that I never have to leave my mother's house. I do not know from where the money would come for a second dowry, so it is not such a difficult wish.

When I close my eyes, I can still see the light from the aarti lamp, burning behind my eyelids. I focus on the light as it merges in the center of my forehead. It is quiet this morning. I am the only one awake at this hour and I sit in silence for a very long time. As I breathe, I feel the lamp light glowing around my body. My skin is tingling as it did when Amma rubbed me with sesame oil. It has been so long since I felt my Amma's touch, and now I am feeling touched all over. I am so bright; I am suddenly afraid there must be fire. When I open my eyes to look, it is only the small flame of the aarti lamp burning, and I am just the same as I was. I am simply a girl doing her morning puja before God.

But I feel changed. I feel the glow inside me now, everywhere inside me. I know now that God is with me, and that the Divine Mother has heard my prayers. My boon will be granted. I will not be a servant in my mother-in-law's house. I will never leave my Amma's side. I know this altar is mine now, that the Divine Mother has wrapped me in her holy light, that I am divine.

I begin to make sounds, like chanting without words. I know they are blessings from the Divine Mother. "Ma," I call, and then I begin to chant to her in all her many names, chanting the name of the Goddess, Saraswati, for whom I am named, and Lakshmi, the Goddess of abundance, and Parvathi, Shiva's consort, and wonderful wild Goddess Mother Kali, and terrible demon slayer, Durga. And soon the household is awake and gathered around me, and I stand in prayer, swaying still with the fullness of song in my heart. When I open my eyes, Appa is bowing at my feet.

All day I am filled with the blessings of the Divine Mother. On the way to the wedding hall, I stop. Tears come to my eyes as I step on an ancient crack in the surface of this dry sunbaked road. I am so young in this body; yet, in this moment, I am caught in the current of an underground stream of wisdom that has been flowing since the beginning of this world. Only this body is new. The cracks in my path tell me of this and of many other secrets existing deep beneath the surface of this earth we call reality.

As the wedding guests arrive, they are brought to me, one by one. I do not know what words to speak, and yet the words come from a place inside me that my mind does not recognize. I listen to the words, hearing them for the first time, just as the guests hear them. Each guest *pranams* at my feet. Even the swamis and saints in saffron robes bow down.

It takes a long time for the wedding ceremony. My sister is beautiful in her red sari trimmed in gold. She is fragrant and sweet as the roses and jasmine twined in the locks of her hair.

As I look around I see God everywhere—in the weary old woman who sits toothless and grinning in the corner, in the beggar with one leg who waits at the door for the guests to remember him, in the little one, unused to wearing pants who has pulled them off to do his business in the corner of the tent. I see God in my beautiful sister and in my mother's sister, and in each chapatti and each sweet that was made with so much love and attention for these guests on this special day.

There are many musicians sitting together, but only the *tabla* player is beating his drums. Now the veena player begins to pluck the strings. The room is bright with excitement. My father calls for a dance, and several ladies rise. Three women and a girl about my age begin the slow circle on the ground in front of Lakshmi and Shankar. "Dance, Saraswati," Appa says. "It is why God gave you legs."

I have never danced in public before. I am shy at first, moving slowly, pacing my movements with the others. We move with precision, each lifting her hands and raising and stamping her feet to the pattern of her neighbor's movements. I feel the peace of moving in harmony with my sisters and forget there are others watching. The tempo of the music increases, and we circle faster and faster, our saris and skirts fluttering as we spin. Suddenly, I am pushed into the center of the circle and dance my own dance as the women circle me

> with the graceful rhythm of their limbs. I dance until my hair unwinds from its braid as my head moves by itself on my neck and my hands fly into *mudras*. Then my eyes flutter back, my body trembles, and I am on the ground, shaking in the embrace of my Lord Brahma. Light shoots up through the top of my head, and I am with Amma. I am in bliss. I am the Goddess; I am Saraswati!

. . .

WENDY PUTS THE MANUSCRIPT down on the nightstand and takes off her reading glasses. She feels more awake now than she did before she started reading. What is she reading? She's never read John of the Cross, but she thinks maybe she should. This manuscript ... it's like reading the old testament. All those miracles, the burning bush—the fire that burns but does not consume, the tablets carved by the hand of God. It's exciting and disturbing in equal measure. It feels right to be reading it here while diving more deeply into her practice—meditating three times a day with the swamis and devotees and community she loves. She'll ask Ramesh to send the original back to her in Rhode Island, so she can hold the small red book in her hand again, even if she can't read the words. It has the weight of love in it. Love and trust. Why would she possess it, if Saraswati hadn't trusted her? It feels like she's been given a second chance.

Her long hours at work provide too many distractions to meditate more than once a day, let alone give this story the mindful attention it's due. Her private practice consumes her in a way that would not allow her to sink into this story. Now, she has five days to read before she joins the yoga and mental health program next weekend.

She's excited about the workshop—how to integrate appropriate yoga practices into her clinical work. Yoga helped her survive the divorce and has contributed to her emotional wellbeing ever since. Why shouldn't she be able to share a little of what transformed her life with her trauma survivors? She thinks of 52-year-old Jeffrey who can't get out of bed in the morning. She would like to teach him something he could do right there in his bed, so he starts his day with more energy. And 37-year-old Carla, who calls her between sessions, always in crisis and usually angry and blaming someone. What might she teach her to self soothe? She wants to finish this diary or whatever it is ... fiction? memoir? ... before her focus lands back on her clients and how what she learns this weekend can deepen their work together.

She was happy to see the program for therapists and yoga teachers listed in the Yogaville catalog. She could have taken the same program closer to home, but Yogaville, and its temple and shrines nestled along the James River in the foothills of the Blue Ridge Mountains in rural Virginia, is special. Those fleeting moments on her mat at home that take her beyond the boundaries of her mind, seem limitless on the grounds of this ashram. A few years ago, when she tried to explain the healing potential of yoga to her colleagues, eyes would roll, and the subject would be changed. More and more though, they are curious and a few of them have even become yoga teachers.

As much as she loves to visit, she would never move in. Ashrams, like every other organization, have their politics. Can we ever be entirely clear, she wonders, free of unmet childhood needs, or of our own self-interest, despite prayers for an "ego as pure as crystal?" And she loves that about humanity—loves the push and pull that makes life interesting. As long as she's a visitor here, who adorns herself with an "in loving silence" badge in the dining hall, she is immune to the push and pull of ashram life. This is her retreat. For Saraswati. And for Becky. In her heart's mind, everything she does is for her daughter. But that's not the way it has looked to others. Not to her family. Not to her friends. Certainly, not to Becky's father Aaron. Becky is the only one who knows. And to Wendy, Becky's knowing is all that matters.

In the morning, Wendy lies in bed. Instead of going to the early meditation, she ponders the vivid scenes she read the night before. Could these truly be the words of a young girl of what, eight or nine? After the initial hurdle of first grade, when survival meant training her mind to seek shelter somewhere, anywhere, other than here, Wendy was reading and had a good vocabulary by eight. Still out-to-lunch in second grade and barely there in third, she had mastered reading and it had mastered her. She was enslaved by those childhood mystery series about the Dana Sisters. But she could not have expressed herself clearly about anything, much less life and death and transcendent states of Samadhi. And Becky at eight, smart as she was—could she have been so precise? Becky, grown now, despite or because of her brilliance, was still beautifully child-like at 29.

Unlike Becky, Wendy had been an introverted child, burrowing into the corner of the bed after school with a gothic novel, and then drawing into a sketch book her imagined Nancy Drew or Heathcliff or the mad wife confined in the tower. Becky didn't escape into reading or drawing as a child, but as soon as she could walk, she danced alone around the living room until she dropped, sometimes so dizzy she banged her shin into the coffee table, and once her head on the Queen Ann side table, so that she had to get stitches in her brow. Becky danced to "Beauty and the Beast" and "Miss Saigon," the call to dinner unheard. She and Becky were both like that—tuned out or tuned in, depending on your perspective. Except for the terrible time when she was ten, Becky has never stopped dancing.

The trance of the dance, the absorption of art. Creation. The flow. Saraswati's description is familiar to Wendy. Had she been born in India, maybe her absorption in the things that didn't seem to count in Sharon, Massachusetts, would have been considered holy. Instead of ... what had her parents called her? Not space cadet. But something like that. Scatterbrained. Absent minded. She remembers those report cards in elementary school. Daydreaming, inattentive, distracted. Slow. She does not pay attention in class. Today, she would be sent to the school psychologist. She might have been labeled, just as Becky had been when she was ten and therapy had been suggested for her supposed ADHD. Becky's teachers wanted to subdue her angry outbursts, her speaking out in class. But, oh, there was good reason for that.

Ritalin had been recommended by the medical director, but thank God, the therapist, a former colleague at the clinic from which Wendy had been forced to resign, had a different perspective. After watching Becky fidget and kick a Lego construction her last client had left in the corner of the office, Sarah had the brilliant idea of putting disco music on her boom box and leaving the room to use the bathroom. When she returned, there was Becky dancing, bright eyed, smiling. Really, she hadn't stopped taking dance lessons since. There were still more years of disruptive behavior, alcohol and drugs, and on-going therapy, but the dancing never stopped after that.

Wendy rubs her eyes, as though she could rub out the vision of ten-year-old Becky sobbing, her arms thrown around Wendy's neck and then pushing her away. Where were you? Enough of this! Wendy throws off the covers and climbs out of bed. If she doesn't wash her hair, she can make the second meditation that begins at 6:20. But she'll skip the yoga class, so she can fit in a little more reading time before noon meditation.

CHAPTER
Four

1938

I am not sure where I am, but it is light again, and there is my Auntie by my side, offering me water from a cup. I ask her if it is morning.

"It is two mornings since your sister's wedding," she says.

I recognize Amma's aarti lamp and the *ghee* pot and I know that I am home on my own mat. I lift my head and Auntie helps me take a sip.

"Your father thought you had died, but I knew you would come back. Where did you go, child?"

"I do not know. It was peaceful and quiet, and I was happy." Once I saw Amma, felt her hand rest on my shoulder. Then I felt a gentle push, and here I am again without her. I do not tell Auntie that Amma was there.

"How do you feel?"

I move myself carefully, testing each joint, each muscle. Everything works, although I am stiff as a reed. Amma's hand on my shoulder. If I close my eyes, I can almost feel it there. She spoke to me. The melody, the rhythm, I remember. But not the words. I have lost the words. I want the words.

"No time for tears, Saraswati," and Auntie is wiping my face with the edge of her dupatta.

Soon I am up, and Auntie helps me bathe and dress. I have had two days without labor, so there is no time for puja this morning. Auntie gives me some chai and idlis, a real treat, and then I sit down at my place with the leaves she has already cut to size in the days I slept. She places a big pile of tobacco in my lap.

. . .

SO YOUNG TO BE motherless. Wendy thinks Saraswati must be about the age Becky was when she and Aaron separated. Saraswati had her Auntie. And her sister. Becky had Martha, the fourth in a long chain of nannies. Becky had Penny next door. Becky had Linny and her other friends. But the day she needed her mother most, Becky did not have her.

Motherless children. The fragile, essential bond between mothers and daughters—it cuts across continents, cultures. Donald Winnicott, the British psychoanalyst, had proposed the theory of the "good enough mother." Did she have one? Did Becky? It's like an ear worm. Wendy knows she's beginning to ruminate. Never a good thing for the default of depression she carries in her genes. But she can't help it. Jewish children in Europe separated from their parents, sent into hiding in barns or attics or taken to camps, parents in one line, children in another. Separation. Death. By 1945, as many as 1.5 million Jewish children dead. Oh, God, I'm spiraling into the dark. I should have practiced yoga this morning. I can't miss any more practices, she thinks, as she pushes herself up from the chair. Let in the light! Let it seep through these wounds—mine, Becky's, Saraswati's, the great grandchildren of survivors with Holocaust genes mutating their DNA. I'll hike, I'll meditate, I'll breathe, I'll chant, and come back to this narrative tonight.

1941

The sister of my mother has gone back to her family, so I do not see her very often. In the morning, I offer puja and then make the food we will eat for this day, while Appa and Ganesha sleep. As soon as there is enough light, I begin to roll my beedis. I am proud of Ganesha. Just five years of age, and he cuts perfect leaf squares for my beedis. I give him 5 paise for 100 leaves. This way he has learned to count. I tell him his name should be Hanuman instead of Ganesha, because he is such a little monkey. He makes me laugh and laugh until I sometimes spill my tray. But if he cuts the leaves for me, when he comes home, and bundles the finished beedis, I can sometimes make 2000 a day.

Lakshmi comes today with Bindu, her precious little one, nearly two years old. It worries me that Lakshmi looks so tired, and she has a cough. She only rolls beedis now and then, so it is surely not the tobacco that irritates her throat. She works very hard in the house of her mother-in-law, who is not loving at all to Bindu. Older Sister whispered to me that she feared her mother-in-law would feed the baby poisoned milk, so set she was on a male child, but Bindu is strong and healthy. Now Lakshmi is with child again, so we are praying for a boy.

Lakshmi is here now, and we are not doing any work. No grinding, cutting or rolling today. It is like a holiday. Since her marriage, so rare! We simply sit and talk. Bindu crawls from one lap to the other, reaching for the gold around my neck and in my nose.

"I have heard," Lakshmi says, "some news about Appa."

"You have heard news? I cook his meals and wash his clothes. I see him every day. How have you heard news, and I have not?"

"I heard my husband and his father talking while I was serving them."

"So, tell me. Is it bad news or good?"

"Shankar told his father that Appa will take another wife."

"But he has me! Does he think I do not take care of him?"

Lakshmi puts her hand on mine. "I do not know what he thinks. You are nearly eleven years old. Perhaps he means to marry you off." Lakshmi's eyes are bright. "Just think, Saraswati, a husband of your own."

I pull my hand away. "I do not want to marry! Appa knows that. I want to stay here. There is Ganesha to see to and puja each morning at Amma's altar. I have no reason to leave."

"No one said you must, Little Sister." Lakshmi's arm circles my waist and I put my head on her shoulder and feel a tear roll across my nose and into my mouth.

Lakshmi wipes my face with the edge of her sari. "I know. I know," she whispers. She looks around at our little house. When I look up, there is a sad expression on her face. I know she misses it, misses Amma, misses me and Ganesha and Appa. Bindu is crawling toward the altar, reaching for the aarti lamp, and Older Sister lets go of me to reach for her. "I am so grateful you are mine," she sings, as she rocks her baby in her arms.

With Bindu at her breast my sister is radiant with happiness. This is not a happiness I will share. There are some things you know. Soon, I could carry a baby in my womb, give birth, suckle a newborn in my arms, but I will never do so. If Appa marries again, there will be more children in this little house, none of them mine. "Did you hear them say who it was?"

"Shankar said Appa had talked to Subhash about his daughter."

"Shakuntala?"

Lakshmi nods. "She is fifteen, like me. She goes to school. She will be like a sister to you."

"No one could take your place." It is my turn to wrap my arms around her shoulder, and she leans back into my embrace as Bindu nurses.

When Lakshmi leaves, I light the lamp for Shiva aarti, although it is only mid-afternoon. Om Jai Shiva Omkara. Only God knows what is best for this life. All glory to Shiva. Change is coming. Oh Shiva, great destroyer, I rest in your bliss. I lay myself at your divine feet. Om Jai Shiva Omkara. Your will, oh, great destroyer, not mine. I chant the aarti prayer and then pranam on my knees, praying to my Lord Shiva, great master of the dance, master of destruction.

I hear the damaru, the drum beat of creation, even as the fire in your hand touches my life, dissolving all that is familiar and known. You, Nataraja, oh glorious Shiva, keep all things changing, ending and beginning. What is ending of this life, and what is it that begins? What is my *dharma*, if not to be here in my mother's house, serving my father and brother in love and devotion, and serving you, oh, my Lord?

In my head, I hear the beat of Shiva's drum, as I rock on my knees, and I feel the heat of His flame burning in my chest, my feet, my fingertips. My whole torso is alive with the pulse and glimmer of the fire, and I move with it. I roll on the floor, my body a tiny ball, as though I could tamp the leaping flames, but I cannot. My legs kick out, the tingling energy pitching me forward and back at the waist, my pelvis rocking, heat rising. My feet stamp and kick at the ground as I lie on my back, and then roll to my belly where the heat is so great, I think I will explode in yellow light. I press my belly into the floor,

> tamping the heat with the earth that supports me. Om Namah Shivaya. And then I am up and dancing, the fire in my heart leads me around the room. There is so much I love in this house. I pick up the beautiful chapatti stand and hold it to my chest as I dance.
>
> And there is Shiva, my Lord, and I hold the small brass statue in my hand, and his sparks sear my skin, shimmer sacrum, pelvis, yoni. The drum in his hand beats in my chest. New fires, little leaps of flame, take my breath away. I dance him around the room on my own two legs. Om Namah Shivaya. Fill me with your fire. You are my Lord, my master.
>
> Suddenly my legs quiver, and I cannot hold him any longer. Every cell of my body is vibrating, and I stumble and fall to the ground. A warm glow fills me, not a fire at all, but luminous as the sun. Each light-filled breath is God's gift to me. There is splendor behind my eyelids, and there is peace. I know that Shiva has heard me, is with me still. Whatever happens, I will be safe and loved by my Lord. Oh, Shiva, you will not forsake me. Om Namah Shivaya.

. . .

WENDY REALIZES THAT SHE has been holding her breath again. She lets out a deep sigh, as she sets the pages on the floor beside her chair. She remembers chanting at the ashram years ago, standing, rocking, filled with light, and a sense of timeless, all-pervading love. It had seemed like the antithesis to her marriage. She recalls the inner vision of firelight—a dancer whirling in the dust around the fire, her movements a flash of gold and green and ankle bells. And now, the image of Saraswati's dance churns in her—sensual, erotic—like the lightning bolt of the 16th century poet Mirabai, who ran naked through the streets, chanting her love-crazed praise to Lord Krishna.

She knew then what was missing in her marriage. After the visit to this same ashram over twenty years ago, she had succumbed to Cal's yearning looks at work, his innuendos, his outright declarations by email: *God, I love you so much. Talk about obsessed—I can't delete the "deletes." They're the only thing of yours that I have constant access to*, and her own desire—how alive she felt and how young. After that horrible trip she and Aaron had taken across Massachusetts to the New Hope Inn in Lenox to "save" their marriage, she had been receptive to Cal's alluring whispers, his pleas: *Please don't say no. I'm not ready to accept that we will never touch, that I can never hold you (yes, maybe even bathe you!) that we can't do the things that lovers do. But today, all I'm asking of you is to meet me for lunch. Just lunch.* Two days after that ashram visit, the memory of that horrible weekend still festering, she met Cal for lunch and many more lunches after that. It doesn't do her any good to think of Cal. It suspends her heart in uncertainty and grief, even now. Better to remember the clear decisions she has made in her life. Even if they were wrong.

And she is back in Aaron's over-heated car, the blur of the winter landscape rushing past. There are trigger moments in a marriage, she believes, when there's a flash of knowing that all the effort, the therapy, the memories of happier times are not enough to carry you through. It must have been 1995, because they were divorced by '97. There was the watershed moment she'd heard her clients talk about. The moment she knew for sure that she would not remain married to him. And then, of course, the knowledge dissolved in a murky sort of hope. She kept trying for a while longer, which was the way with her back then.

"Any water left?" he had asked.

Without turning to look at him, Wendy unscrewed the cap and handed the nearly empty bottle across. This was the part of the drive that dulled the senses—endless miles of snow-patched hills sparsely populated by barren trees, a leaden sky. In the distance, an abandoned barn, roof caved in, weathered siding, a broken-down corral fencing emptiness. Everything gray, especially at this time of year. The middle of February. The middle of Massachusetts. The middle of their lives. Three months ago, Aaron had turned forty, and in a few months, she would follow.

As he stretched the bottle across the console, he kept his eyes on the rise and arc of the road ahead. A simple question. She hadn't answered "here" or "a little," nor had she smiled. Just the thrust of the bottle. Mechanical. Dumb. He was handing it back the same way.

Wendy screwed the cap back on, as she registered his face in profile. Labile, she would call it in her clinical mode, emotion always shifting beneath the mask of failed dominion, the German Jew in him from his mother's side. Emotion he rarely expressed. Even now, the Litvak cheek, so much like his father's, round, clay-colored at its peak, quivered with a feeling she couldn't name but regretted all the same. As if she were the source of the pulse at his temple. The tension in his jaw, the push of his thick lower lip out and in against his teeth—about her? She hadn't accustomed herself to the buzz cut he came home with last month. When she'd married him, his auburn curls framed his long Lincoln-like face and stood away from his scalp like mahogany shavings. Now he was prickly as a cactus. Stiff. Agitated.

Aaron's head swung away from the road. "What?"

"Nothing."

"I hate it when you gawk. That blank look and your mind's in China."

"Sorry." She cracked the window an inch. It was close in the car. The heater. His irritation. Hers.

"You just spaced out on me again. Sometimes I feel so shut out of your life."

"I'm here, honey."

"Then please tell me what you're thinking."

There it was again—his desire to walk around inside her head, as if it were some unexplored swampy acreage he owned. His acute attention had pleased her once. She imagined the tall curve of his body like a lean question mark, striding through the marshes of her mind. Back in her twenties, when she barely knew herself, his deep inquiry had penetrated the fog of her unknowing, had helped her understand and even define herself. But he seldom gave her the same privilege. What bugged her was his faith in his possession—that he could read her moods, discover her thoughts. It was a piece of the story he told himself about their marriage—for him a single word—happilymarried. She could feel his expectations, even as he watched the road ahead and stole wary looks at her. New Hope. Even the name of the inn a cliché. "Nothing special," she said.

She wished she could remove the turtleneck from under her jumper without completely undressing, but all she could do was unbutton down to the belt and sling out of the arms.

"What are you doing?"

"Aren't you hot?"

"Turn off the heater in the seat."

She'd forgotten about that. Her five-year-old Subaru had no such amenities. Oh, who cares? She lifted the turtleneck over her head, struggling to pull out of her sleeve and free her left earring, stuck on a thread at the shoulder seam.

"Wen-dy!" He was almost tsking.

She was small breasted, and, as usual, not wearing a bra. Fifteen years ago, he might have pulled off the road. A few years ago, he might have raised his eyebrows, pretended to ogle, laughed. Now he tsked. Later, at the appropriate time, teeth brushed, face washed, pills taken, he might want to make love, which, given their sex life lately, or lack of it, was the point of the trip. Wendy shrugged into her corduroy sleeves and leaned forward to touch the smiley-face sticker Becky had stuck on the wood-veneered glove compartment. The fact that Aaron allowed it, this imperfection on his BMW, endeared him to her, almost made up for his prudishness.

He glanced over. "I shouldn't have let her do that. Will it come off without a mark?"

She shrugged, laughed. "I think it balances the car's Teutonic character."

"It's not the car you object to, it's me."

"Only when I can't find my lemongrass tea in the morning." She gave his arm a playful punch, as though she were kidding about the fact that he had been up in the middle of the night, reorganizing the tea shelf. Again.

Though it was only 4:00, a mass of gray clouds had moved in, obscuring the sun, and he turned on the headlights. She gazed over her shoulder. Was he right? Behind them, the hills were fading into the horizon, where, though it had become too cloudy to see it, the sun was low in the sky. Maybe it was about him.

As she turned back, light from a highway lamp glazed the glass, and the momentary reflection of her eyes made her think of Becky.

Those big eyes that pulled something out of her, always a little more than she knew how to give. Thank God, at nearly eight, Becky wasn't as clingy when Wendy left for clinical trainings or for the ashram—the only place she no longer felt the pressure to paint. Becky was happy to spend a weekend with a friend now. Until lately, Becky had clung to her neck when Wendy tried to kiss her goodnight, not wanting to go to sleep, demanding a story, then another. A circle of insufficiency was the way she saw it, because if Becky felt sufficiently loved, those scenes wouldn't happen. Bad mother. She could blame herself or she could blame the long matrilineal chain of insufficiency.

"What are you thinking?"

"About Becky."

"Tell me."

She remembered a younger Becky, floating in the bathtub, gazing up, her eyes trusting, serene. "Nothing special ... about giving her a bath when she was little. It's a soothing image." When the self-critical thoughts assailed her, Wendy often went back to the unforgettable moment nearly bursting in her heart—Becky's hair spiraling out like some Ophelia, firm little torso—wide shoulders, narrow hips. How beautiful she was at two. Still was.

"She was perfect, you know, with that long torso I've always loved about your body." Wendy noticed his face soften and a little tug at his lips, almost like a smile, and realized how little she complimented him these days. Her Gottman score, five compliments to one criticism—the ratio for couples likely to stay together—was going down.

"There's something about my body you love?"

She knew he was on to her, had noticed how she avoided looking at his undressed body that still had that Mick Jagger length and leanness, but not its appeal. "You've got a great body," she said the way her next door neighbor Norma had said it to her when she came back freshman year with all those dorm carbs riding on her hips, and her mother had insisted she go on a grapefruit diet.

"What made you think about bathing Becky, now?"

"I don't know. It's one of those moments I go back to when I'm being hard on myself. I cried when I looked at her. I felt this weird feeling of longing and love and, at the same time, this feeling like I was going to disappoint her."

"Guilt, maybe."

Her right hand gripped in a fist. Does any mother not feel some measure of guilt? A client had asked her that just last week.

"You were still trying to paint," he added.

She looked out the window, feeling the fist in her belly now. Trying to paint. She didn't know whether she was feeling angry because she'd tried and failed, because she hadn't tried hard enough, because the word "trying" was wrong, because she was painting, not trying, and she was good but not good enough, and she'd quit and she shouldn't have, or maybe because she should have quit a long time ago, should never have started, in fact. Maybe the whole problem was that she had an artist's sensibility, an artist's longing for immortality or, what was it that Freud had said? —that the artist consoles himself by creating fantasies that fulfill his repressed infantile longings? And what were hers? Whatever they were, in the moment of creation, they were fulfilled. But she just wasn't good enough to make a career of it. Or maybe she was angry because he had said it—trying to paint—and he was the one who had led her here, to this cliché of happilymarried that did not—why not? —allow her to paint? Well, of course she couldn't be serious about her art with a child to raise and a full-time job that wrung her out so that there was little energy left to give to art, not her own, anyway. Someone else's maybe. Yoga had become her passion once she'd rolled up what was left of her empty canvas.

But damn it! Painting or not painting—it was her business, not his. It was intolerable to even hear him speak of it. Trying to paint! She'd never told him of the time she'd come up from a painting to realize that the sound in the background, constant but unheard, had been Becky crying, waking long ago from her nap. Or the time Aaron was away, and she hadn't bothered to brush her teeth or change out of her nightshirt. Just picked up the paintbrush and started right in on the picture in her mind. That was the day Becky missed her school bus. She sat beneath the easel in the basement studio, eating left-over tuna noodle casserole and looking at the pictures in Wendy's art books.

Wendy has a flash of Becky's tear-stained six-year-old face the day she was locked out, Wendy's last as a painter. Layer upon layer of paint. Weeks before, Aaron had said the painting was finished, to leave it alone, had even taken a photograph of what would soon be covered up. But Wendy had been driven. The sheer power of the brush in her hand, the moving forward and back to see the five-foot canvas, the physicality and texture of the new paints she had ordered—vermilion, terre verde, caputi mortem. Her palette thickened by days of thinking in cobalt, then ochre, then again in sienna. But the wailing of six-year-old Becky comes back to her now. The last day of her life as a painter. How had the backdoor, always left open during the day, become locked? Becky had stood, apparently for a long time—twenty minutes? Even a minute was too long—pounding on the door, crying. Of course, Wendy had heard. How could she not? But she hadn't. And then suddenly, as though coming up for air, she'd heard.

In the car with Aaron, she told herself that it was her decision, not his. She couldn't justify the self-indulgence anymore, when, in all the years she'd been painting, the closest she'd come to a solo exhibition had been her thesis show in college. And of the five group shows in which she'd exhibited, two were non-juried Women's Sacred Art Exhibits at the Unitarian Church.

Here at the ashram, the only art is the stunning beauty of the mountains at sunset, the temple, the lake, the polished brass of the icons, the shrines, and the Guru's beloved face in tinted photographs hung in every room. For a long time after Cal, the ashram and her yoga practice had almost been enough to fill the empty space of his absence. Now, there is this pulse in her hands, the urge to feel the fine texture of sable in her fingers, and the yearning for the smell of turpentine. It has been too long since she has even looked with the keen absorption of an artist at the world around her. Can she translate what she sees onto paper? Can she even really see anymore? Musicians do finger exercises before they play. After years of absence from a violin, a violinist doesn't pick up the instrument and play a rondo. Yoga and meditation have tamed the fire to paint that had burned in her. She senses the little red book will implode her life once again. Aaron had said it. Maybe he was right. When she rolled up her canvases, she unmasked an abyss of longing that not even Cal could fill.

"I don't want to borrow trouble, but I think when you stopped painting, other problems surfaced. Do you blame me for making you quit?"

"You didn't force the issue. I decided."

"Then why do you seem unhappy?"

"I'm not unhappy." It was a small lie, really: just another basted stitch to hold the seam together. Is that what was happening? Were they coming apart? Would her growing feelings for Cal rip through the fabric of her marriage?

Had she changed since she stopped painting? Maybe, yes. But it seemed to her that Aaron had changed too. She couldn't put her finger on how exactly or when. It had been a slow erosion of curiosity over the years. Wasn't he more compulsive than ever? There had been a time when she appreciated his need for order. She could relax a little, let him sweat the details. Plus, she thought she understood him. How else was an eleven-year-old boy supposed to cope with a mother like Bea? A mother whose undiagnosed mental illness had him talking her down from the rooftop ledge of a Memphis hotel on a visit to his grandparents? His idiosyncrasies seemed a window to his wounds, and it was through his wounds that she could love him. But lately, she had only to look at the hard lines of his face, as she was doing now, to sense the layers of scar tissue covering those wounds. Just last week, he'd written to the school superintendent, supporting a new values curriculum that, among other things, banned the proposed diversity program. What had happened to the poet, the leftist, the passionate lover, the man she'd fallen in love with? Even back then, his pencils lined up vertically by his tablet and his jeans hung in rows. But after business school, out on his own, charting clients' profits and losses on the program he'd designed before QuickBooks took over the market, the poetry ran dry and the politics veered right. That's when he began taking his jeans to the cleaners, adding starch to his shirts and insisting that dinner be a sit-down affair at 6:30 every night. There was so little passion these days. She thought he loved only the idea of her.

Washed out black and white images rolled past the windshield. Even the upholstery of the car was gray. The only color, the smiley-face sticker, and she stared until it blurred, and her eyes closed. They rode in silence for several minutes, maybe longer. She couldn't be sure that she hadn't fallen asleep because the sound of his voice startled her.

"You're like a wall I can't break through." He turned his face from the road for a moment, and she met his gaze. She recognized the clench of his jaw, girdling rage.

"I want to be attentive, honey. I don't want to think about work or anything else while we're away." She hoped this could happen. Away from their ordinary routines, maybe the spark of connection would ignite, maybe it would rekindle feeling, love even. Really, she did want that with Aaron. But as soon as she said it, her mind latched onto an image, unbidden: the look on Cal's face yesterday when they happened to walk out of the building at the same time. They'd stood for a moment, talking by her car. Her lips twitched into a smile as she remembered the longing she thought she saw in his eyes when she told him that she and Aaron were going to the Berkshires this weekend.

In that instant, Aaron's hand surrounded hers, and something froze inside. Closing her eyes, she prayed to be able to feel something when he touched her. She felt the car slowing and opened her eyes into the descending dark.

"Gas," he said, pulling off the highway onto the exit ramp. "Gas will be cheaper off 90. I thought we'd take that rural route off 20 and gas up before dark."

The car rolled to a stop alongside the gas pump, and she opened the door. "I'm going to get a snack. Want anything?" She gestured towards the convenience store window where a florescent glow from within lit a path from the pump to the door.

A grimace traveled one side of his face. She took that for "no." More than no. Some commentary on no, like you shouldn't have to ask, like you should know by now what I want, like you're incapable of giving me what I want. Or maybe she was reading all that in. In that moment, she was incapable of giving him what he wanted.

Inside the store, Wendy faced the narrow aisles crammed full of processed, edible substances in glaring packages, and her mind went blank. She wanted something. What? Nothing here. Something. Avoiding the cashier's gaze, she headed toward the back of the store to the door with the skirt sign. In the bathroom, she splashed water on her face, and when she came out, she was able to focus on the rack of hanging snack food. Too much sodium, too much sugar. A bag of pretzels? Then her attention was drawn to a stack of oranges in purple mesh bags on the floor in front of the cashier. Aaron loved oranges. Loved peeling and eating. It was something she could give him.

"You sell produce?" She looked into the bloodshot eyes of a skinny young man whose hoodie covered his hair and was tied under his chin.

"Owner's daughter sent those from Orlando."

"Navels?"

"Don't know."

"Any good?"

"Don't know."

By the look of him—pasty complexion, the bluish gray rimming his eyes—it had been a long time since he'd eaten anything fresh. She bent and picked up a bag, holding it as if it were a bundled infant. The weight of it and the way the spheres pushed into her belly and chest reminded her of that stage in Becky's life.

"You want 'em?"

"Uh ... yes." She reached into her shoulder bag for her wallet and extracted her credit card with one hand, without letting go of the bundle. As he rang up the sale, she was aware of the light citrus scent, and it made her think of all the times she'd peeled oranges for Aaron, then of a particular time on the beach at Plum Island, the day after she'd sat for the social work boards. Bundled in layers of winter clothes, on a blanket pushed back against a sheltering dune, they'd fed each other orange slices between kisses. As she signed the charge slip, she imagined her fingers bringing an orange slice to Aaron's lips. Something like hope made her offer the cashier an orange.

"Guess it won't kill me." He reached out. His face was the same drooping gray sack it had been before, but, for an instant, his eyes seemed to reflect the brightness of the orange in his hand. "Thanks."

As she pushed through the door, heading toward the circle of light where the car was parked, she felt lighter, not tired anymore. She sensed that more than her cramped muscles had relaxed. She wanted to see the look on Aaron's face when she slid a slice of orange between his lips. For the first time in—what? Two years? —she wanted to do this.

"Oranges?" A real smile twitched on his lips as she climbed in.

"Can I peel you one?"

"I can do it." He reached out, but when he saw her face, he let his hand drift back to the steering wheel. "Oh. Okay. Thanks."

He started the car and drove onto the road. "I think that left up there is the back road we took before."

"How can you remember—what 12 years ago?"

"Where's your sense of adventure, Wendala?"

Right here, she thought, as she covered her skirt with a tissue—my fingers in your mouth. "Can you smell the citrus? Kinda reminds me of those picnics we used to take on the beach." She could feel him turn from the road to look at her as she peeled slowly, bending over her lap, concentrating on removing the fibers, suddenly hungry, breathing the orange smell filling the car. Was it arousal she was feeling now, as she imagined her juicy fingers touching his lips? She had the first clean segment of orange mid-air, on the way to Aaron's mouth, when he shouted.

"What the ...?"

"What?" In the middle of the road—something white and wavering. A flag? No, vertical. A banner? It was moving. "Can you see? Aaron, slow down."

"I am."

"Is it a person? Stop! It's a person!" The person—woman or boy or small, thin man, she couldn't tell—was running toward their headlights. "Aaron, stop!" Then she saw the white flash of nightgown. "It's a woman!"

"Honey, she's crazy," Aaron said, and accelerated.

"Please, slow down, Aaron."

As they drew nearer, the woman's mouth opened wide in a soundless scream. Wendy pushed frantically at the window button, but it wouldn't go down. "Open the window! Please!"

He swung the wheel hard, throwing Wendy off balance. Pieces of orange rolled onto the floor.

"She's saying something!" What she heard was the quick catch of each other's breath and the sound the tires made as Aaron swerved to avoid her.

She craned her neck as they passed and saw the woman turn, too—saw her wild, feral eyes, the henna hair frizzing out from her head, the arms flapping like empty coat sleeves. Then it was just the night again outside the window and Aaron, driving on the wrong side of the dark country road.

Wendy flung off her seat belt. Now turned fully around on her knees, all she could see in the glow from the taillights were a few yards of blacktop and a dash of yellow down the center. "We should go back."

"Honey, I saw her. I know that look."

"Maybe someone's chasing her." In her mind the story was reeling out—a drunken husband, a rapist.

"She wasn't running from anyone."

"How do you know? It looked like a distress signal. Her arms were waving."

"Wildly. She was demented, Wendy. If it were a flat tire, you know I'd stop. But that woman looked dangerous."

Dangerous. It was the word he'd used to describe his mother. Out of control, he'd said, and he just a boy of four. Terror reigned for a time, cracking through the absolute order of the household. Wendy had never seen that side of Bea, but of course she was medicated now.

Wendy settled back into her seat, forgiving him a little. But not herself. The image of the woman still fresh on her mind, the words "thou shall not stand idly by" rolling through her mind, beating against her temples, until everything was quiet, and the thought was gone and so was she. From somewhere else, she watched the car's headlights flash against the ribbon of road unfurling in front of them.

"And we have dinner reservations," he said, pointing to the dashboard clock.

She nodded numbly. "Dinner reservations."

She felt a piece of orange under the toe of her boot and ground it into the mat.

They drove on. The woman's wild eyes, her mouth in a scream—the image there in a flash and then not. Inside the silence between them, was he seeing her too? Or his mother? After a while, she began groping through her bag.

"What are you doing, honey?"

She felt the antenna of her Nokia. If she did something, the creeping fog of numbness might dissipate. Even her limbs felt heavy. "Calling the police."

"Good idea but I don't think you'll get through," he said. "It's a dead zone."

She ignored him, pounding the digits. "You're right," she said after a minute, tossing her phone back into her purse. "Not even 911 works." She grabbed the peel with the few remaining segments still attached. Juice dribbled on her dress, and her hands were sticky.

She thought she saw a light, and she strained to see. "Are there gas stations out here?"

"Maybe not until we get back onto 20. We may as well wait until we get to the inn."

"Up on that hill! There's a light."

"That's a farmhouse, Wendy. Do you want me to get shot?" He paused, looked over. "I thought you were peeling me an orange."

She felt the weight in her hand and remembered she'd had a crazy notion she would feed him. "I did." She took another tissue and laid it on the console between them, then picked the orange pieces out of the crevasses of the seat and set them there. "It's ready."

CHAPTER Five

WENDY SHAKES HERSELF out of the past and sees that it's already 11:40. If she doesn't leave now, she'll be too late for noon meditation in the temple. She could hitch a ride, but her body and her mind need that twenty-minute jog down the mountain trail through the woods. She's been sitting in one place for far too long, and she feels the stiffness in her lower back as she stands. She promises herself more reading time this evening. This afternoon is filled with a yoga workshop that she doesn't want to miss.

As she settles in on a cushion in the temple, she prepares for thirty minutes of silence. Without mantra chanting to ground her, there is no distraction from the flood of memories of that passionless weekend with Aaron and the ride home.

The homeward drive with Aaron, east on 90, had seemed even longer than the one going away. In the warmth of the morning, the snow had melted, and where there had been a dash of brightness on a hillside, there was only a darker brown, a heavier gray, akin to the numbness that had hijacked her mind. Cows huddled against the brooding sky. Aaron talked in spurts about having another child. A son. Adam for his great grandfather Adolph who had changed his name when Hitler came to power. Or Martin for her grandfather Marvin, of recent memory. "We have a system in place now. Childcare. Housekeeping. If I go to work for Dad, you can quit, and we'll be able to afford someone who baby-sits *and* cleans. Maybe you can take up painting again."

She let him ramble on. What was there to say? The dull ache in her heart was wordless. Now and then, images flashed like the shards of the mirror, the hand that held it between her legs, his tears, hers. "I can't even think about another child, right now. That system is built on a shaky foundation."

"What are you talking about? We have shared values, common goals. We love each other. Marriage, family—it's a structure." His palm hit the leather laces around his steering wheel. "It's not about passion! Without that structure there'd be chaos. Otherwise we're animals."

He'd survived his childhood this way. She knew that. What had happened to her compassion? She had an image of it swirling down that bathtub drain. "You sound like your father."

"My father is right about some things."

"Were you happy when you were eight? Ten? Fourteen? Did structure work for you, Aaron?"

His eyes were bulging, his face red. "How dare you use my childhood against me? You're not my therapist!"

"I'm sorry." But she wasn't really. Not one bit. "It's like you forget how bad it was."

"There were good times, too."

"Your notion of family is idealized. It's not your lived experience. You *suffered* at the hands of your family."

"Just because my childhood was difficult, doesn't mean Becky's has to be. Or Adam's, if we have our son. Maybe the family we're creating is the corrective to what we suffered as children."

She looked at him and thought about all the ways she'd felt isolated and alone as a child, and all the ways she felt isolated and alone in her marriage. "I don't think so."

They took Exit 26 towards Weston from 95, so they could pick up Becky at his parents' house. It was Sunday night. Dinner would be waiting. His mother would have slow-cooked a brisket, and they would dine, as always, on the Rabin's best china, using the gold-plated, bamboo-patterned flatware. Wendy had never seen gold-plated flatware until Sunday dinners in her in-laws' home.

As they pulled into the circular driveway of Italian pavers, her head began to pound. "Do you think we could just pick Becky up and leave? Tell them I'm sick?"

"Of course not."

"But I *do* have a headache."

"Since when?"

"A minute ago."

His lips curled back. "Get over it."

"Hey, hey, hey!" His father greeted them at the ornate front door, opening his short, beefy arms wide. "The love birds are back. How was the get-away?"

Sam Rabin was compact as a prizefighter and low to the ground, with a barrel chest and short, thick legs, the counterpoint to his wife's imposing height. He loved his family, including his daughter-in-law, with a protective ferocity, precisely because they were *his*. As a child, Wendy had loved him back, loved the way, when she and Aaron were kids, he'd been the adult to set up the horseshoes or bring out the bocce balls. He'd noticed and cheered when he'd seen her pick up ten jacks at once, and he'd paid her five dollars for the "darn good" likeness she drew of him when she was thirteen. And yet, over the years, she'd grown wary of Sam, afraid that his powerful love, when breached, could turn to powerful hate. When Aaron went to work for Rabin Trucking and Warehouse Industries last time, she'd watched him fire a secretary who'd worked for him for years—some slight misunderstanding that mushroomed into betrayal. Yet, even now, there was something about the pitch of his enthusiasm, his all-out, no-holds-barred love that satisfied something inside her, and she stepped into his open arms. "Nice," she said.

"Great food," Aaron mumbled. He didn't smile.

With one arm still around Wendy, Sam patted Aaron on the back. "Looks like you need a vacation from your vacation."

"Wendy's not feeling well. We won't be able to stay long."

"Aww." He squeezed Wendy's shoulders. "Let's talk to Bea. She has a remedy for everything." He walked her into the den where Bea and Becky were watching TV. "Wendy needs a picker-upper," he announced.

"Hi, Mom. That's okay. I'll be fine after a big hug from my baby." Wendy wriggled free of Sam's grasp to reach for Becky on the sofa as her mother-in-law unfolded all five feet and ten inches of herself from her chair. "Hey, Sweetie. How was your weekend?" Wendy asked, leaning forward so that her lips pressed against her daughter's wispy curls of auburn hair.

Becky rose and wrapped her arms tight around Wendy's waist. "Mommy!"

Wendy breathed in earth, mushrooms, flowers, sunshine, all there in Becky's hair. For an instant, she wished she never had to let go. Then Becky pulled away.

"I'll get dinner on," Bea said, stomping toward the kitchen. From the way Bea held her helmet of beauty-parlor blue, her chin pointing into the air, Wendy could tell her mother-in-law was in her usual stew about something. This time, she didn't feel up to the effort of finding out what it was. Ordinarily, she could take a breath and give herself enough time to empathize. As a therapist, motherless children moved her the most, and Bea was not only motherless (her mother died giving birth to a seventh child when Bea was six), but she'd grown up in the middle of the kind of family other Jews disowned, a dirt-poor family from Memphis. *There are Jews in Memphis?* Ever since she'd come north, Bea said, she'd been asked this question as soon as she began to speak. And if Jews had migrated to Memphis, hadn't they been merchants of one sort or another, peddlers whose sons owned the department stores their fathers had founded and whose grandsons would eventually sell out to a major chain and retire in Boca Raton to play golf? But Bea's father hadn't been a ragman who started a textile mill or a junk man who founded a trucking and storage business like her husband. He was the one thing that "didn't exist" in the Jewish community—a raging alcoholic, a jazz man who could play a mean sax, but who couldn't hold a job. Where once he'd fronted a band, by the time he was forty, he couldn't even sit in with the musicians on Beale Street. The whole brood lived with Bea's sullen and bitter grandparents, who despite the string of disreputable boarders, couldn't hold onto their home. Bea was put in an orphanage when she was eleven. She ran away at fifteen but managed to put herself through secretarial school cleaning houses.

Most Sundays, Wendy reminded herself of all Bea had endured as a child and could follow her sulking mother-in-law into the kitchen to listen and nod, making sympathizing noises as Bea told how the bridge club girls had snubbed her, or how she'd gotten less than her share of credit for co-chairing the Hadassah luncheon, though she'd done most of the work. But today Wendy was happy to let Bea's tizzy build into a raging storm. Let Sunday dinners cease!

"Zadie took me to the aviary." Becky smiled at her grandfather and stretched to pick up a large coffee table book. "And I got this."

"What a beautiful book." Wendy knelt beside Becky as her daughter turned the pages.

Becky pointed to a picture of a yellow-bellied sapsucker. "Did you know that sapsuckers drill holes in trees to drink the sap? Like at about a thousand pecks per minute."

"Cool."

Aaron hung back for a moment to say something quietly to his father, and then joined them. "Hey, Beck-a-Peck! How's the best daughter in the world?"

"Hi, Daddy." She giggled, handed the book to Wendy, and then reached her arms up to Aaron.

He held her for a long moment. "I missed you, darling."

"Did you see my book?"

"Show it to me."

Aaron sat in the leather armchair his mother had vacated and pulled Becky onto his lap.

"Give me the book, Mommy."

Aaron whispered in her ear.

"Please," she added.

Wendy handed the book to Becky. There was no room for her on that chair and nothing else to keep her from facing Bea. She called to her mother-in-law about helping with dinner.

"How are you, Mom?" Wendy said as she entered the kitchen, wishing she didn't have to find out.

Bea sighed. "A seven-year-old has a lot of energy. Darling, my arthritis is killing me."

"My parents will be back from Florida at the end of the month. Becky can stay with them next time."

"No. It's a pleasure. You've spoiled her, though, or the housekeeper has. She only eats bagels and ice and lemons. Lender's Bagel's. Not even good ones from Rosenfeld's."

"She's decided she wants to be thin."

"She's plenty thin. What? Is she anorexic?"

"Offer her ice cream and cookies. She'll eat plenty. She just gets these compulsions. Last month, she was living on hard boiled eggs, but only the whites."

"And you let her?"

"As long as she takes her vitamins. She'll grow out of it." It would make no difference to her mother-in-law if Wendy told her that she worried, too. Had even consulted Becky's pediatrician about it, who'd said that as long as her weight was within normal range and she showed no other symptoms, it was best, for now, to ignore the behavior. His advice made sense to her. Why pathologize what was probably a temporary stage?

Bea made a disapproving noise and shook her head. "Would you put this on the table, please?" She handed Wendy the butter dish.

Sam would be the only one who touched the dish, slathering butter on his potato kugel and Parker House rolls, despite his high cholesterol and the blood pressure medication he complained about taking. Wendy felt guilty as she set it on the table by his place, and then returned for more instructions.

She could see the hurt in Bea's eyes and the slight tremble around the sealed lips.

"What's the matter?" *Now*, Wendy thought, but didn't say.

"I don't know how you do all you do. You're just so busy." Wendy heard the whine in her voice—a hint of Brooklyn beneath the Tennessee overlay. Becky whined like that sometimes, right down to the Southern accent, which Wendy chalked up to her spending too much time with her grandmother and, maybe (and in Bea's eyes, this was *her* fault, of course), like Bea, not getting enough attention, despite being an only child.

"I *am* busy, but I'm here every Sunday, Mom."

"And that's it. Like a hair appointment. We never spend any real time together. I wanted to ask you to be my guest at the Synagogue fashion show next month, but I knew you'd say no, so I asked Rachel. She always makes time for me, even though she's a professor with *two* children and another on the way."

She thought she knew what Bea was leading up to. "Rachel's schedule is more flexible than mine. I have clients with standing weekly appointments who count on me to be there."

"You could call me once in a while, just to see how I'm doing. Ida's daughter-in-law calls her twice a week, and when Jimmy and Michele went to the Bahamas, Michele brought Ida a cocktail shaker with palm trees painted on." Bea's arms crossed her hefty old-world chest, the shelf on which her chin rested when she pouted. She was pouting now.

"I didn't see any cocktail shakers in Western Mass. I'm sorry."

"What would I want with a cocktail shaker? I don't need anything, darling. I was just giving an example of a little consideration, a little thoughtfulness. Here, take the potato kugel."

Wendy stood with the casserole dish. "Michele doesn't work." Last Sunday, Wendy would have hugged Bea and told her how grateful she was. Today, she couldn't.

"How much time does it take to pick up the phone?"

"I'm sorry, Mom. I call when I have something to say. I don't talk to my own mother every week."

"I thought I was getting a daughter when Aaron married you."

"You did. Just not the kind you wanted." She heard the quick intake of Bea's breath and turned to see the pain in her eyes. Wendy tried to smile then, and she reached her arm around Bea's waist. "You may have gotten an imperfect daughter-in-law, but you got a granddaughter who adores you."

"What about a grandson?"

There it was. The Rachel factor. Wendy dropped her arm and walked out of the kitchen without answering. Three kids? Was Aaron's cousin nuts? She set the potato kugel down with a bang, also by Sam's place, and went into the guest bathroom. She splashed cold water on her face, and then opened the medicine cabinet, hoping for aspirin. Nothing. And she felt too angry with Bea to ask her for anything. Why couldn't she be nicer to Bea, tonight? Usually she let the veiled insults and innuendos slide. Good material for the humorous stories she told her best friend Penny.

Becky wanted to sit beside Aaron at dinner, which left Wendy by herself on the other side, close to where she'd set the decanter of Mogen David. She poured herself a glass and drank it down quickly, flinching at the sweet, sticky taste. She refilled her glass and reached for the over-cooked green beans, the only thing, besides the wine, with color at the table. Aaron and Becky were talking about the mating habits of cardinals and why the males were more colorful and showier.

"If a female were bright red like the male, she'd be a target, sitting on her nest," Aaron explained. "She's safer if she blends in with the branch."

"But why does she have to sit on the nest? Why don't they share that responsibility?"

Sam laughed. "You've been listening to your mother and her friends."

Becky looked at Wendy, who rolled her eyes. "No, I haven't."

"Aren't you going to eat something besides green beans, Wendy?" Bea said. "What kind of an example is that?"

Wendy ignored her mother-in-law. Becky's plate was heaped high with potato kugel. "No bagels tonight, Becky?" she asked with a smile.

"Take a few green beans, and try a little brisket," Aaron said.

Becky made a face.

"Make Bubbie happy," Bea whined. "I've been cooking all afternoon."

"Nuh-uh. You were watching studio wrestling with me."

"Don't talk back to your Bubbie," Aaron said.

Bea smiled at Aaron. "Your cousin Rachel is pregnant again."

"Mazel tov to her," he said.

She turned to Wendy. "She's your age, dear."

"I know." In fact, Rachel was two years younger than Wendy.

"Time is running out," Bea said, "if you know what I mean."

"You'd like a baby brother, wouldn't you, Becky?" Sam said.

Becky nodded but said nothing. Wendy watched her face redden and remembered the conversation they'd had a few days ago about where babies came from. "The sperm in the father's penis enters the mother's vagina and travels up to th—," "Yuck!" Becky interrupted, covering her ears. "I don't want to hear." Later she'd come to Wendy, who was working on insurance forms in the living room and asked if Wendy had really let Daddy do that to her.

"You only had one child," Wendy said to Bea.

"But he was a son."

"What's wrong with girls?" Becky wanted to know.

"Nothing, sweetheart," Aaron said, covering her small hand with his large one. "Girls are wonderful, and you're the most wonderful."

"But girls get married," Bea said. "They don't carry on the family name."

"Well, I'm always going to be Becky Rabin. Nobody's going to make me change my name!"

"You absolutely don't have to, Sweetheart," Wendy said. "It's your choice."

Bea rolled her eyes. "Your mother is different. Girls usually do. That's the normal way."

"I think you may mean 'the traditional way,' Mom." Wendy paused, smiled. She should let it pass, but already she could feel the fists in her lap. "Not 'the normal way.'"

Color flushed into Bea's face. "I know what's normal and what isn't. I've lived a few more years than you have, darling."

Wendy ground her feet into the plush carpet beneath her. She clutched at her training as a therapist as it dissolved. "On lithium," she muttered. She could feel Aaron glaring at her, but she wouldn't look at him.

"How dare you?" Bea whispered, tears hovering on her lower lashes.

In that moment, Wendy wanted to take the words back, but Sam was already pounding the table, the dinner knife upright in his fist. "I won't have such talk at my table!"

Wendy could hear his breath, hard and rapid. And his face—*my god!* His face was beet red. "I'm sorry." What if he had a stroke, right now? She looked from him to Bea, whose mask of control was back in place beneath her clenched jaw. How much she and Aaron resembled each other in that moment. "Really, I'm sorry. I don't know what got into me."

"What's lithium?" Like a chime, Becky's voice changed everything. The adults at the table seemed to wake from their individual nightmares into the bad dream of a family dinner.

"Medicine that helps people think clearly and balance their energy," Wendy said.

"Lots of people take it," Aaron added.

"Now eat your green beans, honey pie." A brittle smile cracked Bea's cheeks, and she turned it toward Wendy. "You want to grow up pretty, like your Momma, so a smart man like Daddy asks you to marry him."

"Not me. I'm never getting married."

Bea gave Wendy a sharp look, as though Wendy had put the words in Becky's mouth. "But darling, you make Bubbie so happy. Don't *you* want to have a baby when you grow up? A pretty little girl to make your mother happy?"

Becky shook her head and looked at her plate.

"Well, your mom's going to have to get busy then," Sam said.

"I am busy. I have a heavy caseload and a household to run."

"If Aaron comes back into the business as our CFO, you won't have to work."

"Wendy doesn't *have* to work now," Aaron said.

"I love my work."

Aaron gave her his first smile of the evening.

"Can I please be excused?" Becky murmured, still staring at her plate. It was exactly what Wendy wanted to say.

"But you haven't eaten a thing!" Bea said.

"I'll feed her at home."

"I'm not hungry. Please, Mommy?"

"I'll come with you." Wendy rose and dropped her napkin on the table. She had to get out of here before she said something else awful and Sam keeled into his kugel.

Aaron stood, too. "Where are you going?"

"Becky and I can wait for you in the car. Please, give me the keys."

His jaw clenched, and he reached across the table. For a moment, she thought he might shove her back in her seat. Then he drew his arm back. "Sit down, please. Both of you. If you're not going to eat, you can at least keep us company." His voice was low and over-articulated. She knew that voice and the blast of rage it often preceded.

Wendy sat down again and nodded to Becky to do the same.

Aaron softened his voice. "Honey, please take a few bites," he said to Becky. "I worry about you when you don't eat."

Becky pushed her fork into the kugel and began to whimper. "I'm not hungry."

"Aaron," Wendy said quietly. "I think we need to leave."

"Not until Becky has eaten something."

"Little girls who cry at the table don't get dessert," Bea said.

"I'm not a little girl." Becky's lower lip pushed out just like her grandmother's.

"Come on, Beckala. Take a bite for your Bubbie," Sam said. "A couple of bites and you can have ice cream for dessert."

Wendy watched her daughter's trembling hand try to manage a forkful of cheesy potatoes. As Becky raised her head to bring it to her lips, Wendy could see the tears rolling down her cheeks and knew she wouldn't be able to swallow. "Please, let her be. Who cares if she eats her kugel tonight? She's not starving."

"Leave the girl alone, Sam," Bea said. "The mother has spoken."

Wendy rose. All around the table, she saw hard eyes, faces slammed shut against her.

Becky lowered her fork and began to sob silently, her chest heaving. Wendy moved around the table to hold her, and Becky let herself sink against her mother's skirt, crying loudly now.

"I guess we'd better leave, Dad," Aaron said, standing. "I'm sorry, Mom."

"You're damn right, you better leave!" Sam's voice was a low growl.

It was an awkward departure. They had to stand there in the front hall, waiting for Bea to help Becky gather her things from the guest room. Sam breathed audibly.

"Are you okay?" Wendy asked, not meeting his eyes.

"Where's your nitro, Sam?" Bea said as she entered the foyer with Becky's backpack.

Both Sam and Bea turned their cheeks away when she tried to kiss them good-bye. No one spoke as they walked to the car.

Wendy helped Becky buckle into her car seat, then walked around and opened the other back door.

Aaron craned his neck around as she started to climb in. "She's not a baby. Are you, precious?" He smiled at Becky.

She shook her head, but her face was quivering, and Wendy could tell she would begin to weep again.

Wendy bent forward and kissed her cheek. "You graduate from that car seat next month, Sweetheart."

Becky's face brightened. "On my birthday?"

"Yup," Aaron added. "All you'll need is a seatbelt to be a legal child."

"But can Mommy sit with me now? I'm sad and mad."

"I see that you're sad and mad, and I'm proud of you for talking about how you feel. We can talk more when we get home. Right now, I'm going to sit up front with Daddy." Wendy craned her neck to address Aaron. "Honey, would you push the trunk release, please? I want to give Becky her present."

"When we get home," Aaron said.

"Please, Daddy. I won't cry anymore."

"She won't be able to do anything with it in the dark," he muttered to Wendy. Then he leaned over the seat. "No more crying, Miss Pecky. I've got your word for it?" Becky nodded, and he hit the trunk button.

Wendy went around to the back of the car then climbed in front with Aaron and handed the paper bag over the seat. "Here, sweetheart."

Becky ripped the coloring book out of the bag. "What does 'ana-to-my' mean?"

"Anatomy. It's the parts of the body—bones, muscles, nerves, organs. You can learn where everything is in your own body as you color."

"But I don't have my crayons."

"It's too dark now, anyway," Aaron said. "You can color at home."

It began to rain as they merged into the highway traffic. Aaron was silent, staring straight ahead. Only the sound of the wheels against the wet pavement disturbed the quiet. As the dinner scene replayed in her mind, Wendy was shocked by what she'd done. Something in her had rejoiced, if only for an instant, but then it had all collapsed—their faces, the family dinner, her confidence. From the look on Aaron's face, it would take more than an apology.

Wendy glanced over the seat. "She's sleeping."

He continued to stare straight ahead. She watched the landscape passing. In the glimmer of oncoming headlights, she could see the taut line of Aaron's jaw.

He took the Newton/Watertown exit, and they drove past the familiar scenery on Washington Street without speaking. They passed a low-rise building that had once housed her father's real estate agency, now a laundromat. And there was the clinic where she worked, where tomorrow she would see Cal. Where, for a brief time, none of this would matter. But it all mattered. She knew it did.

Though Aaron was looking straight ahead, she had to tell him when the light turned green on the corner of Washington and Centre.

He scowled at her with that "who's driving?" look, and then turned back to the road. He drove faster than usual through the business district on Centre Street, swinging wide onto Pearl.

She closed her eyes as they passed Lincoln, her elementary alma mater, now Becky's school, a few blocks from their house. There had been thirty-six students in Wendy's first-grade class. Miss O'Reilly. Short, blond hair, tight skirt over a tighter rump, red lipstick. Pretty Miss O'Reilly. Wendy had been in love. Just as she'd kissed the television screen, in love with Miss Jean from

"Romper Room," she wished Miss O'Reilly was her mother. She had Miss Palumbo for second. She loved Miss Palumbo too. But Miss Sweet in the third grade was nothing like her name. She yelled at Ralph Simms, the boy from the foster home, when he didn't pay attention. For the same reason, she yelled at Wendy, who, that year, definitely preferred her own mother to Miss Sweet.

Aaron turned onto Cedarhurst. A few minutes later, they were pulling into the driveway, silently unloading the car. She wondered if he'd speak to her after Becky was in bed.

He carried their sleeping daughter up to her room. "I'll tuck her in," he whispered.

Later, when Wendy emerged from the bathroom, Aaron was lying face down on the bed, still in his clothes. He turned his head to look at her.

"You're going to have to apologize to my mother," he said.

She pulled the clip from her hair and let it tumble down her back. She reached for the brush on her nightstand and stood brushing out the tangles. "I shouldn't have said that, I know. There's no excuse for hurting your mother, but if I don't apologize, we won't have to go next Sunday. I can't take another family dinner with us the way we are, with your mother digging at me."

He rose to his elbows. "I have never, in my life, been so humiliated. Your behavior was unconscionable. You are not the woman I married."

She sat down hard on the edge of the bed. "Your mother tells me what to put on my plate, nags me to make her another grandchild, even as she says I'm a bad mother."

"She never said you were a bad mother."

"It's always implied. You should have heard her in the kitchen."

"What's gotten into you? It's never bothered you before."

"It's *always* bothered me before. I'm usually working hard to be understanding. I'm sorry. I just couldn't muster the compassion today."

"I'm asking for a simple apology! It's a small price to pay for everything they do for us."

"Tell me you didn't ask your father for another loan."

He rolled onto his back. "When I get that payment from Papercraft, I'll pay him back. Do you realize how much they owe me?"

"Every time you ask him for money, they think they can control our lives. Pretty soon, you'll be working for him, and I'll be calling your mother twice a week."

"Look, since when is a note to my mother such a big deal?" His tone was different, now—softer, pleading. "Wendy, please?"

She felt herself stiffen as he stroked her back. "It's a huge deal. I can't take another potato kugel."

"I'll tell her to make noodle kugel."

Wendy laughed—a momentary analgesic. "Worse," she turned to him, almost ready to smile.

"It's not about food. It's about family," he said.

"I know." She nodded, sighed. "Can't I take a time out from Sunday dinners for a month or so?"

"For the sake of your feelings, you'll destroy our family life?"

She flinched, as though he'd drilled through to raw nerve. Her jaw tightened against the edge of truth.

"Becky needs her grandparents," he continued.

"Of course, she does. But why do I have to go?"

"Because you're my wife."

I should be unpacking my hand mirror right now, she thought. The Novocain is wearing off.

The temple bells bring Wendy out of her reverie. Another busy meditation of memory. Has she come to the ashram nearly twenty years after the divorce to finally face her feelings without numbing out? Maybe that's the true gift of Saraswati's little red book. She sighs as she rolls off her cushion and climbs to her feet. Bea had been harmless, really—an easy target for their dying marriage. Wouldn't she have more understanding for her now? If only for Becky's sake. She would have been a better mom today at nearly 60, even if she could never measure up as a wife.

She walks slowly up the mountain trail, careful of tree roots and rocks. No more stumbling. So many mistakes in one human life. Can she ever forgive herself?

CHAPTER *Six*

 1941

I must have fallen asleep, for I am being shaken by the tiny hands of my brother, who is crying. When I look down at myself, I can see why he cries. My hair is quite wild, and my salwar kameez is undone, the top nearly over my head; the bottoms askew. Quickly, I adjust my clothing. "Dear Ganesha," I say to him as gently as I can, "do not be afraid. Your sister is fine. I slept, and I was very hot."

He rubs his eyes and climbs into my lap, just as he did with Amma. I cannot help wondering whose lap he will find if Shakuntala comes here. I rock him and sing the lullaby that Amma sang to me. Soon he is napping in my arms. It is time to prepare the rice for Appa's dinner, but I do not wish to disturb Ganesha. I do not wish to disturb myself.

I must have fallen asleep again, because Ganesha is still on my lap when Appa arrives. He too looks frightened when he sees me. I follow his gaze around the room and see the spilled can of lentils and the basket of rice that has been knocked on the floor. "What is going on, Saraswati?" he says. Ganesha looks at Appa and begins to cry.

"Hush, Ganesha," I whisper. "All is well." I turn to my father. "Do not worry, Appa. I will clean the house now." I push Ganesha off my lap, climb to my feet and reach for the broom.

"Your hair! All tangles and knots. How did it come unbound and loose around your shoulders, daughter?" My father takes my arms so the broom slips from my grasp. "I want to know what happened in my house!"

Will he believe me? Will he bring the doctor, or worse, will he send me away, cast me out like a demon, so he can move his darling Shakuntala in? "Appa, I do not know," I say. No, that is wrong. He will think I am crazy. I look directly into his eyes, and he does not avert his gaze.

"I am waiting, daughter."

"I did Shiva aarti, and while I was praying to my Lord, he ... he came to me."

"How do you mean that?"

I shift my gaze to Little Brother, who stares at me with wide eyes, and then I wrench away from my father. "I do not ... I cannot ... speak of it."

He steps back, and then surveys the room slowly. "Fix yourself, daughter, and fix this house." My father leaves.

As I adjust my *salwar shameez*, I notice it's straining across the new roundness at my chest. Will he send me away from all that I love?

. . .

WENDY LETS THE PAGES she has read drift to the floor. Once in Sedona, Arizona, after the divorce, when she and Becky were camping high off Schnebly Hill Road, she had awakened before dawn, left her sleeping daughter a note and climbed the mountain behind their tent. She was on her mat in bridge pose, chanting

Ram, as the sun rose when it happened. Only the sun touching her, a moment of light, of enchantment, and she had come. She has never told anyone, but sought out the poetry of mystics—Mirabai, of course, but also Hildegard of Bingen and Teresa of Avila, and Rumi. What does it mean, this ecstasy? In her clinical training, such episodes had labels, were symptomatic, pointing to mania, hysteria, or religiosity—what her textbooks called a form of obsessive-compulsive disorder. She has never felt closer to the divine.

And Becky—as Wendy rises from the chair to get ready for bed, she remembers the rapture on her daughter's face dancing solo at the Jewish Community Center, and on the outdoor stage where the students performed at Jacob's Pillow, and at the 92nd Street Y, and in a loft performance space in Chelsea, and around the living room in every home they've ever lived. Becky must have experienced these moments too, so transported by the creation of new choreography for her dance troupe, that she's immune to distraction or disturbance or mundane items on her many lists like doing the dishes or laundry or returning a phone call. Wendy figures it's about 10 to 1 these days. Ten attempts on her part to reach out to Becky until one of them is answered. When Becky doesn't respond, she worries, and she tries to turn worry into prayer, which she believes would do a lot more good than the disaster fantasies that blossom in her mind when the silence has gone on too long.

She'll call Becky tomorrow, she thinks, as she turns off the bedside lamp.

It is 4:40 am when she opens her eyes, and Wendy is grateful to be able to shower before the first meditation. As she enters the hall, she picks up a cushion and wraps her moth-eaten Indian shawl around her. It's the same white wool with red embroidery she had folded in her backpack when she met the temple dancer. She settles in, ready to welcome the morning with the ashram residents. For a moment, she gazes, unblinking, at the slender *ghee* lamp burning in front of the *yantra*, the beautiful symmetrical pattern of color that hangs above the altar. She closes her eyes as the first morning chant begins. With everyone else, she does the *pranayama* and *kriya* breathing practices until the room settles into silence, broken by an occasional cough, a deep sigh, the belly rumble of the woman behind her, and then her own. Before the end of practice, they will all rise for *aarti*, and one of the devotees will gently sway the lamp to honor the Guru and the Guru's guru, the *yantra*, and the statues of Shiva, the destroyer, and Ganesha, the wise elephant god of new beginnings. Wendy loves this part, waiting gratefully for the leader to wave the light of the aarti lamp in her direction. This morning, especially, Wendy looks forward to *aarti*, imagining the lamp in Saraswati's small hands.

Year after year, even before her divorce, Wendy has come to this ashram. This is where she took her first yoga class. She has not become a disciple, although she loves the community living here and those who are drawn to visit. The Guru died two years before her first visit, and yet she feels his presence on the land and in the eyes and actions of his devotees. "Love All. Serve All." He offered this simple instruction that shapes the welcome she and every guest receive. From each visit, she brings home a book, a DVD of a *satsang* talk, a CD of the Guru chanting. Almost as if he is alive, she finds herself talking to him, asking for guidance. A day doesn't pass without a petitioning prayer for protection for her daughter. She prays to God, but the Guru is there too, like the partner you text at the end of a trip to say you've landed. For herself, most often these days, she asks for the trust to love deeply and openly and to work the same way.

She enjoys the work she does as a therapist. But sometimes the darkness of a client's story penetrates the room. Lately she's been trying to let in more light. Yoga works for her. Why not add it to her treatment plan for someone like Karen with a history of trauma and substance abuse? Or Geoff who can't sleep more than four hours a night?

For a long time, before she found yoga, making art seemed necessary—the antidote to terror. She couldn't have articulated it then, but now she sees that somehow painting kept terror reigned in, wild beneath the surface but contained. When she stopped, something raw and unprocessed like sewage seeped into her marriage and poisoned the life she'd known. Her yoga practice has cleaned the sewers. If she painted now—color, line, image—she's not sure, but she thinks it would come from a clearer place. And maybe true art is like draining the swamp of unanalyzed terror. She thinks of Van Gogh, Pollack, Munch, Schiele, Dali. Maybe she's too sane. Too female. Too happy. She's thought about setting up a studio again, a place big enough for an easel and canvas stretched long and wide. On her 57th birthday almost three years ago, after years without making art, she bought herself a sketch pad. What came to her were ancient hand gestures abstracted in rings of fire. Her efforts embarrassed her, and most of the pages remain empty. She needs to work from nature or join an open studio and retrain her hand to capture her vision—what is actually seen. And then, when she can do that, she can trust the given to be revealed through the view from the spaciousness within.

Startled from her reverie by the *mahamrityunjaya* mantra rising in the room that accompanies prayers for loved ones in need, she sends out a prayer to Saraswati and the spirits of all the devadasi. She hasn't accomplished anything of what Saraswati had asked of her. She asks now to know how to honor the gift of the little red book.

1941

Father is home now, and I have kept the fire going all this time. He asks that *mahaprasad* be served to the guest he has brought with him, so I take the coconut pieces blessed by the Gods from our altar and put them on a plantain leaf. This guest is a Brahmin priest, dressed as such with the markings on his forehead, and he cannot eat the food I have cooked on the fire. Ribs poke out from his bare chest. I feel his dark eyes, studying me as I serve him, and I think that Appa has told him something about me. As I complete the service and prepare to remove myself, Appa asks me to stay.

"What is your name?" the guest asks.

"Saraswati."

"Can you sing?"

"I sing devotional songs, Sir." I think it best not to mention the film songs I used to sing with Lakshmi.

"Can you dance?"

"I have no training, but yes I believe God has given me the ability to dance."

"Turn around," he says.

I do so, feeling his eyes all over me, slippery as sesame oil.

"Fine. Now sing something."

"What would you like, Sir?"

"Anything. I want to hear your voice."

I close my eyes and my Amma's voice comes to me, singing a divine chant to the Goddess of our village. I share Amma's voice with our guest.

He nods and smiles. "This is excellent," he says. "Your father is quite right. There are knots in your hair."

"You may go now, Saraswati," Appa says, and I go out to tend the fire, squatting beside it as the men continue to talk.

A few minutes pass and then the guest comes out of our house. He strokes my hair, lifting a knotted lock and twisting it through his fingers. "You will be quite beautiful one day," he says as he lets it fall. I back away from the firelight, and he passes on his way. No man but Appa has ever touched me before. I shake my head vigorously as though I could shake off his boney hand.

I hear my father call me from inside the house. "Come, child," he says. "Bring my dinner."

I enter with his food, set it before him and retreat. I go to Little Brother to check that he is sleeping comfortably. When Appa has finished, he calls me to clear. "When you have thrown away the leaves and washed my spoon, come back, Saraswati. I wish to speak to you, my dear."

I am comforted by his tone. And yet I am afraid, for I did not like the stranger, and my father may have sought his advice about me. It could not be that I am to be married to him, for a girl of my caste cannot even cook his meals. How could I possibly serve his ancestors? I once heard from a friend at school that some men take women, but do not marry them. I do not think my Appa would let him take me.

"Dear child," my Appa says in a very solemn voice. "Chandrakant, the priest has seen the knots in your hair. It is a sure sign, he says, that you belong to the Goddess. You are to be dedicated to God. This is a great privilege for you and a great honor you bestow upon our family."

"I am to become a *devadasi*?" I remember the beautiful woman dressed in silk and adorned with jeweled ornaments, who danced and sang at my sister's wedding. When she entered the wedding tent, my father had bowed to her.

"But Appa, I am of a different caste. How can this be?"

"The priest himself will arrange it."

"But who will sponsor me before the *Rajah*?"

"So many questions, Saraswati! Is not your Appa responsible for your well-being? I thought this news would please you."

I bow at my father's feet, then rise to sit on my heels. "I am humbly grateful before your decision," I manage to say. I am confused and excited and also afraid. There are so many questions. "I don't understand this news. Please let me ask questions, Appa."

"Very well, but do not expect answers."

"How will I learn?"

"Chandrakant will arrange it. He will be your *acharya*."

"But he is not a devadasi."

Appa sighs. "In religious matters only. He will arrange your adoption by a devadasi who is childless and has no daughter to whom she can pass on the tradition. She and your dance master will teach you all you need to know."

"Would I live here, then, and visit my teacher?"

"It will be the other way around."

"But Ganesha needs me."

"He will have a new mother, since I am to marry."

My lashes are not strong enough to catch the runaway tear. Appa holds out his arms, and I go to him. "You shall be a most auspicious woman, my child. You will dance the sacred rituals in the temple. You will be honored with gifts of gold and cattle and land. None but a devadasi can walk about in the village. You will be able to visit us here at any time. You will not marry any mortal man, so you will never be a widow. You, my dear Saraswati, shall marry God." He pushes me back, so I am at arm's length and he can look at me. "I have long thought that this is right for you, my child. Your fervor in prayer and in dance will be honored in this ancient tradition. I believe you were born to be dedicated."

I nod my head. "This ... can it be true, Appa? But if it means I must leave you and Little Brother, and all the things that were Amma's ... I ... I do not want this honor."

"Amma would be so happy for you. She would bless you in this. As a devadasi, you will not only be serving God, but you will serve your family. The abundance you receive will support your brother's education more easily than the thousands of beedis you have been rolling. And you will be able to support your Appa in his old age."

"How is this possible?"

Appa looks into my eyes and then away. He squeezes my hand. "These are the things you will be taught," he says.

. . .

WENDY SHUDDERS AS SHE takes off her reading glasses. This honor she's been offered, this opportunity to be educated ... is she being trafficked? Absurd how protective she feels about this little girl, when she hadn't been able to protect her own daughter. She remembers when she was ferocious about protecting Becky. The time before she wasn't. Becky must have been in first grade then.

She stood barefoot in her blue plaid nightgown, choosing her clothes, imagining how Cal might see her, when she heard a sound that brought her running down the stairs to the front window.

What she saw was the yellow school bus, huffing exhaust like a felled elephant, lodged at an angle between the telephone pole and the Stein's front gate. And scattered like multicolored marbles in the snow—the neighborhood kids in their blue down vests and hooded red parkas and purple ski caps.

She bolted through the door. There was her neighbor's gray Volvo station wagon stopped behind the bus. That was her neighbor Gregory Stein leaning over a small form. *Blue and red and silver!* Oh, my God! Had Becky worn her Patriots scarf this morning? Could that be her? *No, please God, no. I'll never paint again.* Don't let it be her. As she ran through the slush of week-old snow that covered their adjoining lawns, she saw Gregory—what? *Lifting?* Oh, God, yes—*Becky!* out of the snowbank lining the driveway.

Or was she getting up on her own?

Becky brushed the snow off her stadium coat and swatted at her scarf. "Hi, Mommy."

Thank God! Wendy pulled her daughter to her. Over Becky's head, she watched the other children scrambling out of the snow, laughing, pushing each other through the gaping door of the bus as the burly driver shoved through them onto the driveway.

"Going too fast," Gregory said, "Lucky you didn't hit anything."

"Or anyone," Wendy added. She thought of the potential target of children who regularly waited at the curb in front of Stein's driveway.

"Black ice." The driver checked his distance from the pole, gauging his back up maneuvers. His white navel framed in black hair was visible between his blue tee shirt and jeans.

Back on the bus, the small—*were they frightened?*—faces pressed against the glass.

Wendy's heartbeat rattled in her ears. "They must be terrified."

"Hell, no. Curious, is all," the bus driver said. He gave her a look like *she* was the crazy one, and then hefted himself onto the bus.

Gregory's hand was on the roof of the Volvo. He looked annoyed, anxious to be gone.

Her daughter was fine, pulling away, smiling, talking, already moving toward the school bus. Then why was *she* shaking?

"Linny's waiting," Becky said. "I gotta go."

"But honey ... don't you want me to drive you to school?"

"It's okay, Mommy. I forgot my homework, but I got it." She held up a wet sheet of lined paper—the vocabulary words they'd gone over last night—then ran for the quivering bus.

At the snap of the doors folding shut, Wendy's knees buckled, and she leaned against the car.

"Jesus, Wendy. What's wrong with you? They're all fine. I need to get going."

As the bus rumbled off, she took a deep breath, straightened. "We should report this. The principal, the school board, the bus company. Somebody."

He opened his door. "Not now. I'm late for work." But he stood for a moment, grimacing at something behind her.

Then she felt a blanket being draped across her shoulders and looked around to see her best friend, Penny Stein. Penny's nose wrinkled into her forehead; her wide lips puckered tight like a grandmother kissing a grandchild's cheek.

"God. You're barefoot," Penny said.

Wendy looked at her bluish feet.

Gregory climbed into his car, mumbling something she couldn't quite hear, but she thought she caught the word "hysterical." She watched the school bus round the corner and disappear.

"Come!" Penny nudged her. "In the house. I'll make tea."

Like a little linebacker, Penny pushed Wendy's blanket-wrapped body up the walk. Wendy had been avoiding this. Her best friend's kitchen. The cup of tea. There was no way to lie to Penny.

And she didn't lie. She told Penny about Cal.

That was years before the affair had even begun, when she was still in control of her senses, but not her heart and certainly not her body's response when he passed in the hall, casually, intentionally, brushing against her arm, or gazing for a second too long during a meeting.

She hadn't given in to the call and response of his attention and her desire until later, when Cal had seemed the perfect antidote to those restless mornings after Becky left for school, before she saw clients. Those were the early hours when she used to paint. They'd made love on the foldout couch in his office, meeting before the receptionist arrived, hoping to be done before the other therapists and staff gathered around the coffee urn in the break room. But although she was careful to reapply lipstick and straighten her clothes, there was always someone lurking about when she opened the door to the hall. Lurking and smirking. They had to stop.

"Don't worry about it," he would say. "I'm the boss. No one will do anything." But she knew he worried too, worried most about what it would do to his wife and his grown children if he left. They lived in a cloud of guilt and desire.

Countless times, she had called a halt, asking for no contact; afraid for him, for her, for their families, their professional lives.

Damn, his email read, after one such attempt. *I know I said you had to be the one to end it, but how can I let you go? Just tell myself that the most important thing in my life (I mean that) is gone? How do I do that? How do I avoid seeing you, thinking about you? How do I do that? I love Denise, but I have never felt anything like what I feel for you (I really, truly mean that). I know it's wrong on many levels, hell, what can I promise you? I don't even know how much longer I'm going to be on this planet. But somehow, someway I would have made this work because I have never felt so right about anything in my life. My first reaction was to walk down the hall, open your office door and take you in my arms. Staff be damned! You have no idea (or maybe you do) how much I want to see you and hold and tell you that it will be what it should be.*

Quite simply, I just love you Wendy, that's all. That's all it's ever been.

She would read an email like that and her resolve would crumble, along with rational thought. She was dizzy with love, drunk with it, addicted. God, she even tried a love addict's anonymous group, despite her fears of running into a client. But she could never hold to the 90 days of sobriety. Their "separations" never lasted more than a week or two. The yearning, oh the yearning. The shimmer on her skin being near him in a meeting. The way her breath caught when he looked at her. The memory of their intimacy, the sense of absolute oneness in his arms, she was crazed. They were crazed. It's over, she said, but she always went back to the couch in the morning, to the weekend conferences in Philadelphia, in Atlanta, Washington, D.C., the trainings in Boston and in Phoenix.

The seed had been planted the day she interviewed at the clinic, when she looked at him for the first time and had that irrational thought, *we are for each other*. Tiny wings of disbelief and wonder had fluttered in her chest. He was older by ten or maybe even more years. Later she would learn, by nearly twenty. But he had the vitality of a younger man. He rode his bike to work when it was warm enough and exercised every day. He ran 5Ks, and in his younger days, marathons, triathlons. They danced around their feelings for all the thirteen years she had worked at the clinic, worked for him. She was married. He was married.

But he began to send her poetry—"*We are each of us angels with only one wing, and we can fly only by embracing each other," the way I figure it, you've got my other wing*—leave music mixes on her desk, invite her to long lunches where he told her that he couldn't live without her, that he had known it from the moment they met. She held off for years, thinking about quitting and then not, because if she left the clinic, she wouldn't see him, sense his nearness. She woke up each morning with the longing fresh in her heart. Seeing him would be enough. It had to be. There was Aaron. There was Becky. And it had been enough until the weekend with Aaron at the New Hope Inn. Only days after that, she found the Rumi poem on her desk. He'd highlighted the lines: *Lovers don't finally find each other/They've been in each other all along*. It was exactly how she felt. At lunch that day she agreed to go away with him to a week-long trauma training in Boulder—the clinic would pay. And that was it. The affair began.

They rode a roller coaster of stops and starts, her ending it, his desperate emails and calls, her caving in. There was nothing casual about their affair for either of them. She believed he wanted to leave his wife, that he thought he could do it, but his sense of duty was too strong. After one break-up, he wrote her an email explaining all he planned to do. How he had another talk with his wife Denise about his feelings for her. How he was going to see his lawyer, his cardiologist, his orthopedist, call his best friend in California, what he planned to say to his daughter in college in Boston, his son working in New York, and on and on. She held onto the words at the end of the message—*you are not responsible for the end of my marriage because I fell in love with you. I MADE THE OVERTURES, NOT YOU. Bottom line, I want you, I love you, I need you, and that's just the way it is. I want us together—in Florida, in Arizona, Mexico, Italy, wherever the hell we wind up. God, I hope you get this email; I'll have no way of knowing since you've elected to cut me off. Be good, be careful, be mine sometime, somewhere. solo tu*

Even on that morning in his office in early November, when she felt she had no choice but to end it, leaving the clinic if that's what it took, and he stood, unfolding his six-foot body from the couch, which she had not let him pull out, the future seemed unbearable without him. The rush of sensation in that moment was nearly the same current that ran through her when she'd entered his office for her interview all those years ago. Only now they had a history, memories of pleasure and pain. And moments, indescribable moments of oneness that the language of love could not frame. She knew she would have to resign from the clinic. But she didn't.

She'd tried to settle back into the job, avoiding times when they might find themselves alone. She tried too to settle into her life in Newton Village, to be a good mother, even if she wasn't a good enough wife. But Cal wasn't done with her yet, and when she didn't respond to emails or messages left on her cell phone, things began to change at the clinic. It was hard to pinpoint at first. And it was slow to happen. But as current clients terminated therapy, only certain kinds of cases were assigned to her, cases that required extra supervision, which meant consultations with Cal that she should have scheduled but didn't. She had once treated a variety of people who had come to her in the throes of transformation or grief or trouble—kids, couples, women leaving marriages, families. Now her case load was weighed down with suicidal teenagers and borderline women who followed her home and called the house at night.

She'd handled it well for a while, but then a seventeen-year-old anorexic slit her wrists after a session. The girl didn't die, but questions were raised—why hadn't Wendy seen this coming? Why hadn't hospitalization been discussed with the family? Worse than the defense of her treatment to Cal and the review board at the clinic, was her own guilt. She hadn't protected her client.

Six weeks later, another client's parents filed a complaint. Their fourteen-year-old, who had already been expelled from both public then parochial school was chanting Om and humming like a bee, practices he said Wendy had taught him to calm him down, which were, in his parents' mind, if not the work of Satan, definitely against their religious convictions. Weird stuff that had nothing to do with therapy. When she was forced to meet with Cal to discuss her treatment of the client and the family's complaint, he said there were certain conditions under which he would defend her. His smile told her all she needed to know about those conditions, and she stood to leave. He came around his desk and grabbed her arms. "Wendy, please. Come back. I can't live like this. I love you."

She struggled free of his grasp. "Come back to a few minutes on a pull-out couch? Sneaking around the clinic? Feeling guilt and dread?"

"And what else did you feel?"

"Love. I loved you, Cal. I still do." She turned away, not sure if she could say what was taking shape in her mind, surprising even herself as she spoke. "You made empty promises. I know you believed you could make the fantasy come true someday, but you can't. We can't have a life together."

"You're wrong, Wendy. Somehow, I know we can."

She turned back, tears streaming down her face. "Then call Denise now. Tell her you won't be coming home, except to pack your bags."

He turned away. "That's ... not ... possible."

"Heart-breaking, I know," she said, thinking of all the people they would hurt. "But possible."

There were tears in his eyes, and he brushed them away, looked down at the floor, let out a low moan. "Not for me."

She reached for the doorknob with her back toward him, so he couldn't see her body shaking. "I resign." She stumbled out of his office and straight into Barb, the office receptionist.

"I was just going to knock. Your husband's on the phone. Do you want to take it in your office?"

She was still crying when she told Aaron she had resigned, that the pressure was too much.

"That's good," Aaron said, "because I just got a call from your boss's wife. She says you're having an affair with him."

The worst had happened. She didn't know what to say, so she told the truth.

Yes, and it had been over for six months.

She thought they would go into counseling together, that he would understand the dissatisfaction she'd felt after she gave up painting. But as well as she thought she knew him, she was wrong.

"You are morally bankrupt, Wendy. You will never get custody of Becky," he said before hanging up on her.

It hit her then, although she and Aaron moved toward and away from each other like an accordion for another year—*happilymarried* had been exposed for the lie it was. She had torn her family apart.

Bereft, humiliated, unmoored after the divorce was final, she had gone to India in 1997 to see Guru Nityananda one last time. She had not been home to protect Becky. But then, neither was Becky. She was at ski camp in the Berkshires.

CHAPTER Seven

1941

Two days have passed. Chandrakant comes once more. Again, I serve him the coconut mahaprasad from the altar, and again he stares. I feel his eyes slide down my body like oiled hands. He strokes my back when I bend at his feet to serve him the coconut. When I look to Appa, I see he has turned away. I wait outside by the fire. My future is in the hands of my father, whom I trust, and in the hands of Chandrakant, whom I do not. When I hear the motions of Chandrakant's leave-taking, I back away from the fire into the moonless night, so he cannot touch me again. I watch him stop by the fire, and look around for a moment, and then walk away. After some time, I enter the house.

Appa smiles at me. "Tomorrow you will meet your new mother," he says. "Varani is a most beautiful devadasi. She is well favored by the king. Even though you are a little old already, your dedication is assured." He looks away, but I see his chin tremble. "We are fortunate you have not yet become a woman."

Never has my father spoken to me of such things, and I do not know where to cast my gaze. "Tomorrow I leave, Appa?"

"My child." He takes my hand and draws me into the circle of his arms. I feel the warmth of my Appa's love, before he pulls back, his hands on my shoulders. "You will be able to visit us here. She does not live so far away. Just behind the temple. She has a fine two-story house, much better than this one."

"Should I gather my things?"

He releases me. "You need not take much. She will provide you with finer garments than what you have, and she will give you your own bowl."

"But who is paying for all this, Appa?"

"She wants a daughter to teach and to love. She will bear the expense. You will pay her back many times over when you become a devadasi."

"What about the dedication and the feast and the celebration?"

Appa does not answer right away. "Chandrakant will take care of it."

"The priest? Why?"

"He, too, will be repaid." My father claps his hands. "Enough! Prepare yourself for your departure."

Ahh, ahh, I am so afraid. Where is my dear sister? My Amma? There is no one with whom I can speak. I sit before the altar. Appa must not see my tears nor hear my lament. All that I have is here before me. My Amma's altar here, the aarti lamp, the pictures of Goddess Lakshmi and Lord Ganesha. The little statues of Saraswati and Nataraja. I must take something. Amma always said Saraswati was mine, and I was Saraswati's. We are one. We go together. I shall hide her in my bundle. "Be with me, oh divine Goddess," I whisper as I look into her cold metal face. She does not respond. What will become of me? I am so alone.

. . .

ALONE. SHE SET THE pages down, remembering leaving Becky for that month in India. She shouldn't have left, not when Becky still needed reassurance that it was not her fault; that though Mommy and Daddy weren't going to live together anymore, they both still loved her. It's what she said, what she and Aaron both said, and what the therapist they hired for Becky said.

Maybe Becky would have believed it if she hadn't been alone after the assault, if Wendy had been there with her rather than traveling on a train in Southern India.

There are some memories she cannot entertain for long, and this is one of them. When she got off the train in Chennai, she'd gone to an ashram and was offline, meditating, praying, chanting and not where she needed to be. She hadn't learned what happened in the *safety* of ski camp until two days later when she had gone to an internet café in the city to check her emails. She couldn't have prevented what the assistant camp director, a man in his twenties, had done to her ten-year-old daughter, nor how the counselor had discovered them and begun to scream; nor how, in that moment, Becky believed that the counselor was screaming at her. That she was the bad one. But Wendy should have been there every second of the day for the next week or month or year or whatever it took until Becky could go to sleep with the light turned out; until the nightmares stopped; until Becky began to laugh and dance again, until Becky stopped screaming at the walls. With the diary tucked in her backpack, Wendy had gone straight to a travel agent to change her flight home. Even so, it was another three days until she could hold her daughter in her arms and tell her yet again, "It's not your fault."

For the first time, Becky pulled away from her. "Leave me alone!"

Wendy shakes herself out of the memory, too late to stop the tears, too late to interrupt the familiar refrain. *What kind of mother leaves her child at such a vulnerable time?* It doesn't matter that years of therapy have provided the answer—one who was herself unmothered, one who has never been able to grieve her own mother's death. There is something missing in her, and in her mother, and in her grandmother, and in the whole matrilineage of daughters who didn't get enough. She had thought she would be different. How full of love she is for Becky. She is that fullness. It's one reason she kept Aaron's surname after the divorce. She didn't want anything, *not anything,* to separate them. Her mother could never have felt this way ... could she? She reaches for a tissue on the nightstand, wipes her eyes and looks up at the Guru's picture that hangs on the wall across from the bed. Years of spiritual practice have shown her that there is something full to the brim in her. She is more than this emptiness, this fullness, more than these concepts. She thinks of a line from a Rumi poem—*Out beyond ideas of wrongdoing and right doing there is a field. I'll meet you there.* She is that field.

As the years passed, there could not have been anything worse for Wendy than the terrible clutching in her heart when she reached for Becky, and Becky turned away. It happened more than it didn't. Now and then when Becky was hurt by a school friend, or when she was sick, or the time she stayed home on a Saturday night when she had expected to go out with a group who for some reason hadn't included her, she sometimes settled in, rested against her mother's chest in the old way, the familiar way, the way of childhood and of longing that seemed to satisfy them both. But those moments were rare, and Wendy moved through her days with the hope, slight though it was and almost unacknowledged, that another moment would arrive. Maybe just a gaze: eyes meeting, a kind of communion, as though seeing the horizon of sea and sky at sunrise.

There was so much else in her life after the divorce, especially after she and Becky moved to Providence. So much to contend with: building her private practice, supervising graduate students, part-time teaching at Rhode Island College. Just the day-to-day buying of groceries for the two of them and the cooking of meals was wearing her out. She tried to offer Becky yoga, to provide something stable when the foundations of Becky's home life—her house in the suburbs, her Dad coming home, her school, her friends—had been kicked away. Wendy knew, oh she knew, but refused to see when she was furiously packing up their lives, that grounding was what Becky needed. No amount of root chakra mantras could help a girl who needed, not her mother's way, but to find her own way home.

There was too much to think about most days. Wendy didn't think about what wasn't there anymore. Not very often. But she felt it nearly every moment of the day, in a way she couldn't articulate—that nagging absence. It was the space on her chest where Becky used to lay her head. It was the space she never found on her own mother's chest. But oh, thank God, had found it in Norma's eyes, the place she came home to herself, every day after school, to see that, yes, no matter what was happening in her own home, with Norma, she found herself again and knew herself loved.

Some people, she understands from her clinical work, never find that and spend the rest of their lives searching. When they occasionally discover it, they are so unused to receiving themselves in the mirror of love, that look in another person's eyes, they run away. Being loved like that and opening the heart to the terror of loss (because everything, everything, *everything* changes) is more than many of her clients can bare. She can barely bare it herself. But she found it with Becky, and for a time with Cal, and maybe she would find it again. For now, what she knows is opening to the divine every morning on her mat. And maybe it's more than she deserves but it's hers, and maybe it's enough.

She picks up the manuscript again.

 1942

I have not called Varani "Amma," as she asked me to do. There is only one Amma in my life, and she lives in my heart. How can I call another by her name? I hope she will forgive me for addressing her only as Varanima. She has been good to me in the short time I have been with her. I have beautiful new clothes, and she combs my hair with coconut oil. She says she will leave one small knot in to remind me of who I am. She says she paid dearly to have me as a daughter, so I am grateful that I had some value to Appa, and he did not have the burden of another dowry. Now that I am twelve, my marriage might already be arranged! When he visited me last with Ganesha, he told me this, so I am happy to be Varanima's daughter. My funny little brother loved playing with my new gold bangles.

Varani has many beautiful things in her house, and she has jeweled ornaments like a *maharini*. The house has a second floor where the cooking is done, and where we sleep, unless she has a husband visiting, and then I sleep downstairs. Her husbands are wealthy *sahibs* who are always kind to me. Chandrakant, the temple priest, comes daily to visit us, to teach me the Sanskrit songs and sacred texts, and to inquire about my progress in the dance. Varanima sighs and looks away when I make complaints against him. "You must be reverent, Saraswati. Without true reverence, you cannot learn. He is your acharya, your true teacher, and like a ferryman, you need him to guide you across the waters of unknowing. It is he who arranged this adoption, and he who will pay for your dedication ceremony."

I reach for Varani's hand. "What is my duty to him for this service he provides?"

Varani takes my other hand in hers and looks into my eyes. "It will not be so difficult. You will have lots of wonderful lovers who bring happiness and sometimes a bit of gold or a cow. My first husband was the King's father, who was very old at the time. Chandrakant is not so old."

"Chandrakant is to deflower me? He is to be my first God?"

"Unless the King requests you first, and then Chandrakant will be second. It is better to have an older man for your first, Saraswati. He will be tender and gentle, I am sure. And he will honor you as the Goddess herself. A young man would be rough and clumsy in his need. You will have younger men when you are ready." She pulls me to her bosom and embraces me. "You will stay young this way, my little one. I will teach you our secret of preventing birth. Only look at your sister, to see the effects of marrying one man and giving birth to his children. Lakshmi is not yet eighteen. She has borne two girls and lost another, and already she looks old and tired. Chandrakant is a temple priest. He will bless you and keep you young."

"I shall perform as you teach me, Varanima," I whisper.

. . .

HONOR AND SHAME. Wendy puts her hands to her eyes and remembers the image she saw on Facebook—a close up of the

Statue of Liberty with her face buried in her hands. Maybe the monks here at the ashram have the right idea. Is there a path that includes embracing sexuality that is honorable and without shame? Maybe that path is marriage. That's what her queer friends think. But that path has eluded her. Certainly, her own marriage was not without shame

There was that conversation before the end, when she still hoped to put the affair behind them, to talk about their unmet needs, to stay married. But there's the moment in the relationship, she thinks now, where you suddenly know it's beyond repair. You turn a corner; you hit the wall. There's the trigger—maybe a gesture or a word. She's heard it so often from her clients. The part of you that has been trying, maybe numbing out in the process, not letting yourself feel certain things, denying, denying, denying until that moment comes and you know. It's over.

She can pinpoint the exact time it happened for her. They'd had a lively discussion about sex over a bottle of wine at Aladdin's earlier that evening—what she liked, what he liked, talking more openly than they ever had. She thought they were trying to repair what had been broken by her affair. His face had softened, and he was smiling more than he had in several months. She told him. "Do you think we could try something different?"

"You mean like role playing, like master-slave?" His eyes were bright. He seemed to be enjoying the direction of their conversation.

"Maybe," she said. "I was thinking more along the lines of ..." She smiled and wiggled her tongue. "I would love it if you ..." The sudden change in his face stopped her. "Actually, master-slave might be fun." She gave him a playful look, grinned. "As long as I can be your master."

He laughed then, but their earlier ease was gone. The taut lines on his face had returned. "Deal," he said, and they clinked their now empty glasses.

Later, as she lay in the tub, Aaron knocked then entered. He sat on the toilet lid as she stood and wrapped the towel around her.

"I'm sorry, Wendy." He looked down at the floor. "There are just certain things I can't do. There's a sense of, I don't know … taboo or repulsion." He rose. "But it doesn't mean I don't love you. That I don't think you're beautiful. May I?" He said, as he pulled the towel away.

She stood absolutely still, ashamed of her needs, of having told him, and confused.

"I love you," he said. "Come. Please. Let me show you." She remembers how he led her, almost as though she were blind, from the bathroom onto the bed and the familiar posture beneath him.

"No," she murmured, but he did not stop. Too numb to resist, she let him mold her movements. Clay in his hands. Senseless and inanimate. He was surprisingly gentle, touching her breasts, licking and sucking her nipples. Though he banged at her body with his erection, he could not penetrate. Her unlovely genitals stayed closed against him, hard-boned and dry.

"I'm sorry," he sobbed when he gave up. "I'm so sorry. Please, Wendy, don't leave me. What would I do?" She rolled over and he wrapped his trembling body around her back.

She believed he did love her, or perhaps the idea of her, the wife. The passive one who rarely raised her voice. The one who loved his daughter too much to leave. She thought the affair with Cal was finally behind them. Twelve years of marriage, of fidelity, nearly a lifetime of friendship. But it felt rotted at the core. Like a dirty secret. Tenderness forever stained by her desire, his repugnance. They settled in the quilts, and she listened to his weeping subside into long breaths. She saw herself rising, packing her suitcase, finding a way out. To the ashram. To India. Back to Cal. But her limbs were heavy and her muscles weak. Like a hangover. Weakness like an overdose, a creeping paralysis. This staying. It was dangerous. A terminal disease.

She heard the sound of his sleeping and felt the sensation of his warm breath on her back. Maybe he would be enough, he and Becky. He was just a man, desperate in his terror, trying to hold on. She was the one who wanted too much, who expected something more of love.

When she remembers herself in those final days and nights with Aaron, she sees the catatonia, the way every action felt as though she were moving through mud. If she hadn't woken up one morning thinking about murder and then about suicide, would she have been capable of leaving? Would she have gone through with it all, if Cal hadn't come back into her life just long enough to catapult her out? But Cal, despite his promises, despite packing his bags and moving to a Crescent Suites motel for exactly seven nights, five of which she'd shared, had gone back to his wife.

Was it too much to ask? Even now, she wants something more of love. Love with honor. Love without shame. Love with good sex.

For the last few years, she has been the extra person at the table of her coupled friends. She isn't ashamed of that, she thinks, as she goes into the bathroom to get ready for bed, but sometimes she wants it to be different. She often thinks about protecting Becky, prays each morning after meditation, but there is no protection for *her*, not in the flesh anyway. Mostly, it's enough. She relishes her independence, her women friends, how easy her life seems these days. But sometimes, like when she gets a bad feeling about the upcoming election, or after hours spent waiting in an airport for a delayed flight, or the time she was attacked in print by a colleague for recommending body-based treatments for trauma in the social work courses she taught at Rhode Island College. She wants someone to come home to, someone with whom she can share the bad news, someone who will watch her back and scratch her belly when she rolls over with her paws in the air.

The thing is, someone like Varani, or like Saraswati when she becomes a full devadasi, they're care-givers of a sort, like geishas, consorts to powerful men. And who watches out for them? Who listens to their failures? Who rubs their tired feet? She needs to stop feeling sorry for herself. Millions of women do not have anyone watching their backs. She at least can take care of herself. Then why the occasional envy of her married women friends? It's too much time alone in the evenings, she thinks. When she goes back to Rhode Island, she'll make an effort. She'll call friends to go to concerts and plays and she'll have dinner parties, like Becky, who stays too busy to feel lonely.

Becky claims to be an ethical humanist with no need for Wendy's prayers. Don't waste your time, she says, which is precisely why Wendy prays for her. Becky would never utter a prayer herself. She claims her choices are made rationally, based on compassion and reason and not on any sort of deity or religious code. "What kind of God would ..." is how she starts a sentence each time there's a public disaster or a private tragedy, including her own.

Being an atheist must be easier, Wendy thinks, than trusting a God who allows the abduction of 276 Nigerian school girls by the Boko Haram, who allows thousands of Syrian refugees to drown crossing the sea to Greece, hundreds of Latinos to die of thirst in the Sonoran desert trying to get to the unwelcoming US, who allows innocent black men to be lynched, tarred, feathered, shot, who lets millions of Jews and homosexuals and gypsies die in the gas chambers, and who allows one ten-year-old girl to be molested. *What kind of* ... Wendy shakes off the association—how close Becky's question is to her own.

Given the state of the world and the trials of her own family, it's not clear why or how Wendy could possibly believe in God, but she does. She climbs into bed and pulls the covers up to her chin. Neither benevolent nor malevolent, God is the spaciousness that embraces all the diversities, the infinite oneness she finds when her own distractions dissolve in meditation. The unity that is always there, she thinks as she turns off the light, even if she and everyone else are too busy working out their own stories to notice.

CHAPTER *Eight*

THERE HAS BEEN TOO much looking back, Wendy thinks, as she settles in for early morning meditation with the others. This morning, she intends to stay present, here and now, embracing whatever arises. She'll nip memory in the bud. Label it. Return to her mantra. Mantra will be her portal into a deeper experience of being home in her body, home in the moment, home to awareness aware of itself. And even as she's promising these things to herself, speaking aloud with the others the commitment to cultivate "a mind well-disciplined, calm and clear," she is recognizing a familiar state of mind—disorganized, agitated, fed by worry, fueled by fear. She presses the tips of her fingers and thumbs together to deepen her breath. Hakini mudra. She thinks of it as her magic carpet, along with her mantra. Her breath is now nearly imperceptible. Now.

When the leader chants "Om," it comes to her from a great distance. She is surprised that forty minutes have passed. She is engulfed by a soft, sweet ease as she rises from her cushion with none of the usual stiffness. Her mind is focused and at peace. She can't wait to get back to the translation.

1943

Now the dance master is here. He has been teaching me the *shuddhanrtta*, the dance that I shall perform, offering myself to the God Ganesha during the afternoon *Cayaratcai Puja*. He is hard with me, and I must repeat it many times. It is such a small piece of the service, and yet we have been working on it all month. He offers puja to Ganesha, so I know something new will be taught today.

"You have the dance for your puja ceremony, now, Saraswati," he says as he offers me coconut *prasad*. "You will now learn the dance to be performed for your debut—your *gajjai puja*, when you shall adorn yourself with ankle bells for all to worship."

The dance master spreads chaff on the floor and I stand in the center. "This is the beat for the first series of movements," he says. "Ta tey tey tat tat tam." He claps the beat for me and then he asks me to repeat it. He shows me the movements for the first line. "Now stand as though you stand before Shiva," he says as he kneels and clasps my ankles in his hands, moving my feet to the rhythm we recite together. We work for many hours on the first few lines of the text. I learn the arm movements and hand mudras for each word. When it is time to finish, I bow, offering pranams to him. Varani brings in betel leaves, a gift of white linen for a fine *dhoti* for him, and part of his master's fee.

After he leaves, we sit down to a vegetable curry that Pushpa, our cook, has prepared. Often after my sessions with the dance master, Varani instructs me on subjects that only a devadasi can teach. Today she watched the last moments of my practice and has some advice. "Where the hand goes the eye must go, where the eye goes the mind must go, and where the mind goes, *there* is the feeling." She rises from her mat and demonstrates this with a hand mudra, a rapid movement of her eyes, and then the intense culmination of the gesture. "You have a broad palette to paint the meaning, the *bhava* of the dance. You have body, limbs, hands, face, eyes, and you must use them all to evoke *rasa*, true spiritual feeling in all who observe, and foremost within yourself."

It is truly art, I think. Like a statue of a *deva* come to life. She laughs when I tell her this and makes me rise and practice the mudra and eye movement with her.

I pretend to not understand, and cross my eyes, stick out my tongue and make animal noises until we are both rolling with laughter.

"Now dance," she says, as we rise from the floor again, "so that all who behold you are drawn into your world!"

When we sit down, she touches my cheek. "Little angel of God, you are learning very well. You have true *abhinaya*. You express meaning in every movement, every gesture. I am much pleased. All who behold you will be seduced into the true *rasa* of the dance."

I absorb her words as though I breathe in steaming ginger, and I feel the tingle from my head to my toes.

"I reported your progress to your father, when I saw him on his way to the palace this morning."

"How is my father?"

"He is well. His marriage to Shakuntala takes place in one month."

"May I go? Will my sister go? Oh, please, may I go, Varanima?"

"We two shall go together, child. Your father has asked me to grace his marriage by tying the golden *tali* round the neck of his bride. As you have not yet begun to bleed, you may come with me."

"Thank you, Varanima! My sister has not come to see me since she lost her boy child. I so miss her, and my dear brother, who grows up without me."

"You shall see them all, my dear, and perhaps they will see you at your dedication. I inquired at the palace today. Your application has been approved, and an auspicious day has been chosen for your dedication."

"But I know so little. I am not ready." I stick my tongue into my cheek and roll my eyes in a rapid circle to prove it, until Varani is laughing again.

"It is in two months' time. Your eyes will know where to look by then! Today we begin a new song, and another lesson in the union of love."

"But I have not begun to bleed."

"Dedication, first. We will celebrate yet again on that most wondrous occasion, when the heat rises in your body. It is a great gift the Goddess Rhamba provides, this flowing, this heat, but we must balance it with cooling forces. It will be up to you to live in harmony with the universe by eating rightly and choosing the right lovers."

"How will I choose?"

"At first it will be done for you, and then I will guide you. You will know in your heart and your mind who is right. A wrong match is dangerous, not only for you, but it can destroy the balance of the entire universe. Swami Chandrakant is your acharya. He shall be first, unless the King desires you." She pinched my cheek. "And you are growing into such a beauty, Saraswati, I think that he might."

"But how will he know me?"

"We shall go there after your dedication. You will perform for him and look into his eyes. He will decide. You have such lovely eyes. Just don't play your little tricks with them. How can he not desire you?"

"But I am a child. A baby." I make gurgling baby noises and then pretend to wail like an infant with my tongue out.

"Enough, Saraswati!" Her voice is stern, but there is laughter in her eyes.

I look down at my curry and rice which are untouched. "I am afraid."

Varanima smiles, covers my hand with hers. "Don't worry, little one. When your blood flows, the heat will rise in you, and there will be no more fear. It is all art. All sacred dance." She begins to explain the *Eight rasas*. "They are tastes," she says, "juices, in any art, in every art. The ruler of all the tastes is the erotic. Now eat. This is not a fast day. We must begin our instruction." From the back of a cabinet she brings out a bottle I have not seen before. "Try a little of this liquid." She pours. "There may be patrons who will serve it."

I taste the amber liquid in my cup. It is fiery in my mouth and smooth as I swallow.

"Drink slowly, Saraswati. We do not want intoxication."

"But why must I learn to drink alcohol? Religious people do not drink it."

"Not every patron will be a Brahmin. If you are to please the King, who is Kshatriya and the wealthy Vaishyas, those of the merchant caste who may be as husbands to you, you need to know those things which please them. Sometimes it is fine wine, sometimes cigars. I am showing you the best, just as my mother showed me. My patrons have instructed me well, so you have the benefit of their knowledge. Life is to be enjoyed in all ways. These things which I teach you are to enhance your knowledge of offering pleasure. There is the pleasure of intimacy between a man and a woman, but there is more to pleasure than sexual union. The senses are our conduits for pleasure. That is why there are always fresh bouquets of flowers by our bed. That is why I have been letting you wear my jewels and dressing you in fine fabrics. Can you not feel the pleasure of silk on your skin? Can you not see how the rich shades of green and gold suit your coloring and your hair? In all ways, a devadasi must know what is fine and beautiful in the world. She must find her style and express it tastefully. She must appreciate art and music, so that she can be a companion of joy and pleasure to her patron, not just on his mat or in his bed, but under his roof in every room of his house."

When I finish the whiskey in my glass, I feel sleepy and happy with the picture in my mind of a bed of silks and satins, a handsome prince leaning over to kiss me. As my eyes drift closed with the beautiful vision, Varanima puts something wet and smelly to my lips. I startle awake. "Ach!" I push her hand away.

She grins at me. "It's a cigar." She puts it between my index finger and thumb. "Try it. If you are with a man, you should know what is in his mind."

. . .

WENDY PUTS THE MANUSCRIPT on the desk and gets up from the chair to stretch. Some might call this sexual slavery, but she feels herself accepting the culture of pleasure that Saraswati is devoting herself to. Besides, it's a means for an Indian woman to gain power and prestige and even assets. Or it was.

She remembers the time she and Becky each took a puff from one of Aaron's cigars, both of them laughing, gagging. There were fun times with Aaron, right? Why doesn't she think of them instead of the times they made each other miserable? She tries to remember and what she comes up with are moments of fun in tandem, parallel, but not really *with* each other—the vacation in Paris where he went off to explore architecture and she went to museums; the spring bike ride in Maryland along the tow path beside the old canal. They had stopped at stone foundations covered in moss, where he wrote in his notebook the calculations and a formula for another accounting program he was developing; where, into her sketch book, she drew mending walls and moss and the knurly tangle of vines. They enjoyed good food, fine restaurants, theatre, concerts. Perhaps they had more in common than many couples. But they didn't play together, not even in bed. Bed. That was the biggest problem. There just wasn't a lot of feeling in what they did in bed—no spirit of adventure, no discoveries, and she never had that heart-stopping feeling of oneness she had experienced with Cal, of utterly and completely dissolving into each other. She and Aaron were planned, choreographed, perfect. There was little room for the messiness of emotions. Even at the beginning. She had thought then that it was because they were grown-ups. Together, they had arrived at a place of maturity. But even the Rabbi, in their prenuptial counseling, must have sensed something missing. "So, you are best friends," he said, repeating what they had said. "Marriage takes more than friendship. Passion is the glue." Aaron had laughed, winked, "No cause for worry there, Rabbi." But Wendy had paused. She didn't think the Rabbi was talking about whether they knew how to bring each other to orgasm. If that's all it took to make a good marriage, Cal would never have happened.

So much for not dwelling in the past! Why does reading this manuscript keep drawing her into the vortex of memory?

It's 7:00 pm. She might reach Becky if she's not rehearsing tonight. But if she's not rehearsing or performing, Becky is usually at a friend's performance or a celebration of something or other, or a reading. Unlike Wendy, Becky does not spend time alone. Most of their conversations take place as she walks the streets of New York City with interruptions to buy bananas or granola bars or toilet paper at a bodega she is passing.

Wendy throws on a jacket to head out to the parking lot. Reception is bad in this room. It's bad out there, too, but it's worse in here.

"Hi, Mom, I only have a minute before I go into the subway," Becky says by way of greeting.

"Thank you for answering!"

"What's up?"

"I've been missing you. We haven't talked in a couple of weeks."

"I'm fine. The troupe's been invited to dance at a women's festival in Asheville next month, so I'm really busy."

"Did you make a new dance?"

"Two, actually. One for the troupe and a duet for Cassie and me."

"That's a lot of rehearsals."

"Yup. I'm running late for one now."

"Okay, sweetheart. Let me know when you're performing in Boston, and I'll come up."

"I would love for you to come, Mom! I'll send you the link to the website for the festival. The schedule should be on there, or it will be soon. Gotta go. I'm at the station. Love you, Mom. Thanks for calling!"

"Love you, Becky." She isn't sure Becky heard her because she's no longer on the line. Even these brief moments cheer her though. Just hearing Becky's bright voice, Wendy gets a hit of her vitality, like a shot of vitamin B. Becky has more energy than anyone she knows. When Wendy visits her in New York, Becky has an agenda from hell—an impossible list of readings, performances by friends at bars, coffee houses and off-Broadway venues in SoHo, Chelsea, Brooklyn, museums uptown, sandwiched between visits with Becky's friends and walking, talking phone calls, which are often interrupted by other walking and talking calls and texts. The only time they actually talk is when Becky's alarm goes off, and Wendy gets up from her morning asana practice to give her a wake-up massage. Or on the subway home, when Wendy can barely keep her eyes opened and Becky, lit up by the evening's performance, is bubbling like a percolator with stories and observations and critiques.

It wasn't always easy. There were difficult years when Becky preferred the company of her friends, her grandparents, anyone but her parents, especially Wendy, with whom she was stuck most of the time. Even Wendy's meditation practice was a source of conflict. Meditation helped Wendy ride the turbulent waves that threatened to overwhelm her during the divorce. But to Becky, meditation flattened her mother out. She constantly tried to break the surface of the still pond of her mother's emotions. Wendy tried to explain the difference between being reactive—the flare up of out-of-control emotions triggered by a situation—and being responsive—the thoughtful response, from a calm and balanced center. "It doesn't mean I don't feel the hurt or the joy or the anger or the love," Wendy would say. "I feel it within the context of a wider field that lets me know that this emotion is just one piece of the puzzle. That puzzle is bigger and stronger than I will ever understand. I know the emotion will change, the circumstance will change, that everything changes."

Becky would have none of it. "The only thing that doesn't change is you, Mom," she said at fifteen. "You're a zombie!"

Becky craved the drama of passionate emotions as proof of her mother's attention, her mother's love, and she spent years throwing matches into water she hoped would burn like gasoline. And now and then, to Becky's great satisfaction, it did.

Wendy was living in la-la land, fourteen-year-old Becky told her, escaping from what was real. What was real was the new black rose tattoo on her shoulder, the nipple piercing, the purple hair, the leather cuffs, the kohl around her pretty blue eyes. *Look, Mom! See what inventive new ways I can find to mutilate myself while you meditate.*

Things improved after the abortion. Wendy remembers sitting beside her daughter who, for the day, had stripped off the Goth. Becky wore no makeup and had dressed in her nicest jeans with the violet cashmere sweater Aaron had given her for her fifteenth birthday a few weeks earlier. The moment Becky's name was called, they reached for each other, and just like that, Wendy was mom again, a *good enough* mom.

Within a few days, Becky asked if they could shop for new clothes. She chose earth tones—greens, golds, mauves—and nothing black. Her old friends were taking risks with drugs now and making leaps from which some would never return. Becky asked to go with Wendy to the ashram and began to practice yoga and to take her dance classes more seriously. That spring, she was chosen for the summer dance program at Jacob's Pillow, and she asked to transfer to a high school with specialties in the arts.

"Dance is my prayer," she would say.

"It's a beautiful way to pray, Sweetheart."

"Then why do you need to sit in front of that altar with those idols and candles and shit?"

"There's a picture of you on that altar."

Becky rolled her eyes. "Yeah. Me and the Guru."

Wendy laughed. By that time, she knew not to take her daughter's criticism too seriously. They were in the dance of separation.

Back in the room, she feels the tonic of her daughter's voice still lifting her spirits, and she picks up the manuscript again.

 1943

Today begins the festival of *Dhanurmasotsava*, and now that I am thirteen, I am old enough to accompany Varanima. She has wrapped me in her beautiful silk, even though it is not yet my time to wear the sari. This is a time of great celebration, for tomorrow brings the wedding of my father, and I will see Lakshmi and Bindu and baby Shanta, and also Ganesha once again.

Now that we are dressed, Varanima takes me into the sleeping room. Here, there is a real bed with what is called a mattress. When she is not with a patron, we often share this place of sleep. From beneath the bed she brings a book with beautiful drawings of men and women in the attitudes of love. These she has explained to me, but I have never before seen the paintings. I wonder if my legs will move into such strange positions. We have been stretching and opening my hips and thighs with yoga postures each morning, but some of these positions look impossible. When I tell Varanima this, she laughs and says, "Love makes all things possible."

"Not with Chandrakant," I say.

"Oh, you won't need to be fancy with him, Dear One. Your virginity is enough."

"Ugh!" I shiver. "I am not giving it to him!"

Varanima smiles, shakes her head. "No, you probably won't." She points to the book. "Now, which one of these seems difficult?"

When I point to a picture, she helps me unwrap my sari, and guides me onto my back and into *halasana*, the plow pose. My toes are touching the floor over my head, and my chin is tucked to my chest. Then she helps me bend my knees and press my head through the opening between my legs. "There. See how flexible you are, dear? Like a little snail." She laughs. "Your body is young yet and can do anything for love."

"Maybe for love." I roll up to sit beside her and wrap the end of the sari material around me. "That doesn't include oily old men!"

"You have time to prepare yourself. Your dedication is one month away, and for that all you need think about is the dance." Varanima reaches her arm around me and hugs me to her, placing a kiss on my brow. "*The gentle breeze of afternoon brings the soft fragrance of your rosebud heart.*"

"Jayadeva?" I guess.

"Very good," she says, and then cups my face in her hands. "I '*drink your smile like a moonbeam cluster out of your moon-bright face.*'"

"Shankara's *Saundarya Lahari.*"

"Excellent," she says, in the soft rumble of a whisper I have heard late at night when a guest is in this bed. "You will speak these words to your lord."

I jerk my head out of her hands. "No!"

Varanima is a good teacher. I do not wish to practice the art of love with anyone else! Never that wrinkly old temple priest. "I won't, Varanima! Not Chandrakant! Not any man!" I am trembling now, and when she draws my head to her chest, I do not resist. I bury my wet face against her breast, and she is rocking me, making soft sounds that have no meaning. I would give her anything, everything! Only here. Only her. Never to leave. Please, *Amma*, never to leave. The thrumming in my ears is softening now, and I never want to move away from her, never want to move from this moment to dance before the King.

. . .

WENDY BRUSHES AWAY the tears. *She's only thirteen!* How could this be happening? She's learning the *Kama Sutra?* Wendy takes a deep breath. A different time. A different culture. Lakshmi was married at fourteen. It's another chapter in the denigration of women. She leans forward and covers her face with her hands. There's something else. It's her own life too. It's a mother's loss, daughter loss. Scenes are flashing through her mind, and she goes to bed that night assaulted by memory.

There was the morning she came out of a dream with a disquieting image in her mind. She saw herself with a gun, shooting him, shooting herself. They didn't own a gun, and she told herself it was just a dream, that her subconscious was working out her anger, but she couldn't stop trembling. She had to leave. Staying would provoke them both to terrible moments they would regret. It already had. She remembers packing a bag that afternoon, thinking she would pick Becky up after school, maybe go to her parents or take her on a road trip. But Becky wasn't there when she pulled up to wait for her, the car idling by the front door. There were her friends. There was Linny. But Becky wasn't with her. She turned off the engine and went inside where the school secretary said that Aaron had come for her an hour before with a story about an orthodontist appointment.

Wendy climbed back in her car, confused. There was no orthodontist appointment on her calendar. Aaron was at work when she left. But the housekeeper had come in when she was packing. Crying and packing. She hadn't told Martha she was leaving, but something must have worried her. Something that made her call Aaron. Or maybe it was Penny. Before she decided that she shouldn't involve the neighbors, she'd left a message, asking if she might sleep in the Stein's guest room tonight. She called his cell, but it went straight to voice mail. There was nothing to do but drive back home, see if they were there. She waited all evening. No calls, nothing. And Aaron and Becky did not come home. When she called Martha around 7:00 pm, the housekeeper told her that yes, she had been worried, seeing Wendy crying like that, throwing things in a suitcase—hers and Becky's, so yes, she had called Aaron. She hoped it was okay, because she was thinking that Wendy needed some help, that maybe she was too upset to be traveling, traveling with Becky.

"She's gone! He picked her up during school and took her away from me."

"I'm sorry. I ..."

Wendy hung up. She called Penny, her parents, even his parents, and if they knew where they were, no one would tell her. They did know! They had to, because no one seemed surprised. They were more concerned with calming her down, reassuring her that Becky was and would be fine, wherever Aaron had taken her.

So, she stayed in the house, waiting. When she called the police at 10:00 pm, the sergeant told her that if they were married, if they were both Becky's parents, then it was not a police matter. Not yet, anyway.

She did everything she could think of for the next three days—showing up unannounced at his parents, her parents, school, Becky's dance class, calling friends he might visit out of town.

At 4:00 pm on Friday, her phone rang. "Can you come to the Rabin's now?" Her father asked.

"Becky's there?"

"Why else would I want you to come here?"

"Thank God. I'll come get her."

"Believe me, Wendy, I've been negotiating this visit with Sam all afternoon. You'll visit her, but you can't take her home. Be grateful you can see her."

The wet drive through rush hour traffic to Weston took longer than she expected. One of her wiper blades was smearing raindrops across her windshield like petroleum jelly, and her windows kept steaming up.

By the time she exited the bumper-to-bumper traffic off 90, the rain had tapered off, and spectacular shafts of angled evening light cut an illuminated pattern along the streets. She craned her neck to see if she could find a rainbow, telling herself, when she couldn't, that even the intermittent flashes of icy light boded well for their reunion.

It was after 5:00 pm, when Wendy reached the Rabin's. As she pulled up the long circular drive, Becky leapt from the top step of the front porch and came running. Wendy was opening the car door, with one foot on the pavement, before she'd properly parked. She left the door open as she bounded toward Becky, and the two of them threw themselves against each other. Becky jumped, wrapping her legs around Wendy's waist as she had when she was a much smaller girl. Wendy staggered with her weight but did not let go. "Oh, Becky. Oh, my darling, Becky." She babbled, she purred, she hummed. The sudden rush of love made her incoherent. After a moment, Becky eased her feet to the pavement, and they tottered back and forth along the perimeter of the spindly rose bushes that lined the drive, holding hands, both of them ignoring the damp cold and the darkening sky.

"Don't cry, Mom." Becky stopped, reached into her jacket pocket and pulled out a crumpled tissue. "Here."

"Oh, my sweetheart. I'm crying for happiness. I missed you so much."

They walked up and down the driveway past what looked like her father's Cadillac or one of Sam's—were both her parents inside? The "Great Adventure," Becky called the kidnapping. Surely, Aaron's words. Becky told her about all the places they'd gone—the 18th century village in Mystic, where she watched workers building a wooden ship, the harbor front in Old Lyme, and how they'd stayed in a hotel with an indoor pool and a video arcade in the lobby. And all the while Becky was talking, Wendy felt sure they were being watched. She kept glancing toward the house, but the high multi-paned windows that rose from the living room past the second-floor landing were dark. The whole house was oddly dark.

"I'm cold, Mommy. Can we go inside?"

"How about we get in the car?"

"Daddy says we're staying here tonight, but I want to go home with you."

As casually as she could, she walked with Becky to the passenger side. "I'll talk with him about that." Jump in the car, she thought, and drive away from here, from Weston, from Newton, from the whole Northeast. To Arizona. California. Keep driving to a place where it didn't snow at the end of February. Where rainbows emerged after evening showers. Trust, she thought. "Get in the car," she whispered, then dashed to the driver's side.

"Don't get in that car!" Sam's voice rang out, and Becky stopped, transfixed by her grandfather's command. He was barreling through the front door, one arm raised, as though he were leading a charge. And he was. There were people behind him. Her father! Then she saw her mother and Bea coming through the door.

"We want to get warm." Wendy ducked into the Subaru and leaned across. "Quick! Get in!" She could see that the four of them were nearly to the car and that her mother, bad back and all, had sprinted out ahead.

Becky bent down and swung her left leg in. "Let's go home, Mommy!" she cried.

Her mother reached Becky first, had hold of her right arm. "Come inside, dear. The house is nice and warm." She was smiling. How could she be smiling?

Wendy grabbed for Becky's left hand, and for a moment there was a tug of war and Becky screamed, and Wendy let go. Her mother's arm was around Becky's shoulders now, pulling Becky, stumbling, from the car. Then Bea was there. The two women had her surrounded.

"Come on, honey," Bea drawled. "You and Mommy can talk in the den."

Suddenly, Wendy felt a pull at her shoulder and turned to see Sam, gripping her arm.

"You slut," he growled. "You don't deserve her love."

Wendy wrenched her arm free. He stumbled back into a rose bush, and just as she slammed the door and locked it, she heard Becky cry out and the passenger door close. The next thing she knew, her mother was sitting beside her in the passenger seat, and Becky was standing by the side of the car with her father's arms around her. They looked, for an instant, as though they were dancing. But they were struggling. "What are you doing here?" She screamed at her mother. "Let us go home!"

"Sweetheart, sweetheart, sweetheart." Her mother placed her hand over Wendy's on the gearshift.

Wendy wrenched her hand away. "Tell me what you're doing here!"

"Calm down. We're trying to help you. You were allowed to see Becky. You know she's okay."

"*Allowed*? What are you talking about? She's not going to be okay if she doesn't go home with me now!"

"Honey, you betrayed your husband. Aaron was wrong to take her away, but he's out of his mind, right now. Let us try to help."

"Help me by collaborating with a crazy man?"

"Just listen to yourself. You're out of control. If you could see your face."

"Of course, I'm upset. You're all against me."

"No, we're not, honey. We want what's best for you and Becky."

"I'm what's best for Becky! I'm her mother."

Then her father opened the door on her mother's side and leaned in. "Don't worry, sweetheart," he said. "It's all been taken care of. I talked with Sam. It wasn't easy. He's enraged and intractable. But we worked out a compromise for now. She's going to spend the night here, and Aaron will take her to school in the morning. She'll be home tomorrow night."

"Where is she? Where did she go?" Wendy looked around frantically. In the growing dark, she saw Bea and Sam moving into the house, but she couldn't see Becky.

"She's inside."

"She'll be upset. I need to talk with her."

"Don't worry, honey. I'll talk with her," her father said.

Wendy grabbed her mother's hand and squeezed. "Please, Mom. Don't do this to us. Let me take her home."

The taut lines of her mother's thin face drew to a point at her pursed lips. She stared straight ahead. "That's not possible. You have no idea what's been going on today."

"Let go of your mother's hand. You're hurting her."

When Wendy did as she was told, his tone softened. "Honey, I'll talk with Becky. She'll be fine. Don't worry about it."

"Dad's very good with her," her mother added.

"She was sitting on the front steps waiting for me. She isn't fine. She wants to go home with me now!"

"We'll take her out for ice cream," her dad said. "She'll calm down, and I'll tell her that you'll see her after school tomorrow, that you'll spend the evening with her."

"The evening? I live there."

"But you're looking for an apartment. The whole arrangement I negotiated with Sam to bring you back into Becky's life is contingent upon your moving out. You know, you can stay with us until you find one."

"This has nothing to do with you and Sam!"

"You know what Sam's like when you cross him. And right now, he and Aaron are completely aligned. You're going to need our help." He reached into his pocket. "Here, let me give you the key to our place. You know the security code, right?"

Wendy imagined revving the engine, plowing through the rose bushes and the privet hedge that ran the length of the house and through the front window. Front wheel drive. She could do it. "I can't believe you're on his side."

"We're on *your* side, dear, even though you ... well, you know," her mother said quietly, patting Wendy's arm. "When you come to your senses, you'll realize that."

"Cookie, honey, get out of the car. Let Wendy go home now." He opened the passenger door, and her mother stepped out. "Drive safely, sweetheart," he said, leaning in again. "We love you no matter what you've done. You're welcome to stay with us tonight." Then he closed the door.

She drove numbly, unaware of her surroundings. Stopping at red lights, moving on green lights, driving for miles without seeing anything but the patch of pavement her headlights illuminated. It was as if she'd come unplugged, and only the automatic, battery-operated functions continued. It was 6:45 when she pulled into her driveway.

That night, unable to sleep, she wanted desperately to hear Cal's voice. It had been eleven months since she'd felt his arms around her—that brief moment of protection that carried her through the days and nights of their affair. He'd called yesterday and in the punishing hours of seeking Becky, she hadn't listened to the voice mail message. It was likely the same as all the rest of the messages she'd saved. Messages about how unfair it was, how he knew he was the agent of destruction, but he couldn't help loving her, wanting her. Unhooking from him meant deleting them, but she couldn't. She never responded, never even picked up when she saw the flash of his name on her screen. But that night was different. She climbed out of bed at 2:00am and went downstairs to the kitchen, where she'd left the phone to charge.

Her breath caught as she listened. This message was different. He's left, he says. Oh, my God! Two nights ago! He's staying at Crescent Suites in Waltham, room 217. He's told Denise that he's done masquerading and wants a divorce. "Wendy, where are you? Call me when you hear this message, any time. I need you. Wendy, I love you."

Her body trembled as she put the phone down, and she reached for the counter to keep from falling. Then she picked it up again and dialed.

They spent five nights together. She couldn't get enough of him. How good it felt to fall asleep with his body wrapped around her back. Days she spent looking for an apartment, consulting a lawyer, deciding what to take from the house and what to leave, and then picking Becky up from school at 3:15. She took her to flute lessons, dance class and to the library and the park. Every other night, she made dinner and stayed until Becky was ready for bed. Aaron stayed late at the office on those nights, so it was just Becky and her and Martha. Some nights, Becky was tearful, begging her to stay. "If you don't love Daddy anymore, you could stay upstairs with Martha."

Wendy didn't cry as she kissed her daughter goodnight, but as soon as she got in her car, the tears came, and she wept all the way to the Crescent Suites where most nights Cal waited. Twice she came in before he did, and he told her he'd gone home to do a chore or to talk Denise down from her hysteria. He said they were talking, that she wanted him to go into couples counseling and that he was considering it. He had to stop at the house every day, he told Wendy, because he couldn't leave her with all the chores, and there were always maintenance issues with the house and the pool.

On the seventh night, no one answered her knock on the door to 217. When she used her key, the place was a mess—a lamp turned over, Wendy's clothes thrown around, and bedding on the floor, but Cal's belongings were still there. She pulled out her phone to listen to the message that had come in while she was driving. He said he'd gone back with Denise to avoid something worse. Denise had shown up with a gun, he said, threatening to kill him, to kill Wendy, and to kill herself. She was drunk and unsteady, and he'd driven her home. In the morning she would drive him over to pick up his things, get his car and check out. He realized now that he couldn't go through with it. Not this way. Not now. But maybe counseling would soften Denise's stance, and it would be easier. Later. He wasn't giving up on their future together. It would just take more time than he'd thought.

She expected tears. None came. Maybe she'd shed all she had over Becky. She was wrong about that, of course. But now, she was dry. Empty. And she had to get out of that room. What if Denise came back in the morning, gun loaded? But she couldn't go home. And she couldn't face her parents right now. Or anyone. If only Norma were still alive. She would go to her.

Numbly, Wendy gathered her belongings and locked the door on the hope she had allowed to grow.

There was a Crowne Plaza on Washington Street. She would go there. That night she dreamt of Norma, whom she had loved since she was three when her family moved next door. She had loved Norma all the way to the grave, after Norma's stroke, and now eleven years beyond.

In the dream, she was that younger Wendy, unplugged from time, even as the timer ticked out seconds, announced them from its perch on Norma's white porcelain stove. Awake before dawn, she lay on her back in her room at the hotel remembering.

She is tracing yellow Formica swirls with her finger. Sometimes she gets dizzy when she crosses her eyes and stares at the table, imagining herself lost in the clouds. She's already a little dizzy now. Norma stands across from her, ironing Joe's shirts on the board that folds down from the wall, letting her mug of coffee get cold. She listens to Wendy with her head tilted, shaking it, making silent "Oh's" with her mouth, as Wendy tells about today in school. How Karen Gilderstern made fun of her poodle purse in the lunch line, the one her grandmother sent her for her birthday last week. How even her best friend Patty, at least she was her best friend until today, laughed in a mean way.

"Karen isn't a very nice girl, is what I think," Norma is saying. "She's jealous of you, so she picks on you to try to win your friends to her side."

"They are on her side." Wendy likes the sound of Norma's smoky voice, and the way she says the word "your," dropping the "o" sound that her mother says comes from growing up working-class. Wendy isn't sure what working-class means, but she thinks it has something to do with breakfast dishes in the sink and drinking coffee out of a mug instead of a Limoges cup like her mother's and doing your own ironing. Wendy's father is in real estate downtown which, her mother explained, means their family is upper-middle, and why she tells Wendy to enunciate her vowels, instead of swallowing them. But she ignores her mother, especially when she sits in Norma's kitchen, dropping as many "o's" as she can.

Norma hangs the shirt she's ironed from a hanger on the doorknob, then sits kitty-corner to Wendy and sips her coffee. Wendy likes the starchy, hot shirt smell. When Norma lights a Chesterfield, Wendy bends to smell the lilacs gathered in a milk-glass vase. Norma tells her they're the first blooms, cut from the bushes that line her driveway, so they're for Joe, but tomorrow there will be more, and she will cut them for Wendy. Wendy hardly knows Joe, since he owns a pub in the South End, and he doesn't get home until everybody in their Newton Village neighborhood has gone to bed.

Funny how Wendy coughs and wheezes when her mother lights up, but sitting here in Norma's kitchen, she likes the clean shirt smell and the scent coming from the flowers on the table all filled with cigarette smoke.

"They won't be Karen's friends for long," Norma says. "You watch. She'll show her true colors, and they'll be back on your side." Then she takes Wendy's hand and says, "You are so precious to me," and it feels to Wendy that love is overflowing the banks of her heart, like the river her grandmother is always talking about that flooded mud and water through her house in Springfield when she was little, dirtying all her pictures and her furniture. But this is spilling something clean and light all through Wendy's body, and she feels it clear down to her fingertips. "Karen can go to hell," Norma adds.

Wendy breaks into laughter. Only Norma and her Springfield grandmother say "hell" in front of her, which is one reason why Wendy's mother never tells anyone she grew up there.

Norma's cheeks are lifted by her smile and pink with laughing. "It makes me happy to see you laugh, funny girl. Not everything's so serious, you know. Not even Mrs. Clean."

Wendy's still laughing at the name Norma has given her mother when the timer goes off. She feels the hands of her mother's watch reaching out for her across the lawn. She grips the ridge of aluminum surrounding the table and hooks her legs through the cold metal of the chair. "Can I stay a little longer?" It comes out as a whisper, because her throat has suddenly shut down tight, like she's coming down with something.

"I wish you could, but your mother wants you home. I'm sorry."

"But it's only 4:30, and I don't have homework. Please. Just five minutes."

"Sure, but if she calls ..."

"I know. I'll leave."

Norma stubs out her cigarette, pushes the ashtray aside, and looks at her. Wendy wants this picture of her neighbor inside her when she crosses the lawn. Norma's eyes are big and moist like the porpoise eyes she saw at Wickee-Wackee Springs in Pompano Beach when she went to Florida with her grandparents and watched them swimming in a glass tank with women dressed in fake fish tails. Wendy could sit here forever, breathing in Norma's kitchen smells. Sunlight comes in at an angle, streaming through the yellow curtained window above the sink where the happy-faced salt and pepper oranges she brought home from that trip are displayed. One side of Norma's face glows with afternoon light, but both her eyes are shining. Without saying a word, Norma takes Wendy's hands in hers, and Wendy swears she feels the pulse of something solid running through them. "Wendy," Norma says, finally.

She is this Wendy. The Wendy Norma sees. She knows her real mother sees a different Wendy. A slow Wendy who is lazy, absent-minded, and messy. She remembers that after the last fight over her dishwasher loading, which caused a porcelain teacup to crack; her father came into her room to tell her that her mother was downstairs crying. He says that she must make a special effort to stop hurting her mother, who is delicate and fine, and also sensitive and fragile. A porcelain teacup, Wendy thought, like the one she hadn't meant to break.

Wendy is a classic, passive-aggressive personality, which she figures means she's constipated, since that's what her mother tells her she is every night when she gets her laxative. Her mother says this nicely but with a weepy sound to her voice, like she says almost everything. She doesn't believe in getting angry, so nobody yells in their house.

Wendy understands she's nothing like her beautiful, whirl-about mother. She knows her mother understands this, too. Her mother told her how she came out squish-faced from the forceps at birth. How she was afraid she wouldn't be able to love an unlovely baby, but of course her fears had disappeared when she held Wendy in her arms that first time. Now her mother grimaces and shakes her head. "How much nicer you would look," she says, "if you lost a little weight and stood up straight."

Norma tells her she looks beautiful and how happy she is to see her, no matter what. Now, she is placing her soft cheek against Wendy's. "It's time to go home. We don't want Mrs. Clean telling us you can't come back because you came home late."

The bigness in Wendy's chest is shrinking, and she feels the fist in her belly beginning to twist and tighten. "I don't want to."

"And I don't want you to, but it's time. Past time. Tomorrow's another day."

"But what if I'm sick tomorrow?" Wendy thinks this is a distinct possibility.

Norma laughs. "I'm cutting the lilacs for you. I'll need your help." She opens the door as she pushes Wendy through it. "Don't be so serious. There's lots to laugh about, kiddo."

Wendy walks sideways across the lawn, so she can see Norma the whole way. Norma stands on her kitchen porch blowing kisses. When Wendy reaches her own front porch, she waves one last time, then turns and opens the door, becoming the Wendy her mother sees.

Wendy rolled over on the king-sized mattress at the Crowne Plaza, daydreaming Norma like an analgesic. Not feeling. That was the point now. Everything in her spiritual and psychological training pointed to embracing what was arising without numbing out, to succumb to the huge wave of grief. But how could she allow emotion to stop her from doing the next thing—getting out of bed, getting ready, continuing her search for an apartment, the supervision meeting she'd scheduled with one of her students? And then clients. Not now. Let the veil of Norma keep her going, moving, one foot in front of the other. Norma, like the morphine she had in the hospital after her hysterectomy. Norma, a safer drug than opioids, alcohol, sex. Maybe Cal had been just that, the drug that kept her moving through this separation from Becky. She didn't trust herself to meditate this morning. Daydreaming Norma was safer.

Those late afternoons in Norma's kitchen and in her yard, playing with snapdragons and cutting lilacs. And times later, when she came home from college, how Norma treated her like a special guest, laying out finger sandwiches and sweets on the coffee table. How they would sit on the couch in front of the big picture window and Wendy would talk or not and Norma would listen and look. It was the looking Wendy always came home to. How seen she felt. How Norma knew her better than anyone else on earth.

Later, when she was married to Aaron, in the times of deepest distress, she would pick up the ringing phone, and there would be Norma, just missing her, she would say, and had to call. And there was the time that she had the sudden urge to call Norma, who had answered the phone in tears. She had just been told of her brother's death. And there was the final time while she and Aaron were traveling in Mexico for three weeks—their one-year anniversary trip—when Wendy had an urgent wish to hear Norma's voice but hadn't called. International calling was too expensive back when there were only landlines. The next day, the telegram arrived at the hotel in Oaxaca. Norma had died the day before. One stroke took her out. She was found on the floor, reaching for the phone. No telling how long she had lain there.

Thank God for Norma. There would not be a God to thank, Wendy thinks, if there hadn't been a Norma. She threw back the covers. She needed to choose between the several apartments she'd seen and sign a lease. She would check out of the Crowne Plaza and stay with her parents for the night.

CHAPTER
Nine

NO WONDER BECKY doesn't believe there's a God, Wendy thinks as she climbs out of bed at the ashram. If your childhood concept of God is formed by the trust you develop in the adults around you, trust that, no matter what, you are loved, and you are safe, then Wendy and the other adults—Aaron, Becky's grandparents, even Martha—had let her down. By that winter after the divorce, the assistant camp director had broken whatever tenuous trust remained. The world was not a safe place. People could not be trusted.

"What kind of God?" was Becky's refrain. "What kind of mother?" Wendy never stopped asking herself.

Where Wendy's default had become depression, Becky had become a fighter, distrusting the system. Whatever system she found herself in, she tried to improve it, sometimes getting fired for her efforts. Becky had been fired or quit more jobs in the eight years she had worked for others than some people held in a lifetime. Whenever and wherever she sensed injustice, she demanded fairness, rallying her colleagues and before that her fellow students to petition, to protest, to walk out.

She can barely make a living with the Rabin Resilience Dancers, her own dance troupe, but since she founded it, no one can fire her. And the company is gaining a following of fans and reviewers. The women's arts festival in Asheville, North Carolina, is the second commission she's received for new work in a year. She's applying to Jacob's Pillow in Beckett, Massachusetts, and she thinks she has a good chance of getting Resilience into their Dance Festival as an emerging company this year, performing for several days in July and teaching master classes. The artistic director remembers her from the year she auditioned and was accepted into the Jacob's Pillow school at 16. She saw a performance Becky mounted in SoHo and encouraged her to send a video. She's already been told she and Cassie, once her partner in life, who remains a featured dancer in the company, have received a Creative Development Residency at the Pillow in April before the season starts. She plans to develop new work that, if Resilience is accepted, will be premiered during the summer Dance Festival.

Becky may not believe in the existence of God, Wendy thinks, but she has been touched by the Goddess of wisdom and music, the Goddess Saraswati.

Before she even gets out of bed, Wendy turns her attention back to the manuscript.

 1943

It is happiness that fills me as Varani, so beautiful, so graceful, ties the golden thread around Shakuntala's neck. One day, I too will tie the *tali* on a bride. One day I will enter the wedding hall, and men will touch my feet. I too, shall be a most auspicious woman. For now, I am happy to be just me, the little sister of Lakshmi, the older sister of Ganesha. "Here, Younger Brother. Come sit with your sister."

Ganesha runs toward me. At six, he has become a real boy, and yet he has the softness and affection of a little child. When I am a devadasi, I shall be able to walk about and visit anyone I wish. "I will soon see you often," I tell him.

"Soon," he echoes back, "I will be big enough to visit you!" Lakshmi joins us with Bindu who climbs in my lap, and her little one, Shanta, whom she carries in her arms.

"When I am a devadasi," I say to her, "we will be like two married ladies. I will be able to visit you."

"I hope so, dear Sister. I pray my mother-in-law permits it."

"Why should she not? Will I not bring honor to her house?"

"She has a somewhat different view." Lakshmi looks away.

"But what, Sister? Why would she not want a devadasi to visit her home with blessings from the Goddess?"

She leans into me with Shanta in her arms. "Always remember that I love you, dear sister, no matter what."

"But what? You must tell me, Lakshmi!"

From across the hall, her mother-in-law gestures, and Lakshmi turns away from me. "I must return to my husband's family. I serve them now, dear Sister." She stands and kisses my forehead. "You are so beautiful, Saraswati. Your hair is thick and rich, and your eyes shine like jewels. You shall be a devadasi queen!"

"Will you come to my ankle bell ceremony and my dedication?"

"It is not permitted."

I did not think I could feel so sad. My tears touch Ganesha where he leans against me. His face tells me he is struggling not to cry too.

My father breaks off his talk and comes to us. "What is this, Saraswati? You must not bring grief into the wedding hall. Please stop your tears at once."

"But Appa," I say, drying my eyes with the corner of my sari, "Why would the family of Lakshmi's husband forbid her to see me?"

My father places his hand on my head. "Not everyone recognizes the honor of the dance. Some think only of the dance you will do with the temple priest or those who stand in his stead. According to the tradition of our caste, we do not associate with temple dancers in anything but ceremonial functions. This does not mean that Lakshmi will stop loving you, my child. But her love, after this, will be held in her heart."

I look into Appa's eyes, and he does not look away. "And you and Ganesha? Will you see me only in your heart, or will you behold me as I am?"

"You will not cease to be my daughter, even as Varanima has adopted you. It is agreed that you will do your duty to both your adoptive mother and to me in my old age."

I fall to my knees and touch my father's feet. "I ask God to grace me with the gifts of divine dance. May I please God, even as I please his servants, so that I may support you in your dotage."

He places his hands on my head. "I add my blessing to your prayer," he says. "You shall always be my most precious daughter. Now, I must return to my guests. Go and greet my bride."

I rise and make my way around the dancers, knowing it is not yet my time to join them. Shakuntala sits on a rise in the middle of the room. The women of her family surround her. When I approach, they close in, so I cannot reach my hand to hers in friendship. "Shakuntala," I say. "I would like us to be sisters." She does not meet my gaze, nor answer me. Shakuntala's mother makes a sign to ward off evil spirits, and several women make a sound through their teeth like a serpent. I turn away.

I make my way back through the laughing dancers. What good will it do to be a "most auspicious woman" when all who see me turn away as though I were unchaste? I wander out into the street where the children of lowest caste *harijans* dance and run to the music coming from the wedding tent. A leper raises his palm to me. I am more welcome here. Suddenly there is a large hand on my shoulder, and I turn in surprise to face Chandrakant. "You will soon receive the honors of this sacred ceremony," he said, his large grin at an angle on his face.

I pull away from him. He is the last one I wish to see now. If he is to be my first, it is no wonder decent women turn away from me. I have a very bad thought about an ox cart. He grabs my chin and pulls me to face him, as though he were a monkey and I a banana. The stumps of his teeth are stained and broken from betel nuts and chai. "You will not turn from me, when I am your first husband. I am your patron, Saraswati. Without me, you do not dance. I am your God."

Chandrakant releases me roughly, and I stumble and fall into the upraised arms of the leper.

. . .

MORE THAN EVER, WENDY has the urge to shelter this little girl. She remembers the light in the eyes of the woman on the train, and how she had felt momentarily sheltered by her gaze. Maybe it's more than light that shines through the crack in everything, she thinks along the lines of Leonard Cohen's song. It's more than light pouring through the bandaged places in Rumi's poem. She thinks of Norma's eyes. Their shelter. Is it the yearning to protect that we learn when we are left unprotected? Becky is skeptical of such lessons. Nothing turns trauma into something worthwhile. But it's the only way Wendy has made sense of her own childhood. She wonders if meaning is something you age into, or not. There are certain catastrophes, particular horrors, to which even Wendy can't find meaning.

Becky has no time for redeeming stories, happy endings, reasons to suffer, and yet, more than anyone else Wendy knows, Becky offers shelter. She has turned violation into service, standing, sometimes as a lone voice, against those who would take advantage of others. Becky has been an advocate for battered women, for women in recovery, for victims of sexual assault and sex trafficking. Saraswati's story, the way she is being groomed as a devadasi to please her patrons—that would trigger Becky. She would call it abuse, and she is probably right. Becky fights whenever and wherever she perceives injustice. She argues with the owner of her neighborhood bodega where she buys her coffee and eggs to-go on the way to the subway each morning, because, she believes, he mistreats the immigrant female workers who run his shop. Aside from her ex-lover Cassie, Becky has auditioned and hired women coming out of rehab, in recovery, coming out of jail. Becky shelters these women, who bring the weight of their stories to the dance and in dancing attempt to let those stories go, to free themselves from carrying the blueprint of their past through the rest of their lives.

Aaron was appalled, of course. It took him six years to meet Cassie, and by then they were no longer lovers. Their artistic partnership was acceptable to him but not their intimacy. When Becky came out in college, it was as if her sexual preference were a direct assault on his values, a rejection, thinks Wendy, not unlike the way he viewed their divorce. It's taken him a long time to come around, to accept Becky as she defines herself. He was angry when she didn't use her Juilliard education to audition for established companies like the Paul Taylor Dancers or Mark Morris or the American Ballet Theater, since she admired Twyla Tharp so much. He would have been happier with Broadway show auditions. Until she started getting the kind of reviews he could hang on the walls of his office, he called her troupe the Jailbirds.

He sends her money now. They both do. Even in Crown Heights, where she and Cassie share an apartment with three other dancers, rents are impossible. But he still hasn't seen The Rabin Resilience Dancers perform. Just last month, Aaron's wife Rachel told Wendy that he liked Cassie when they finally met, and that he was settling into the idea that his daughter was queer. It had helped, Rachel said, that one of his favorite clients and several associates in his accounting firm had invited them to *legal* same-sex weddings and birthday parties for their children.

Wendy hopes to see Aaron in the audience at one of Becky's performances. There is no better venue in the world for emerging dance companies than Jacob's Pillow. Aaron has to respect that.

Wendy stands, rolls out her mat and does postures. She's been sitting for too long, and she needs to stretch and breathe before she can pick up the translation again.

1944

In five days, I will be dedicated, married to my God, but today is auspicious, too. It is *gajjai puja* that we will make today, honoring my new ankle bells, and I will dance my first dance.

Varani's house has been purified. All month we have kept it so, awaiting the *muttirai* ceremony, when I shall receive the brand and finally wed. Today Appa and Younger Brother come, and the many devadasis from the temple. Chandrakant will be here, and the neighbors in Varani's caste. Pushpa and two helpers from the village have been preparing rice and *sambar* for everyone. Yesterday she sat on the dirt in front of the house removing impurities from the rice. She hardly spoke, so intent was she on her duty. And today, my duty is to dance in a way that will not dishonor my dance master, or my adopted mother. It is not a full performance, as I will have during my *muttirai* next week, but there will be musical accompaniment and my ankle bells will jingle for the first time.

Since my Appa's marriage, I asked for Amma's aarti lamp. This, he brought yesterday, in honor of my gajjai puja and my fourteenth birthday. While Varani sleeps, I have come quietly from bed to her altar downstairs. Here, I fill the lamp with ghee and cut a new wick. Now, I shall offer my own prayers. I pranam before the altar to Ganesha and to Divine Mother Kali. I sing praises as my *acharya*, Chandrakant, has taught these many months. I sing of Shiva united with Parvathi. Of Shakti pulsating God into existence. I sing my adoration to Brahma, the creator, Vishnu, the maintainer, and Shiva, the destroyer. I sing to the twin breasts of the Goddess, the sun and the moon, and when my prayers are finished, my voice lingers in the corners of the room, pulling forth the secret dusty prayers of my heart.

There lie the secrets of my own desire. There is the thought of the ox cart that crushes Chandrakant's skull. And there is the memory of Varanima's gentle embrace. How am I to be with God alone, oh Kali, Divine Mother? Must Chandrakant be my first? My husband? My God? You, oh Lord, have sung through me, danced with me, and I have loved you well, without the physical body of another laid by my side. "Let me be dedicated to you alone, Oh, Lord." I feel myself lifted from my knees. "Lord of the Universe," I whisper, "do not let me sink into the world of the physical body. Even as men come to know me, let me find union with you. Do not let me be a lump of flesh, here on the floor before Varani's altar." I stand, reaching my arms toward the sky. "Beloved Lord, come! I am your servant. Let me dance in your arms."

"Who are you talking to, Saraswati?" It is Varani, descending the stairs with a candle illuminating her sleepy face.

I drop my arms. "I was practicing the songs that Chandrakant taught me."

Varani smiles and strokes my hair, which is still loose this morning. "God is pleased with you, little temple dancer."

I shake my head. "Why do I feel that as I learn to please men, I lose God's pleasure?"

Varani places her hands on my upper arms and turns me toward her. "This is your fear that speaks, Saraswati. In your heart you know that each union with a man is union with God. This is your sacred duty. May it also be your pleasure."

. . .

DUTY AND PLEASURE. Do they ever co-exist? Wendy sets the manuscript aside. For those not on a monastic path, you have only to look at the *Kama Sutra* or read the life of Rumi and Shams, or read the Song of Songs, or study Tantra or Kashmiri Shaivism, as she has done in a dabbling sort of way, to know that they can be joined. The teaching for the householder is that pleasure is temporal. It has a beginning and end. What is time bound has limitations, and whatever limits us, blocks our freedom. Whatever constricts us, brings suffering. When we understand that, we don't get hooked. We can enjoy the pleasure of the ice cream cone, but we don't cling to it when it's gone, craving more. It's the clinging that's the source of the suffering, not the pleasure itself. She ponders this as she gets ready to go to meditation. She loved Cal in a way that was limiting, that brought suffering. The strongest passions, like her feelings for Cal, like her painting life, came to her in ways that seemed to be a shirking of duty. Ultimately, duty is what drew Cal back to his wife. She is convinced it was not for lack of loving her, but rather the part of him that would never abandon his commitments was stronger. She had to admire that in him that loyalty.

For her, their love felt feverish and out of control, not the grown-up kind of dutiful love she had felt for Aaron that even the Rabbi had questioned. Will Saraswati find a path unifying duty and love that is without shame? Without limitations? Without suffering? Can this Indian child teach her something that she's never been able to learn on her own? It is almost time for evening meditation, but Wendy picks up the manuscript instead.

 1944

I feel the music in my heart. My dance master intones the rhythms as he moves along beside me, the beat of his symbols guiding me, just as we have practiced all these months. But now there is another musician walking behind me, who sings and claps to a separate rhythm, and a flute accompanies him like a lark in flight. Even as their melodies interweave, I move only with my dance master. My heart unfolds, as I move in harmony with the yearning of the music. I am the yearning. I am the longing, and in the next moment, I am union. Male and female united in me, the seeker and God.

The dance over, I bow my head to those assembled, then pranam to my dance master. There is a buzz of voices around me. "How she feels the music," I hear someone say. "The King will surely want her." When I rise, my dance master bows to me. And then the devadasis surround me with their blessings. Varanima smiles and nods at me from a distance. As the crowd around me thins, I see that Appa is helping Ganesha to the coconut prasad that has been blessed with my ankle bells in the puja. I move toward them.

"You will make a beautiful devadasi, my child," Appa says. "Amma would be happy."

Ganesha has forgotten all about my performance. His interest is in more coconut. I laugh and give him a squeeze, then straighten to speak with Appa.

"Do you think Lakshmi will be permitted to come to my dedication?"

"No, Saraswati, but she will hold you in her heart. She is once again with child."

I turn away so that Appa does not see my tears. "This is not such a good marriage you arranged for her, Appa!"

"Shankar's family takes care of her and her daughters."

I cannot help it. I must say this to his face. I spin around. "And if she bears another girl? What then?"

"No harm will befall her baby."

"How do you know? She belongs to her husband now."

His shoulders slump. "This is true. I can no longer protect her."

"There must be something I can do. After my dedication I will go there myself."

Appa places his hand on my head. "I wish you good fortune in this, Daughter. I praise God for marrying you Himself and giving you this freedom. May the way not be barred."

Chandrakant calls my name, and I turn. When I glance back after Appa, he and Ganesha are moving toward the door.

. . .

WENDY HEARS A LIGHT buzz and looks to see that Becky has sent her a text with the website for the Women's Arts Festival. When she links through, she sees the dates on the home page and gives a little yelp. Damn! The second weekend in November she's scheduled to take another yoga training, this one for trauma, at Kripalu Center in the Berkshires. But maybe she can get her money back. It's after eleven, late for her, but early for Becky, so she hits the call button.

Becky sounds tired when she answers.

"Can you come to the ashram next week? I'm supposed to fly home on Sunday, but I'll stay on a few days if you can join me. I'll buy you a ticket."

"That's crazy, Mom. You know I have rehearsals, and I want to send another video clip of this new dance I'm setting for the company to Caroline at the Pillow. I just spoke with her, and she said as long as it's before the deadline, I can send it to her, and she'll swap out the one I sent last week."

"It's only October, Sweetie. I thought you said their deadline wasn't until February."

"Yeah, well, it's on my mind. I wouldn't be able to relax."

"You know you recharge after you take a break. It would be good for you."

"That's your hideout, Mom. It's not mine. If I'm going to take time off, it's not going to be at your ashram."

"Okay. Maybe something else then."

"All those swamis bowing down to the guru, chanting to gods. Forget about it!"

"Okay, Becky, I get it."

"I mean, it's just too weird."

"I hear you."

"Why do you need to pray to an elephant? You should put all that devotion into finding a husband or at least a decent boyfriend."

"I'm not getting into all that with you now." Wendy speaks quickly, so Becky doesn't interrupt with more commentary on her notion of ashram life or Wendy's lack of a personal one. "How about this? I could fly to New York on Sunday evening; maybe get us a Midtown hotel room for a couple of nights. You could work, but also be pampered a bit. I can try to book you a massage with Gillian. You liked her massage last time. And maybe a dance performance and some good food?"

"Cool. Could you do that? Change your flight and everything? Because I've wanted to see ..."

"I'll check tomorrow. Look at your calendar to see when you might be free for a massage. Are you rehearsing Monday evening? I'd love to watch."

"Why? Can't you come to Asheville?"

"I'm not sure yet. I'm supposed to be in a training in the Berkshires when you're in Asheville."

"That's okay."

Wendy can hear the disappointment in her voice. "I'm going to see if I can cancel, but I want to see the new dances, even if it's in rehearsal."

"I wouldn't have time to hang out with you in Asheville, anyway. At least we'll be in the same room in New York, even if one of us is sleeping."

They both laugh. Though neither of them sleeps more than six or seven hours, it is never the same six or seven. "You called that one."

Wendy is smiling as she prepares for bed. In four days, she'll see Becky. But sleep is far away. She replays Becky's commentary on her relationship history and lies awake, ruminating about the men she's loved since the divorce.

No one besides Norma has ever made Wendy feel adored the way Cal did in the hours they spent together over the years that he promised to create a daily life with her. By the time Becky was twelve and angry at her for loving another woman's husband, Wendy knew Cal would never leave Denise, no matter the promises to her and to himself. It was Becky's judgment of her that gave Wendy the strength to finally let go. No one had ever come close to making her feel the way Cal did, so she gave up looking. She didn't go out on a date until Becky went to college.

After Cal, no one she met seemed worth the risk of disturbing the tender truce that substituted for the sweet bond she'd had with Becky before the divorce. Besides, her expanding clinical practice and teaching schedule demanded so much it seemed best to be present for Becky when she was home, even if being present seemed to mean little to Becky. Still, there were the occasional rent-a-movie, popcorn night when Becky was a teenager. Sometimes rare confidences were shared, usually when Becky felt abandoned or betrayed by one of her new friends, or the times when Becky heard from someone in the old gang in Boston. That always seemed to throw her off balance for a day or two. It took her several weeks to recover when she heard that Sophia, a girl in the old crowd, had died of a heroin overdose. By that time, both girls were seventeen.

After Becky left for Bard, the guy on the Cybex machines next to Wendy, a guy she had seen working out in the same gym at the same time for years, suddenly seemed remarkably sexy. Why hadn't she noticed that before? His name, it turned out, was Mike, and she was aware of how they seemed to rock towards each other when they talked. They danced in the swirl of that attraction, becoming lovers and friends, until Wendy broke it off. Mike wasn't Cal. He was a forensic psychologist with a military background, and enough childhood trauma to make him moody and interesting and funny and resilient. He loved kids and animals, and Becky, home for Thanksgiving, surprisingly liked him a lot. But they were different in too many ways. The crust of his Alabama Southern Baptist childhood had dissolved years before, but his politics were too far to the right of a liberal Jew raised in the Northeast. She loved Mike, she thought, but not enough. Not down deep. Not the way she still, in the deepest most bound up part of her heart, loved Cal. She broke Mike's heart, really. She hated doing that, and so she swore off dating. She had a fling now and then, but she hadn't been in a serious relationship since Mike. She missed Mike more than she could admit, even to herself. But it hadn't taken long for his heart to mend in the arms of a woman with whom he was still living eight years later. His new partner Jill grew up in rural Texas and Wendy tells herself they are a much better match.

It is hard to sleep tonight, though. She keeps asking herself if she made a mistake not staying the course with Mike.

CHAPTER Ten

WITH NOT MUCH SLEEP, Wendy nods off during morning meditation, and when the final Oms begin, she jerks awake and looks around, trying to place herself. She's been dreaming of a temple dancer stomping her feet with arms and hands flowing into mudras. She imagines it's a dream about Saraswati, but in this dream, the dancer is older, maybe as old as Wendy. The woman on the train? Her name, too, was Saraswati, but the difference between the two Saraswatis seems to be more than age. Are they really the same woman? She hopes to know by the end of the translation.

 1944

I have not taken any food since yesterday, but my hunger has faded with the coming of morning light. All night long I have knelt before the altar in prayer. I prayed that my life brings honor to Appa and to Amma. Let me live and dance for God in ways that bring happiness to Varanima. May I bring love and joy to all those I serve. If I must have many husbands, let each be as a God to me as I take him into me. May they be servants of my true husband, my God, whose sword I shall lie with tonight. I giggle suddenly at the silly idea that a sword is my Lord when God is everywhere. I must banish such thoughts, and I remind myself that the sword I shall hold to me all night is the symbol of my true God. I bow once more, touching my forehead to the earth, feeling the radiant energy here in the middle of my forehead. I am on fire on this special day, the day of my dedication, the day on which my brand will say to the world that Saraswati is a married woman, dedicated to God.

I rise for my bath. Pushpa fills the tub with pots of hot water, and steam rises from the surface as she helps me climb in. I hug my knees to my chest, relaxing into the warmth, letting all the impurities wash away as Pushpa scrubs my back with a cloth. When my bath is done, she helps me out, and Varanima comes to rub my body with turmeric and oil. She assists me in wrapping my new silk sari, and I adorn myself with the beautiful gold bangles she presents to me.

"These are the bangles I received from the King on the night of my deflowering. May they bring you to the kingly bed to make love with his son on your own first night."

"Will I dance for him tonight, Varanima?"

"If he requests you to dance, you will dance. A meeting has been arranged, my child. After you dance *pushpanjali* this evening at the temple, the mark will be made upon you. Then you will go to the palace to pay homage to the Rajah."

"This homage . . ." My voice rings high and off-key. "It cannot . . . I cannot . . ."

"What is this trembling, this fear?" Varanima kisses both my eyelids, and then turns me around, so she can braid the jasmine in my hair. "He knows you have not begun your woman's flow and are not yet ready. But tonight, you must look in his eyes. Let him sink into those deep pools, Saraswati, and you will be united together for life."

She finishes the braid, and I lean back against her. *United together for life!* "But God has already claimed me," I whisper. "Can I not be your dutiful daughter-in-law?"

Varani laughs. "What? I am Krishna's amma? I would rather be his Gopi!" Varani gives my shoulders a squeeze and then gives me a little push. "Now you must wait for the sword," she says.

"If the sword is my true bridegroom. You can be mother of the sword, and I shall call you Kali-ma!"

"Humph!" She shakes her head, but she is still smiling. "Sit on the roof, if you like. You will hear the musicians and old aunties carrying the gifts to your bridegroom."

"And what shall my bridegroom give me?" I laugh as I climb the ladder to the roof.

"You shall receive a wondrous cloth cut from his robe, and the bountiful garland of roses from around his neck, and most important, you shall have his sword. After tonight, you can never be a despised widow, for you will not be married to a mortal man."

I climb to the roof. Maybe I am not a true devadasi. After all, I was not born in this caste. Why do I wish never to know the blood, the heat of being a woman? Without it, I can never know my husband fully; never fulfill my duty as a devadasi. They tell me I cannot know complete union with God through the body that has been given me for this brief lifetime until I am fully a woman beneath the body of a man. I look down at the street below. I do not believe them.

The procession is about to begin. There are old women in a rainbow of saris, none of them wearing the white of widows, and there are the musicians in white, who will play for me later as I dance. Now the air is full of drumming, and the neighbors emerge from their houses as my parade moves toward the temple. They don't have far to go, since the house we live in belongs to the temple. Once they are inside the outer walls, I cannot see what is happening, and I close my eyes to meditate, for when they return, I shall not be alone again today.

The sound, now louder than before, and accompanied by the old women's high-pitched *hula-huli* with their tongues, brings me out of my solitary meditation. They are returning, and I can see my Lord's sword held high over their heads. Tonight, he shall be mine. I am to sleep with him between my legs, to bring on the flow of my blood. But what if I hide it under my mat instead? Yes! That is what I shall do!

Varanima beckons me down. She straightens my sari and adjusts my hair, as I melt into her arms one last time. When I am fixed, she sends me into the *puja* room to receive the sword. My Lord in this form is golden and long with many jewels on his handle. He feels as heavy as a log in my hand, and as long and straight as a tree. We are seated together now on the bridal rise with the priest. There are many rituals, but I do not grow tired. My Lord in this sword form is all I shall ever need, and each ritual brings me a little closer to Him. Finally, the sister of Varani's mother ties the golden *tali* around my neck. With this thread I am bound to an all-pervasive God in perfect union, and the ceremony is complete.

A *puja* is offered while I change into the *pyjama* I will wear for the dance and adorn myself with Varanima's jewels. Varanima comes in and places sandal paste on my forehead. It is the first sign that I am now a married lady. "May you be blessed with many husbands," she whispers in my ear.

"Do not curse me, Varani," I whisper back, and she looks at me as though I have struck her.

There is applause as I enter the room, and the guests assemble themselves on the mats. The bridal platform has been pushed to one side, and my dance master beats the *tala* with his cymbals. The musicians join in with a gentle raga, and the singers begin. I respond to the mood of the music with my body, as I stay strictly with the movements and mudras I have learned. I flirt with the sensation and mood of each verse, plunging into its exhilaration, and then rolling into its sadness. The music flows with the beautiful poetry of love and devotion between man and woman, Krishna and Radha, God and devadasi. I am lost in each gesture; each moment consumes me. I am here, oh my Lord, dancing for you. Each turn of my wrist, a love note. Each shake of my head, a caress. Each dart of my eyes, a kiss. I am here loving you, feeling your love pour through me, radiant with your light.

And now the dance is finished, and I bow down to God. All the devadasis applaud me. When I rise from the floor, Appa is there with Ganesha. He is smiling. "Amma would be so proud," he says. And then Varani and all the devadasis surround me with hugs and kisses. "What beautiful *abhinaya*!" I hear. "You are a princess," I hear. "Such feeling! Such *rasa*!" "Surely the Rajah will be your first prince."

Trays of festive food are brought forth, and each guest is served as he sits cross-legged. I am given only milk and fruit. My body must remain pure for my God tonight. I gaze at the women in their silk saris and the men in fine *kurtas*. Everyone seems to be celebrating this union of love, but it pains me that Lakshmi is not here. I shall not have a child of my own, and even this simple pleasure, the gift of knowing my sister's children is denied me. I long to be their loving auntie, to watch the changes as they grow. Bindu's feminine beauty will be not much honored in Shankar's house. I want to hug her every day, and tell her how wonderful she is, as Varanima does with me. And what will happen to Lakshmi and Bindu and tiny Shanta, if the child in her womb is also a girl? Today, I have become a devadasi, God's servant and wife. God has only compassion and kindliness for all beings, including baby girls.

He will not let harm come to Lakshmi and her children. As his servant it is up to me to see that this is so.

Varani's hand rests on my shoulder. "So quiet, Saraswati, sitting alone behind the bridal rise. What are you thinking?"

"I am meditating on God's goodness to me and his harshness to my sister."

"What appears harsh to human eyes, may be the blessing that moves Lakshmi
through many lifetimes. It is not for us to understand or interfere." Varani sighs. "Come, little devadasi. Speak with the friends who are here to celebrate your good fortune."

. . .

WENDY WALKS THROUGH the woods to the temple for noon meditation, thinking how the whole karma and reincarnation thing is used by Hindus the way Christian fundamentalists use heaven. Suffer now for rewards in the afterlife. It makes sense in Saraswati's world, Wendy believes. Becky would be contemptuous of this reasoning. She would be as outraged by Lakshmi's servitude as she would be by Saraswati's.

Becky is scornful of this path through the woods. These days, she has little interest in anything happening outside the City, but the ashram in particular annoys her. Wendy thinks it's because she used to love it, loved to come along for a weekend of practicing yoga, hiking, meditation. She even loved the Saturday night satsang chanting, as long as she was allowed to stand in the back and dance. It may have been the closest she has come to feeling a connection to the divine, and she adamantly does not believe in God. Believing might make Becky feel vulnerable, and at this time in her life, it is not a feeling she can afford. Dance isn't a doorway to the divine, as it is for Saraswati. Dance *is* the divine. Dance is

Becky's god. She thinks Becky would be happier if art were Wendy's god. Ironic, because she turned away from that portal to the divine for Becky's sake. She has a flash of the woman on the train telling her to follow her dharma, and she shakes it off, picks up her pace and begins to chant. Come back to this present moment, she admonishes herself, this step, this mantra.

1944

In the evening, the aunties gather around me, and we proceed to the temple. I perform *pushpanjali* and then I dance my offering for Shiva. The dance master is pleased with my performance. I can tell by the way he makes little "ah" sounds that are not part of the rhythm. My eyes are on the statue of Shiva through every movement. I am so concentrated on my Lord, and I am rewarded by his rapt attention. He approves of me, his newest devadasi!

Chandrakant moves beside me now with the hot brand. It is his duty to make the mark on my upper arm. Even my breathing must be still, and I turn away from the look in his eyes. May I release this fear of the heat. He intones the prayers like a tiger roar and then presses the brand, hot from the fire, into my arm. Tears come to my eyes, but I will not let them fall. The temple servant brings me the silken head cloth and Chandrakant ties it around my head.

The magnificent lamp is placed in my right hand. Now, no matter the stirrings of my heart, I know I am truly a devadasi, for no other female may swing the lamp before God in the temple. I am grateful now for the brand that binds me forever into God's service. There is nothing else I want to do. May I always find ways to praise Him from my heart with my dance and my song.

The musicians begin to play again, and we form the procession to the palace. Neighbors emerge from their houses as we pass. Some climb to their roofs to watch the parade. The musicians are merry and there is song as well as a lively step. Old aunties sit on their porch swings with young ones in their lap, pointing and smiling at me. Shankar's house is on the route to the palace, and I hope that Lakshmi might come out to see me.

We turn up a narrow street and pass houses that have two and three stories. On this street, the lamps are lit in every house, and the people lean from the windows, waving. There are wedding processions nearly every day in this season, but few travel this road on the way to the palace. I have stopped in front of my sister's mother-in-law's house, and although the lamps are lit, there is no one leaning from the windows or on the porch. "Blessings, dear sister," I cry, before I am jostled along by the musicians behind me.

The musicians cease their playing as we enter the palace grounds. Varani gives them each a gift of cash, and then she and her sister devadasi accompany me into the palace. The electric lights are lit all through the great hall. The Rajah has been expecting us, Varani says. There are many paintings in large gold frames. When I whisper that they look strange, Varani says they are from the West. The furniture too, is big and dark and hard. There are chairs for sitting straight, with legs dangling. How painful it must be to sit in such a way.

We are shown into a beautiful room with golden statues of ancient devis and many tables with bowls of flowers. The scent of jasmine is everywhere, even in this room. The Rajah sits in a tall carved chair with many pillows. He sets aside the documents he has been reading and smiles. We bow before him and then I lift my head and give him words of praise, as I have been taught.

"You speak beautifully, Saraswati," he says. "Come sit by me and let me hear your sweet voice in conversation."

Until now, I have only seen the Rajah from a distance during the festival processions, and I did not know how young he is, nor how handsome. As I move to sit on the floor by his chair, I am suddenly aware of the dust on my feet from the walk through the streets. I hope the jasmine has not fallen from my braid. I hope he asks me something I can answer. I gaze at the wall of books behind him and wish I could have stayed in school. There is so much more to read!

"How do you feel about becoming a devadasi?" His voice is low and has a smile in it.

I wonder if he has noticed my feet, or the wrinkles in my dancing *pyjama*. I adjust my costume. "It is a great honor, your highness."

I hear a little jingle of Varani's ankle bells behind me, and I know what she is trying to tell me. I am to look into the king's eyes. I wish I could just dance for him. This is the hardest thing I have had to do today, this looking, this talking. I take a deep breath and letting go of the worry about my dirty feet, I look. He meets my gaze and we do not speak for what seems like an entire evening. It is restful now, this looking, and tears come to my eyes. I do not understand this, but I have no desire to look away.

Still looking at me, he asks what I will like most about performing my duties.

I am calm now. I feel as though I could sit at his feet for hours. "It is union with God," I say.

"How will you do that, Saraswati?"

"Through dance, through puja, through song, and through giving my body lovingly and with great passion to my master here on earth." I do not know where these words have come from, for it is not how I felt this morning. But it is how I feel now, looking into the eyes of this man, not old at all, this manifest God.

"It is we fortunate men who will serve you, my dear one."

The Rajah sighs deeply and nods to Varani. "May I have the blessing of being your first servant?"

Varani nods her head. It was never a question.

"It would please me greatly, if you were," I say.

"Good." He turns to one of the attendants. "Take her to the bed chamber."

I draw a quick breath at his words, though I know this is a ritual, that I am only to run my hand across his bed linen. I rise and Varani follows me into the room. Drapes surround the bed. I see myself wrapped in the soft thick fabric, letting the Rajah unwrap me like a parcel. The bed is so big, it looks like a chariot. I imagine that the Rajah and I will play games in this bed, riding the mattress, as though horses pulled us through the streets. This will be fun. I am so grateful to my divine husband that he has chosen the Rajah for my first lover. I will hold His sword in my arms tonight! When I turn to smile at Varani, there are tears in her eyes.

. . .

WENDY SIGHS, RELIEVED. Maybe it's a love story after all. Why does she feel she needs to defend Saraswati's life against her daughter's imagined judgment? It's almost as if there are two competing voices in her head—the Indian girl's acceptance of her culture's norms and Becky's adamant rejection of them. The low value placed on female life is painful for Wendy to contemplate then and even now: baby girls are aborted, women and girls are blamed for their rape, and indigent beedi rollers still die young. Yet she is absorbed in Saraswati's journey and can imagine herself on the same path a lifetime or two ago. The meeting with the Rajah has given her hope about how this story will end, at least for Saraswati. She looks at the clock and sees that she has three more hours to read before evening meditation and dinner. This week of retreat is passing too quickly. Tomorrow evening, the weekend workshop begins. She wants to be finished with the translation before that, before meeting Becky in New York on Sunday. She gets up, stretches, plugs in the kettle to make herself a cup of tea. Black tea, she decides, so she can read as much as possible without falling asleep. When the tea is ready, she settles back into her chair and picks up the manuscript where she left off.

 1945

The schedule of lessons is tiring. I thought it would not be so after my dedication, but the dance master still comes every day to teach me new repertoire. Chandrakant comes to chant the sacred sutras I must learn, so there is little time for visits. I went to the house of my father last week and shall go again next month. But so far, the way to Lakshmi has been barred. She has lost another baby, and I fear that Shankar's mother will want another wife for him. Varani tells me that only pain will come from a visit where I am not welcome. She tells me it would be bad karma, that my sister would bear the consequences in this lifetime, and it would be my burden in the next. But I think my sister is in danger. I must find a way to get there, despite Varani's warnings. In the meantime, Varani has shown me several spells and incantations that we practice together to ward away all evil from my sister and Bindu and little Shanta. These we do at night, when the servants have returned to their hovels. She is teaching me the rituals that no man knows, for they have been handed down from devadasi to devadasi from the very beginning of time. We will do the snake ritual after my blood begins to flow. There are many secrets that must wait until then, like the conjuring of sexual passion in another, and how to keep my womb from receiving a child.

Now, it is late, and Varani's patron, the wealthy rubber merchant who brings her gold from the city, is sleeping upstairs. I am admiring the gold bangles he has brought for me. He says I am like a daughter to him, which I like better than being a wife. When he arrived, Varani asked me to bathe his feet. She said it would be good practice. Though his face is handsome, his heels are cracked as the earth and his toes are misshapen. And so big. I am glad it is Varani lying with him now and not me.

I lie awake on my mat, listening to the love cries they make, learning how to show the patron I am pleased. When I asked Varani about the sounds she makes, she says it lets a man know of the pleasure he brings her. "Is there much pleasure in it?" I asked her. "Sometimes," she replied.

"Ta tem tem tem. Ta tem tem." This seven beat *tala* is not so easy as the *pushpanjali* rhythm I have been performing at *puja*. When I ask my feet to dance, they slip back to a four count after just one line. I must practice these lines again and again. I feel there is someone behind me, watching, and as I finish the line, I turn to see Pushpa. She is trying to hide her laughter behind her hand.

"What am I doing that amuses you, Pushpa?"

She points to the back of my *pyjama*, and I strain to see behind me. There is something red on the yellow silk. Did I sit on something? *Kumkum* powder perhaps? But it is bright. Blood! It is blood. I have begun to bleed. I fall to the floor. I cannot stop the tears that flow with the blood. My life will forever be changed by this flow, this heat in my lower chakras. "Only God, only God," I whisper.

Pushpa runs out of the room, and in a moment, Varanima is there. She holds me by my arms. "Get up, darling Saraswati, and rejoice! The time of your fullness as a woman, as a true servant of God, has come. We will celebrate when the bleeding has stopped. You will be honored, Saraswati, like the Goddess herself. And then your sweet voice can sing the evening prayers."

"Ma, ma," I cry. "I am not fit for the Rajah. I am not ready."

"You will be, my dear one, when the flow ceases. Take this time now, to know yourself, Saraswati. To know that which changes, and that which is unchanging. You have the gift of six days alone, to see the fullness of the woman you are. Come, my dear one." Varani takes me by the hand and puts me in the room where I am to rest for six days. No one will touch me here. I will eat little and shed the *kumkum* of a married woman that I have worn on my forehead. My *tali* will be removed. I will be alone. Neither Chandrakant nor my dance master will visit me, for I am to see no man's face. My hair cannot be combed or oiled.

I have been in this room for two days. My blood flows now into the cloth that Varani's mother, Mataji, has brought me. When she brings me my flattened rice and fruit, she smiles kindly. It is strange to be so alone, without the chatter of servants around me. I cry for Amma in this room, for when I close my eyes it is her face I see. It is her gentle hand that rocks me to sleep. Sometimes when I close my eyes in meditation, reciting the mantra I received upon my dedication, it is her voice chanting the sound, and then she comes to me, filling the whole room with her presence. She tells me many intimacies of preparation. How she knows these things is a mystery to me, since she had only one husband and was not a devadasi. Yet she tells me the secrets of herbs to purify my body after lying with a man. She tells me how to carry myself. "Straight and tall, Saraswati," she says, "because God is always with you."

She has told me there is a place inside me that is so deep, no husband will ever touch it, unless it is unlocked, and that only I have the key. She gave me the key in a dream, and it is the secret name of God. I am to give the name voice when I am with a husband with whom I seek total union, whom I wish to serve as my God not just for this lifetime, but for an eternity. "I shall never use this key," I told her. I need no mortal man to bring me to God.

"Your blood flows now, Saraswati. Things will be different. You do not wish to use it now but hold the key in safekeeping for when you do."

Now, I sit in wonder over her words. I repeat the sacred mantra she gave me silently and alone. I need no husband to find my God. I have been blessed by Krishna. Shiva himself danced with me. It was Shiva who led me to my *dharma*. It was He who called me to my role, out of my ordinary life as a daughter and sister who rolled beedis all day. For it was on the evening He came to me that the decision was made for me to become a devadasi. He is my protector, my God, my lover, my husband. I have no need for union through any ordinary man. I shall do my duty, and that is all. I have learned the love sighs and touches. I know the positions for my legs, my arms, my feet, my tongue. I shall be a devadasi who brings honor and wealth to her family. But my true union is with God.

Mataji has come to bathe me this morning, and as the water rolls down my skin, I see my nipples pressing forward into the cool morning air. I look down at my body in a way I have not done before, noticing that where there was smooth flat skin, a new roundness has appeared. This is what the Rajah will see, these rounded thighs that only yesterday seemed as straight as sticks, and this tuft of dark hair between my legs. This is the fourth day of my flow, and the first of my baths. Mataji will come again tomorrow and the next day. On the seventh day my ritual bath prepares me for the *rajaguru* ceremony and there will be a very big feast, even bigger than the day of my dedication. The cooking smells have been coming to me for days, but I am brought only flattened rice and fruit. Today, Mataji gave me a little yogurt with molasses for breakfast, but it did not take my thoughts from honey cakes and biryani.

Now, I sit before my statue of Shiva, contemplating the changes that await me. In just three days I shall be taken to the palace. If the Rajah lies with me, then I will know God in the most pleasing of mortal forms, for he is beauteous and strong. It is a great honor to be his desire. But when the Rajah has done with me, I am to go to Chandrakant. Then, shall I know God in the most disagreeable of human forms? It is my shame that I speak of my patron, Chandrakant, in such a way. I bow before my beloved Shiva. "Let me be yours," I whisper, "in each of your human disguises."

As I rise to sit on my heels, I feel a warm glow at the base of my spine. All around me there is radiance, so like human touch, I feel there is another being in my room. My Lord Shiva who sits with me now, letting me know that all is well. His spirit encircles me with the warmth and glow of the sunset, and I know that all will be well with the Rajah. God will be there, for he is everywhere.

It is not yet light, and Varanima and all the other devadasis of the village accompany me to the river in silence. Varanima carries the pots of turmeric and oil. The other sisters carry *mahaprasad* trays of bananas and coconuts, and the fine garments I shall wear when I have purified my body. The sun is rising as we reach the riverbank, but I can still hear the crickets all around us. A frog chants a deep mantra, and I think of Chandrakant's voice. I praise God that it is not to him I will go tonight.

As I stand on the edge, feeling the cool water playing with my toes, I am taken by a sudden fear. The black water will swallow me, and I shall remain solely the possession of my one true husband. It is both a deep yearning and a fearful dread. This water will eat me alive, and I shall become a virgin *sati*, sacrificed for God.

"Go ahead," Varanima says, and gives me a little push. "Wash clean your childhood in this water."

I go no farther.

Varanima reaches down and taking a handful of water, she sprinkles it over me. I feel the cold drops soaking through my sari to my skin and begin to shiver.

"More water will make you a woman who has no need of fear," she says. "Go down into the river, Saraswati. I am here with you." She removes the washing cloth tucked in her sari, and dipping it into the water, she rubs it with soap. Now, she scrubs my arms as I stand. I tremble in the cool morning air. "Where is your courage, daughter? Step deeper into the water."

Suddenly there are two sets of strong arms lifting me up by my elbows and walking me deeper into the river. I am lowered down and pushed into a sitting position. "Ai, ai," they say as they lift their saris out of the water and run back to shore. Varanima unwraps my sari and scrubs the rest of me, then bundles me in a bathing cloth and walks me back to shore where Mataji waits to rub my body with turmeric and oil. All the invited guests help dress me in the fine new sari of red and gold. There is red kumkum for my forehead and the beautiful tali goes around my neck. Varanima looks at me with raised eyebrows. It is time to say what she has taught me. I reach down for a handful of sand. Although there are a thousand grains in my palm, they are all one wet clump, so perhaps I will be spared the meaning of the words I must say. I rise. "May I have as many husbands as there are grains of sand in my hand," I say.

"What?" cries one of the devadasis. "What did she say?"

"Let God hear you, my child," Mataji says.

Varanima gives me a strong look.

I take a breath and raise my arm over my head. "May I have as many husbands as there are grains of sand in my hand." I throw the sand down. Around me the devadasis raise a great noise of celebration, as I wipe my hand on the cloth Varanima offers.

"You are a fine married lady, now," Mataji says. "Tonight, you will know the bliss."

Perhaps he will have drunk too much wine, or he will be tired, I think. Perhaps it is the bliss of the Gods that I will know for just a little longer. We form a lively procession back to Varani's house. The sweepers make music for us, and my sisters warble their *hula-huli*. The mating call of the peacock, I think. We are almost past Shankar's house, but I turn back, just in case. And there she is! My beautiful sister Lakshmi stands watching the procession. Shanta is in her arms, and Bindu stands beside her waving and blowing me kisses. It is such a precious sight, and I know it is a most wondrous omen that all will be well tonight.

When we reach the house, the women welcome me. They wave lamps and shower me with rice, as though I were the object of their devotion, and in this moment, on this day, I am.

Chandrakant performs the *mangala-aropana* ceremony in my honor, and then the feasting begins.

The cook has prepared a bountiful table to last throughout the day for our many guests. All day long the coconut rice is brought out in great bowls, and idlis and masala appear on trays, but I will not partake. I must stay in readiness and purity for my husband, the Rajah. He may wish me to dance, to recite the poetic verses of the great pundits of old, or to sing the ancient lyrics of love. I must be ready to please him in all ways.

It is nearly time. Varanima and her sister will accompany me. An elephant has been procured for the occasion for I am to arrive in a way befitting a bride of the Maharaja. Chandrakant will walk beside the elephant. I think he is most pleased that his devadasi has been favored by his ruler. I am pleased also for the Rajah is young and handsome, and I am told that though he is not yet twenty and two, he is a scholar. I saw the many books when I danced for him. I am told they are in English, Tamil, Kannada, Sanskrit and Hindi. Chandrakant's cousin is the royal librarian, and he has said that the Rajah has added to his father's magnificent collection of the sacred Sanskrit texts, from which he seeks the *darshanas* and teachings of great gurus and pundits. He is most sincere, Varanima says, in his devotion to knowledge of the divine.

I hear the din of my guests as I prepare myself. Is it not a great honor? Will I not be performing my duty to my God and Rajah? Have I not been well trained in the art of love? Then why this great agitation? If there were a secret tunnel in the house, I would hide myself there. I would even take up the broom of the lowliest untouchable, if I could escape this night.

"Do not dawdle," Varanima says as she enters the room. "Saraswati, you have not even done your hair properly. Here, let me," she commands, taking the comb from my hand. "It is a sin to keep the Rajah waiting." She strokes firmly, and then begins to twist and braid, working quickly. "There!" She turns me around to see myself in the silver tray she holds. "You are a princess, Saraswati. He will delight in you for sure."

"I am afraid. I do not wish to go." I hold my belly where there is sudden pain. "Varanima, I am sick."

Varanima's hands come to rest on my shoulders. "Look at me, child."

Her hands are warm, but her eyes are cold. "If you are sick tonight, and do not do your duty, Chandrakant will be waiting for your recovery. You will not have a second chance with the Rajah. Which would you choose?"

"I will go to the Rajah."

"A wise choice."

She releases me, and we enter the room. The crowd parts as we move through to the front door of our house where the elephant waits with Chandrakant.

People come out to stare, and to toss flower petals and good wishes. "Forgive me for my fear, Lord," I whisper to myself. "Give me courage to fulfill my duty. Give me strength to please the Rajah in all the ways I have been taught. Let me love him as I love You."

The marble is cool beneath my feet. As I move through the great hall with Varanima, we are attended by many palace servants. One who wears a splendid red coat guides us to the Rajah. The room we enter is large and filled with chandeliers lit with candles. There is a pool at one end of the marble floor and lotus blossoms float there. The air is filled with the fragrance of jasmine. The Rajah looks as though he has just come from the temple. He is dressed like a priest, in a fresh white *dhoti* wrapped to his waist, and a shawl draped over one shoulder. His chest is bare, as is his head, but his forehead has been painted with white and red *namam*. He is prepared, I think, to do his royal duty with me as though it were a holy act. I am much pleased by this. He sits on soft silken pillows, and there are many servants surrounding him. He watches as I enter and approach. "Thank you, Uncle," he says to the man in the red coat. "You may be seated." All of the company sits down on the woven mats that ring the room. His eyes fall on me. "Saraswati," he says softly and smiles.

I bow before him touching his feet, and then rise to my knees with my hands in prayer position. "Your highness, I am here to worship God," I say.

"But God is everywhere, Saraswati. You need not come here to worship him."

I glance frantically to my right, but I cannot see Varanima. How am I to respond? It is not as we have practiced. I swallow and continue. "Your Highness, I worship you as my God."

"But God is formless, Saraswati."

Can this be true? I wonder. Can God be everywhere, and yet be formless? I want to ask this, but I cannot. I look at him curiously. He smiles at me, and I smile back.

"I see your mind working, Saraswati."

Dare I ask? I give a quick glance to the left, and there is Varanima, admonishing me to continue through her stern expression.

I turn back to meet the Rajah's gaze, and I smile at him with my eyes. "I offer thee prayers and salutations, your Highness."

"Thank you, my little devadasi. But what I would most like is a dance. Would you offer me something fresh and new, something you have never danced before?"

"It would be my greatest delight, Your Highness," I say.

He claps his hands and the palace musicians come forward. I move to the side of the room where Varanima ties on my ankle bells. I have not danced publicly without my dance master before. Nor have I performed an improvisation, but now I must do so to unfamiliar beats and rhythms. I stand on the far side of the room and listen for several moments as the singer establishes the *raga*. There are seven counts to this *tala*. The *mridangam* has already begun to improvise on the *talam*, and although the drumming is forceful, I must concentrate on the beat the singer is keeping. When the venu enters, improvising on the melody, I too come forward, moving my feet with the count of the singer. I let the music flow through my movements, using abstract gestures that suit the rhythm. The singer begins a Sanskrit poem I have never heard. There are many words I do not know. I must imagine each line in light of my body's response to the music. Soon I am one with the *bhava* of the text. I sense the intention of each thread of words, telling a story of love that is beyond the measure of things in this world. I express this love through my hands, my limbs, my darting eyes. I do not know every word of Sanskrit, but I look at the Rajah smiling at me so gently, and I feel the meaning in my heart. The *abhinaya* is flowing through me, drawing him into my body, my mind, my spirit.

When the dance is over there is much applause. I bow at the Rajah's feet.

"Get up, Saraswati. Do not bow to me again. Come, sit." He makes room for me on his pillow and a servant brings another. "I did not know you understood Sanskrit, Saraswati."

"I do not, Your Highness. Only the words in the prayers I have been taught."

"Then you know this one."

"Not in my mind, Your Highness."

The Rajah smiles and reaches for my hand. "In your heart then. That is even better." He turns to the uncle in the red coat and nods. There is a low murmur as everyone is ushered out, and then there is silence. It is just we two.

"Would you like music, Saraswati? Shall I call the musicians back?"

I look down. It is suddenly harder to meet his gaze. "No, Your Highness."

"Are you afraid, dear devadasi?"

How can I burden the Rajah with my fears? "No, Your Highness."

"It is natural to be frightened. Do not be afraid to tell me. I am afraid, too."

I look up into his eyes again. "You, Your Highness? Why should you be afraid? You have been husband to many devadasis, have you not?"

"I have performed my duty with many of your sisters, dear Saraswati, and I was never afraid before." He lifts both my hands. Slowly he turns one over and then the other, and brings each to his lips, placing a kiss on each palm. "You are different. I do not know why."

Could it be that there will be no deflowering tonight? "Your Highness, may I inquire into the meaning of your words?"

He smiles and leans back on one elbow to see me better. "Of course."

"You said I should not worship you as my God, because God is formless."

"This is so."

"But all around us we see the forms of God in our Temple and on our altars. And you are wearing your rosary, your *mala* beads with which you pray your *japa-mantra* to your God. How can you pray, Your Highness, to a formless God?"

"This is an excellent question. In fact, it is the essential question. All these Gods and Goddesses, have you noticed how naughty they are? They are erotic and immoral tricksters, are they not?"

I nod.

"They are sometimes jealous, sometimes angry, sometimes full of grief. Do you think God has so much reaction to the ups and downs of heavenly life? Is God so petty? No, we Hindus have these Gods mainly to make fun of them. They react the way we react. We have made them just like us, so we can poke fun at ourselves. All these deities we praise are simply the symbols of our own virtues and faults."

"Then what is God?"

"God knows no form nor gender nor any word in Tamil or Sanskrit or English that, when used, would limit and define the Absolute."

"Your Highness, I have prayed to Shiva and invoked his presence. I have danced with Krishna. How do I seek this Absolute One?"

"Absolute All, Saraswati." He picks up my hand. "I see more clearly now, how you are different. I shall try to answer your question." He pauses and looks into my eyes. "Do not struggle to catch hold of God. You are like a little fish in the ocean of God. Suppose the little fish says, 'I will swallow God. I will swallow God.' The ocean is big, and the fish is in it. There is no need for him to swallow the ocean. So, you simply allow yourself to be. You do not have to do anything special. Everything is cared for, looked after. You are given everything. There is nothing more you need. If you know that, you are filled with gratitude."

"Can you see the gratitude in my eyes?"

He laughs. "It is about to spill onto your cheeks." He hands me a beautiful white cloth, and I look at it. "Go ahead, Little Fountain. Use it to dry your eyes."

I do as he says and folding it neatly, I hand it back. "You may keep it," he says. "I have other gifts for you, my dear, but this handkerchief is a symbol of me, and it caught your gratitude, so now it is a symbol of us both.

"This I shall cherish most," I say. "Just as the statue of Shiva on my altar is a symbol of God, so this cloth shall symbolize you."

"You are very sweet, Saraswati."

"I feel you are like a guru to me." I bow and touch his holy feet.

"Rise up, Saraswati, and sit beside me. Before you leave I shall give you a *Bhagavad Gita* with a commentary by a great Vedanta philosopher. If you have questions about it, I shall try to address them as best I can."

"Thank you, Your Highness."

"Please return to me tomorrow. Perhaps we will be ready to perform our duty."

"And if we are not, Your Highness?"

"Then you will have to keep coming, will you not?" I feel his hands on my face, and before I realize what is happening, he is kissing my lips, and I am kissing him back. My first man-woman kiss, I think, and I do not wish to stop. But he pulls back.

"Until tomorrow then, my Saraswati, my muse."

"Yes, Your Highness." I look down at my trembling hands. I did not want to stop. I do not want this night to end.

He rises and claps his hands. The servant-uncle with the red coat enters. "Please present Saraswati with her gifts, Basha, and see that she is properly escorted home. Where is my librarian?"

"He is home, Your Highness."

"Ah, Saraswati, my dear, I shall have the book for you tomorrow." He looks into my eyes and then brings his hands together at his heart. "Namasté," he says and leaves the room.

Varanima is alone in the bed when I return, and I climb in beside her. She opens her eyes, and then opens them wider. "What? So early, Saraswati? It is not even daylight. What went wrong?"

"Nothing. We talked together. It was wondrous."

"But he did not take your maidenhead?"

"Tomorrow night perhaps."

"He wishes you to return?"

"Yes, Varanima. I think he is well pleased with me."

"I hope you are right, Saraswati. Chandrakant waits."

"He will wait a long time, Varanima, for I will not take him for a husband."

"But you must. It is already arranged. It need not be forever. Besides, you may have many other husbands as well, ones you choose."

"I will have none but the Rajah."

"I do not think he will take you as his favorite concubine. You are yet a baby, and he is already a man."

"No, Varanima!" I cry. "I can count the years between us on one hand. I am not a baby, and he is just barely a man. Besides, he's a scholar."

Her voice raises to meet mine. "What have books to do with anything?" Her grip on my arm is tight. "Besides, Chandrakant has paid a high price for the privilege of your love."

I pull away. "And now I have enough gold to pay him back."

Varanima raises above me. "The Rajah gave you such lavish gifts, and did not yet deflower you?"

"Beautiful gold, Varanima, and other fine jewels." I pull the cloth from my bosom. "And the finest gift is this."

"What is that?"

"His handkerchief."

Varanima nods slowly, as if she is just beginning to understand. "Maybe you will not have to worry about Chandrakant."

"What are you dreaming about, Saraswati?" Varanima asks, as she pours the sweet batter on the table. We will cut and roll it into cakes for the feast day which approaches.

"Thinking, not dreaming," I say.

Pushpa looks at me and giggles. "It is her husband, the Rajah. She has not finished anything in this kitchen all week. I come behind her to finish grinding the idlis and rolling the dosas."

"He is not yet my husband, Pushpa."

"But you are with him every night. What are you waiting for?"

"I am ready now. It is he who waits."

"But what have you been doing together all these evenings?"

"We study."

Pushpa raises her eyebrows. "He is teaching a tiny girl like you? Whatever for?"

"I have questions, and we look to the *Bhagavad Gita* to see how Krishna addresses the very same problems. And then we look to other sacred texts. It is glorious."

"What problems, what questions?" Varani's tone is harsh.

"The real problem is uniting with a formless God, with boundless pure awareness. Can God be bound to individual consciousness through action, on the battlefield, for example, or through devotion, as in our dancing, or ..."

"Where did you get such notions?" Varani knows I got them from the Rajah. "Bind yourself to your duty! The dance master comes soon to teach you the new dance you will perform at the festival in five days' time. You must put all other thoughts out of your head to learn this dance."

"But it is your dance, Varanima. Why are you giving it to me?"

"You are most favored by His Highness, little one. You should be the one to dance it this year."

"If I must," I say.

"If you must? What is wrong with you? You are a devadasi, not the *maharani*!"

"Yes, Varanima. I am a devadasi. But how many dances do I need in my repertoire to know God? Will not one suffice?"

"One will do in the moment that you dance it but learning and performing keeps your devotion alive."

"Was that the priest's voice?" Pushpa asks.

"Probably the dance master." Varani wipes her hands on her sari. "I will see."

Remaining behind the wall, I wait and listen.

"Welcome, Sir," Varani says. "I am very glad to see you."

"Thank you, Sister. But where is Saraswati?"

"She is at rest just now, Chandrakant. The dance master comes soon. If you wait, you may see her."

"Why has she not come to my hut, Varani? Each night I have waited."

"She is to be first with the Rajah."

"And has he not exercised his privilege?"

"He has not."

"But ..."

"I know it is strange, since she has been going these many nights to the palace, but he has not yet deflowered her."

"Then what is his intention? Another girl is to be dedicated next week. Will he have a harem of virgins at his feet?"

"I think not. He has taken a special interest in our girl."

"My girl. Does he know that?"

I step into the room. "Nine thousand rupees was my price, I believe. The cost of my dedication and the many feasts you have generously provided."

"There you are, Saraswati. You are far beyond the measure of rupees, my dear."

"Then I owe you at least that. I am so grateful to you for all you have done. You are just like a father to me, Chandrakant."

He smiles and reaches his hand out towards me.

"I can never hope to repay you for all you have provided," I pull the gold necklace, studded with jewels from behind my back, "but this, I think, is of value far greater than 9,000 rupees."

He takes it in his hand and studies it carefully. "This is the gift from the Rajah and should rightfully go to your mother." He presses it toward Varani who waves it away.

"It is for you, to pay you back for your investment in Saraswati's future," she says.

"It is not how I wish to be repaid. It was agreed between us, Varani. You dare not break our covenant or there will be trouble for you in the temple."

Varanima glances at me. "Of course, I shall do all in my power to honor the agreement between us, Sir. But I cannot control our Rajah's desire. It may be that other arrangements can be satisfying, arrangements that recognize and honor your abundant contribution to our beautiful Saraswati."

"Nothing will satisfy but this ripening fruit!" He spins toward me with a smile that twists his face. "Thank you for this gift of your gratitude and love, Saraswati." He lifts my chin with his tobacco stained fingers. "I shall see you tomorrow." He does not return the necklace.

There are tears in Varani's eyes, and she turns away from me. "What has been promised before the eyes of God cannot be broken." Her voice is a whisper. "I am sorry, Saraswati."

My body feels coiled and ready to spring. Every day, promises are broken, covenants destroyed. How could she give up? I want to ask her to stand with me. I control the shout in my heart and whisper back. "But what could he do to us at the temple?"

When she turns back, I see how sad she is, and something else. I see the fear in her eyes. My strong Varanima is frightened of that lowly worm. "He could see that we never dance again," she says. "What is a devadasi who can no longer perform the temple rituals and dances, who can no longer march beside the Rajah in the important processionals? What is her life, then, but a life of banishment and shame?"

"And Chandrakant could do that, even if we have the support of the Rajah?"

"He is the chief temple priest. He has a great deal of influence in these matters." Varani puts her arm around me. "If we do not serve God at the temple, we do not have the privilege of living in this house. We would have no home, Saraswati."

"I do not understand why you think he must win," I say, pulling away.

"He is a temple priest and he is a man; therefore, the Gods are on his side."

"The Gods? He has only the icons, the small gods of the smallest minds! I have my husband, my Rajah, on mine."

Varanima grabs my shoulders. My body trembles in the cold of her fierce glare. "You are a simple girl, Saraswati. You do not understand the laws of the universe. If you do not take

Chandrakant as your husband, you will cause pain and suffering for your entire family. You must do your duty! You must obey me in this!"

The rage in her eyes matches my own. I look away and spit on the floor.

"Look at me!" Her fingers press into my skin and suddenly there is no fight left in me. I am limp and unsteady, as the force of her grasp nearly sends me to the ground. "Look into my eyes and promise you will be an obedient daughter."

I meet her eyes. "I am your obedient daughter, Varanima."

"And that you will obey Chandrakant."

"I shall obey my lord and master."

"Say Chandrakant, say his name." She gives me a shake.

"Chandrakant," I whisper.

Her gaze is fixed on me as though I were prey. "Never forget the promise you have made to me and to God on this day, Saraswati." She holds me like that for a moment more, and then she lets me go.

CHAPTER
Eleven

WENDY SETS THE MANUSCRIPT aside and goes outside where the angled light of late afternoon adds a shimmer to the leaves vibrating in the breeze. She needs a walk before she dives back into the translation. It's not just Saraswati's promise that jars her insides, like an itch she can't scratch. It's in her chest. No, her throat. It's Aaron, she thinks. How awful she was to him. And how awful he was to her. Their worst selves. That's what they brought out in each other at the end. Had she stayed with him, she would have fulfilled the promise she made before God, before her family, before her community. To him. And to her mother. *For* her mother. Sometimes—she feels she married Aaron to usher herself into an acceptable adulthood. But it was the beautiful grandchild that changed things. When she gave birth to Becky, she made her mother happy. For a time, it seemed to erase her disappointing childhood—her failure to be the feminine little girl her mother expected.

How many times had her father come to her room after she'd been sent away from the table for a sarcastic eye roll or a caustic word? "How can you hurt your mother like that?" he pleaded. Wendy was a failure as a girl-child, not caring if her hair was perfectly braided, oblivious to the untied bow at the back of her dress. But she wasn't good at boy things either, like catching a ball or running a race. Charm school hadn't worked, except to let her off the hook as a runway model, since she couldn't balance the book on her head or sit, as instructed, with her knees properly touching. Unlike her graceful wisp of a mother, she bumped into things. Her mother told her that she'd been ugly at birth, bruised by the forceps delivery and somewhat twisted—one foot facing forward, the other to the side. Not what her beautiful mother deserved. Until she married Aaron. Then the unexpected had happened. The longed for had happened. Wendy found herself accepted.

Norma hadn't shared her mother's enthusiasm for Aaron, had even tried to caution her, through wary questioning, through sideways looks, against marrying him. Why? She can't quite remember the reason why Norma was against him, but she was. Norma was her first guru, a guru of love, even a barometer of love. Norma, like the rabbi, had sensed something off. That familial love, friendship, companionship was not enough to build a lifetime of intimacy. But so many women accepted companionship as more than enough. So many men too. It seemed that most lasting marriages were based on it. Not the heedless passion she felt for Cal. Arranged marriages were grounded in something other than romantic love, something that grew over time into an abiding and deep connection. At least, that's what they said, those long-married Orthodox women, Hindu women, Moslem women, whose families found them an appropriate match.

She's never entirely forgiven herself for breaking that promise, for breaking her mother's heart. For cracking the empty *happilymarried* vessel Aaron carried in his heart. In some ways, she wonders if her growing need for a creative outlet had led her to push the boundaries of their marriage, of what it meant to make a promise and then give in to a looser, more personal concept of what was "right." Something compelled her out of the marriage. If it hadn't been Cal, would there have been something else? Because Aaron was a good man. Becky loved him. His second wife loved him. Wendy and her boundary crossing, reaching beyond the confines of *happilymarried* for fulfillment, had driven him to the extremes of his personality—his rigidity as a defense against her unchecked flow; his compulsiveness given definition by her inattention, her forgetfulness.

The diary was steeping her in more questions than answers. And that was okay. She stopped on the path. There was bird song. Where was it? She looked up into the glow of oak leaves over her head. There! A cardinal? Singing its heart out.

 1945

I lay aside our books, for Vyasa (that is what my Rajah wishes me to call him) has fallen asleep. My lap is a nest for his long dark hair. His face is smooth as a little boy's. In this moment, I feel the amma to my young son. I stroke his cheek with my fingers, and his eyes open. A little smile plays about his lips, and his arms reach up, pulling me down to kiss him. I cannot taste his lips and mouth as fully as I would wish, so I gently place his head on the pillow and stretch my body out beside him. Now our kisses are full and deep, and he moves his lips down my neck. We kiss until my lips are tired, but I do not wish to stop.

"Sit up, my bliss," he whispers, and he helps me unwind my sari. I have worn no choli on this night, and he holds my breasts in his hands. "My beautiful bliss," he says, and lays me back on the feather bed, and with his hands and lips he caresses me. We lie like this until my nipples grow sore, but I do not want him to stop.

He gently unties my slip and pulls it down, exposing my whole body. I know now that he will deflower me, and I am swimming in love's nectar. I am ready to receive him as I know I always shall. He unwraps his dhoti, and I see that he is long and hard and ready to enter me, but he merely lays beside me, and lets his hands explore me first, touching and probing and rubbing, until my yoni rocks like a cradle and my arms reach for him. Then the glorious lingam of my Rajah, my God, my Vyasa, pushes me hard. I cannot help the cry I make as his rod tears into me.

He rises up, lifting himself from my body, but we are still joined, in our most sacred place. "Do I hurt you, Saraswati?" he whispers.

"It is a hurt from God," I say, and then he plunges into me time and time again. I know the pain will go away, that it will get easier, as Varani says, and one day, I, too, shall find bliss in this holy place with my God, my princely lover.

It ends as it began. My Beloved sleeps, his head on my breast. If I could but always carry the weight of his body upon me, I would be released from worldly concerns, and I would not bother with Chandrakant's demands. Chandrakant. Varanima believes even my Rajah cannot interfere, but if he loves me, he will. He opens his eyes and rolls over.

"Are you all right, my little temple dancer?"

"Yes, Your Highness. I am quite all right." I curl my body against him, and he shelters me with his arm. "I would wish not to do this with another."

"But you are a temple dancer, Saraswati, and I am merely your first conquest."

"So, I am not to return to your bed after tonight?"

"It is customary that you should not return, but as your exalted ruler and your humble slave, I command and beg you to return."

My tears mix with the sweat on his glistening skin.

He lifts my chin. "What is this, Saraswati? Shall I lick them away?"

"I am sorry, Your Highness. I am so happy to know I may come back to you."

"What is here between us, Saraswati, is not customary. We are not bound by the tradition of Maharajah and devadasi. There is something much deeper than a deflowering that has happened here."

"But Chandrakant waits for me. He feels I belong to him as soon as the deflowering is complete. He will expect me tomorrow."

Vyasa sits up. "This is a different story. He sponsored your dedication?"

"And has been my *acharya*, guiding me through my Sanskrit studies."

"What is your feeling for him, Saraswati?"

"It has always been a feeling of gratitude mixed with revulsion."

"You do not wish to welcome Chandrakant as your husband, even for one night?"

"I do not wish it, my Prince, but if you say I must, then ..."

"I have not said that, Saraswati. It is a delicate situation. It might be easier if you were willing to be with him for one night, but I am not saying it will be necessary. I will consult with the palace priest. There may be something Chandrakant wants almost as much as he wants you. I will work on this problem. In the meantime, do not tell anyone you have been deflowered."

> I feel the wetness between my legs, and the sticky sheet beneath me. I could clean myself up and dress as though I had never been unwrapped, but Varani will take one look at me and know.

. . .

WENDY CAN BARELY REMEMBER her own first time. There were so many Saturday nights with Mac in the backseat of his mother's car. The panties had stayed on, but maybe, on occasion, pushed to one side so that there was the penetration she could hardly feel that might not have been penetration at all, that was always followed by the pulling out, the coming against her panties and the worry that the wetness there would travel up her insides—the sperm finding its egg. That's how much she understood at 16. If there had been blood, a broken hymen, she would never have known, because the blue leather of the backseat could be wiped clean, and it was dark. No ritual, no celebration. Shame. Worry. Would she become pregnant? Would he lose respect for her? But oh, had she longed for it, all those nights of touching and kissing and the wetness on the panties could well have been her own.

Mac was her first love and she had wanted to give him everything. But she was going off to college in Vermont and he was staying home to help his father run the family restaurant and attend community college. If she got pregnant, she knew she wouldn't want to marry him and stay home with a baby and live the way his parents lived. But oh, she loved him, and her heart was broken when her friends told her he was sneaking around with an older girl, a senior who put out, that his mother's car was seen parked in her driveway all night. Mac was not her prince, her rajah, but then neither was Aaron. Her prince was the one she couldn't have, the one who still came to her in dreams at night. Cal would be 79 now. She could imagine pushing him in a wheelchair, still loving everything about him. Just a fantasy. Had he left Denise and come to her all those years ago, would he still be her prince today?

1946

The house is peaceful just before dawn. Pushpa has not yet begun the breakfast preparations, nor has Varani risen from her bed for the puja. I had hoped to find a pair of sandals at the door to tell me of a visitor, but there were none. I climb the ladder to the second floor as quietly as possible, and lie down on the bed, facing away from Varanima. She rolls over and puts her arm around me. Her face presses against my neck. "He has made you his wife," she says. "His scent is all over you."

I sigh. I knew it would be impossible. "The Rajah says I must tell no one. I am to return to him tonight."

"There will be consequences, Saraswati. Have you no gratitude for all I have done for you?"

I turn and wrap my arms around my adoptive mother's waist. "I would do nothing to hurt you, my dear sweet mother. You have given me so much."

"It is to Chandrakant you owe the greatest debt."

"And he has been paid in gold."

"We will starve, Saraswati. You cannot reject him."

"You worry needlessly. The Rajah will take care of Chandrakant."

"Only you can take care of Chandrakant. We made a covenant before God."

"Let us wait this day and the next, before Chandrakant knows of my deflowering. Just these two days, Varanima, please. Let us see what my beloved can accomplish with the priest. If he fails, then I shall go to Chandrakant as promised."

"Just two days?"

"Yes, dear, dear Mother, just two days. No misfortune shall befall you, I promise."

She holds my face in her hands and places a kiss on my forehead. "My precious child. I shall pray for a miracle for us all."

I have learned today that Lakshmi is once again with child. I would like to share with her the secret that has been taught to me, but it is forbidden. Besides, Shankar already talks of taking a second wife. If she does not bear him a son, her lot will be even worse, so she must keep trying. The last to be delivered was a boy, but his poor soul had already passed from this world before his body entered it. Lakshmi is in my prayers. It is all I can do.

It was my duty to sing the *Gita Govinda* at the temple this evening. Full devadasis perform the evening ritual in the inner sanctum to put the deities to bed. As I sang, Chandrakant turned to stare at me. His look was full of such venom that I stumbled. I do not know what transpired earlier today, I hope that Chandrakant is no longer my patron, for looking as he does toward me, he would do me harm.

The Rajah's lorry waited for me by the temple gates. Others took note of my conveyance as I climbed into the cab. Now, I bump along the street toward the palace, wondering what my neighbors and the other temple dancers think about the young devadasi who pleases the Rajah. They keep farther apart from me, but I notice them watching me more.

Basha greets me at the door in his fine red coat and leads me to the Rajah's rooms. "Your skin glistens this evening, Saraswati. You have been dancing?"

It is the first time Basha has spoken to me in such a friendly manner. Is there a change in my status, I wonder, of which Chandrakant and Basha have been informed and I have not?

Before we enter the Rajah's chambers Basha turns to me. His smile slides sideways on his face. "Do not forget, Saraswati, that His Highness has honored many new devadasis before you and many will come after."

"What you say is only half true," I say, lifting my head as though I were about to dance. But my hands tremble as I enter Vyasa's room. The Rajah is lounging on pillows, reading an English book. A table with food has been set before him, but he does not eat.

"Ahh, Saraswati," he says as I enter. "I have been waiting for you. Come and eat with me."

It is not right that I should eat with one so far above my caste, lounging together in this manner. It is not right that a ...

"You are terrified, my child. Your presence will not defile my table, and mine will not disturb your karma. We are equal partners, exploring the divine mysteries of the universe. We are in and of the Absolute in equal measure, regardless of your puny size." He laughs and stretches out his hand.

I move to take it and let myself be drawn into his lap. In the arms of my Beloved, I know his uncle is wrong, that none will come after me.

He rolls some rice and dahl into a little ball with his fingers and feeds it to me. "You are like a little bird," he whispers. "A little bird."

I laugh at his play, and I, too, reach into the plates mixing a morsel with my fingers, and then bring it to his lips. He nibbles my fingers as he takes the food. "You are like a hungry monkey," I say, and he laughs. "Can you not tell a banana from a finger?"

"They are both equally delectable, so who is to tell? I must make a study." He pushes the table of food away. "A very thorough study," he says and nibbles my arm. "Ah, this is even more delicious."

"I have been dancing at the temple, Your Highness."

"Hmm. I love salty food."

We roll about on the pillows, laughing. In this way, he nibbles and bites all over my body, exclaiming at its excellent preparation and flavor. "So succulent!" he says, sucking my toes. "So tender," he says, nibbling my breasts. "So well-seasoned," he murmurs, coming up from a dip in my yoni. Somehow, in the course of his meal, he has removed all my clothes and his as well.

It is my turn now to taste the rich flavor of my Rajah. "Oh, so chewy," I say as I gnaw on the muscles of his upper arm. "A bit tough here," I complain, nibbling his toes.

"You are not supposed to swallow, Saraswati. Licking and sucking toes brings the most pleasure."

"For you or for me?"

"Why for you, of course."

Soon we are tasting and nibbling and stroking each other's bodies in every reachable place. Our breathing comes faster, leaving no room for the laughter that has gone before. And now he moves inside me, and my whole body swallows him, deeper and deeper. I want him, and tonight there is no pain, only the thrashing and throbbing of my yoni yearning for the fullness of him, for the deep quenching of my thirst. He pours himself into me for too brief a moment before he rises and pulls away. My hunger is ravenous, consuming him, eating the stars in this dark night. My fingers pulse, opening and closing of their own will. I want. I want.

He returns now, and I see that with each pulling away there is a return. I can relax and wait, and all will come. He falls into the universe of my small body, and together we drown in a boundless ocean. It is union beyond this body and that, a union so deep and full that though we might touch it only for this brief moment, it will be with me always. The whole universe contracts inside me, holding and letting go, and I cry with pure joy. My Rajah gives a cry like death as he falls so deeply into me that I fear for his mortal life.

He sleeps tenderly against me. I watch the rise and fall of his shoulders. I cannot imagine loving any other man, as I do this one. The vow I made at my ritual bath returns to me. "May I have as many husbands as there are grains of sand in my hand." He rolls over onto his belly, and I gently climb on his back. I place my hands on his shoulders and look up to the heavens. "May all my many husbands be manifest in this one man," I whisper. "My true husband, my beloved Rajah."

Vyasa sighs and rolls on to his back, and now I straddle his chest. "We have dispensed with one husband, at least," he says, reaching for my hands.

"But how did you settle things with Chandrakant?" I ask.

"Justly, Saraswati. You need not bother yourself with how."

"I wonder if Chandrakant agrees with your justice. He looked at me with anger while I sang this evening."

"Do not trouble about how he looks. His look cannot hurt you. He is quite satisfied with the agreement we made." He brings my hands to his lips and kisses each one. "As long as I am your Rajah, Saraswati, I will be your protector."

I am suddenly afraid, and I do not know why. I sigh and look away from him.

"What is the matter, my dear?"

My thoughts return to Basha. "Your uncle, Your Highness. Is he unhappy with my presence?"

"Basha," he laughs. "Do not take him seriously. My mother's brother has many opinions, but he will do us no harm. He is often critical of the hours I spend with my books and in meditation. 'A ruler rules,' he says. 'Leave prayers to the priests.' But this I cannot do. Though born a *Kshatriya*, the dharma of my heart is not that of a warrior Rajah, but that of an ascetic. I have given Uncle much power of state, so he need not ridicule the *namam* on my forehead and the prayers that keep me from entertaining concubines and princes. He is happy with his lot."

I lift his slender hand and place it on my breast. "If you are such a holy man, Vyasa, why do you bother with me?"

"In you, my dear one, I find a soul like mine, born out of its caste and longing to live a life of devotion. We are as one in this yearning, you and I, and in this completion."

And then Vyasa pulls me toward him and enters me again.

. . .

WHEW! IT'S GETTING STEAMY. Wendy notices her own arousal. It's been a long time since she's had a lover. She sometimes thinks she should put herself out there on one of those online dating sites, but she's heard horror stories from her friends. There's the occasional fairytale wedding, the result of an internet hook-up, but mostly it's disastrous meetups. The guy is looking for a sugar momma, or he's got some kind of STD, or he looks nothing like his picture, or he's lied about his age. One of her friends dated a guy for a few months who had Fox News going in his house night and day, whose snoring drove her nuts. When she kindly, she thought, ended their relationship, he stalked her, sent texts at terrible times, drove past her house, and scared her into changing the locks and threatening a restraining order.

Wendy doesn't want drama. She's had her fill with Cal. Still, there is this mild yearning, not so much for frontal contact these days, but for someone to watch her back, to pick her up at the airport on her return and make passionate love to her before tucking her in. Someone honest. Funny. Smart. Active. Pleasing to look at without needing to be handsome. And politically aligned. Is that too much to ask?

Most of the time, she doesn't think about it. Her life is full; rich with connections and love. It's a satisfying life, most days. But now and then, like now when she reads about this great romance, well ... there it is. Not the feeling that something is missing, but, well, honestly ... almost.

 1946

Today there is to be another dedication, Varanima has been kind to me. She behaves as if I am already in mourning, as though my beloved is leaving me behind in this material world.

My Rajah told me this morning that he would not deflower the new devadasi. That forevermore, I should have no such worries. I am the only devadasi he will ever need. Still, I cannot say that I am without fear as the hour approaches.

I hear the procession move past our door, but I do not look. I do not want to see the magnificence of my devadasi sister, riding on whatever conveyance has been chosen for this new temple dancer. I will pray at my altar and await the summons to Vyasa.

When I enter, he sits reading as usual. I run to him and fall at his feet, wrapping my arms around his legs. I bury my face against the fine white linen of his dhoti, and I sob. "Oh, my darling baby girl," he says, as he lifts my face and wipes my tears with the fabric. "Did I not promise that you are the only devadasi I will ever know from now to eternity."

Though his presence calms me, it takes me many minutes to settle into my voice. "I believe you, your highness, and yet ... I couldn't help it. I was terrified."

"I understand, my Beloved Sara. Come. Let me hold you." He picks me up in his arms and carries me to the bed. But he does not undress me.

"We mean the world to each other, the sky, the boundless sea," he whispers as he cradles my head in his hands and twines his legs around my thighs. "We are deep inside each other now, even when we are apart."

I await the Rajah's limousine for my visit to Lakshmi. At first Vyasa does not understand why I ask for a car to visit the house where my sister lives. "Saraswati," he says, "I am surprised you want to show such luxury to your poor sister."

"It is not for my sister that I require such finery. It is for Ranju, her mother-in-law. How can she refuse me entry, if I arrive in splendor provided by the Maharaja himself?"

"She prevents you from seeing your sister?"

"She has in the past. But if I come in your own car, she may think I bear gifts."

"She will expect gifts, no doubt, and what, my darling, have you to give, besides what I have given you?"

"Nothing Your Highness. I was going to give her the emerald nose ring."

"But that is for you alone, my dear."

He stands and moves to a cabinet on the far side of the room. I do not dare tell him I have already given the golden necklace with the many fine jewels to Chandrakant in my useless attempt to buy freedom from the priest's embrace.

"Here," he says, returning with a gold cup. "The servants will never miss it. Give her this with my blessings. How can she refuse you, when you come bearing a gift from the Rajah?"

Many people follow the shiny black car as it makes its way down my narrow street. When Varanima sees the fine limousine and the crowds, she decides to go with me. "Fetch my gold *dupatta*, Pushpa," she calls, and then throws the shawl around her head. Although Shankar's house is but minutes away on foot, our journey is slowed by the many people who accompany us. It is like a festival procession with much laughter and song. I imagine myself the Goddess, Saraswati, being carried by devotees for a reunion with my sister, the Goddess Lakshmi. When we arrive, I ask the driver to knock on the door.

"Saraswati arrives bearing a gift for Ranju from His Royal Highness, the Rajah."

He returns to our carriage. "She asks us please to wait."

I smile, imagining the scurrying, and sweeping going on at this moment. We sit for several moments until the front door opens. Bindu runs out, only half dressed, her arms open wide to me. I jump out of the carriage and kneel to hug her. "Bindu, my precious, my little princess. You are such a big girl. It has been far too long since I have seen you." I walk with Bindu's hand in mine, followed by Varanima who carries the cup, wrapped in a soft wool cloth.

Ranju and her sister Bina stand by the door. Lakshmi peeks at me from between the large bodies rolled into shiny pink saris.

Ranju looks at me severely. "You bring a gift from the Rajah?"

I release Bindu's hand, take the parcel from Varanima and unwrap the cup. "Yes, dear Ranju. He asks that you drink from this, his golden cup of love, so that you may rule your house with loving kindness, just as he does his kingdom."

She grabs it from my hand and looks for the insignia. "It is from him! I do not trust the message."

"But the Rajah, amongst all his riches, is a just and learned man."

"This is so," Varani adds.

Since Ranju does not offer the customary food and drink, I move past her into the room to embrace Lakshmi.

As we leave, Varanima follows me into the coach.

"I will protect my sister and her children," I say.

"But you are a small girl, Saraswati. They will curse you. It is you who needs protection."

"As long as I am in favor with my beloved Rajah, I have the power to help. Did you see how Ranju grabbed the cup? She is too greedy to do Lakshmi or her children harm."

"So, you will offer more gifts? Are you going to give all he provides for you and your family to that evil woman?"

"If necessary, I shall adopt the girl babies, just as you adopted me."

Varanima places her hand on mine. "Saraswati, no child who carries Ranju's blood will ever be a devadasi."

I look into Varanima's eyes. "Then I shall find another way to keep my sister and her children alive." I turn away from her then, thinking of Chandrakant's angry face, and the eyes of the men who stare at me when I dance before the Gods.

Now, I go often to see my sister and beloved little Bindu. Ranju does not welcome me but neither does she bar the way. She knows where I spend my nights. Everyone in the village knows, and I walk freely along the streets, talking to my neighbors and the vendors in the market. Even Chandrakant seems to have lost the glare of hostility. He merely nods and looks away.

On the seventh day of each month, Vyasa celebrates the anniversary of the day I first danced for him. I go to him every night when I am not in my time of the moon, and sometimes we remain together during the day. We walk through his beautiful park, we meditate, and we talk long hours. Whole days have passed as we sit in his library reading and discussing the sacred texts. We dine together often now, and I laugh when I remember my fears. He even says I may come when it is my time of the month, that our relationship embraces all the ways we arc human, including my menstrual blood. But Varani forbids it. She thinks I am risking God's wrath. "What you are doing can throw the entire universe off balance," she said yesterday.

"You speak from the world of illusion, of matter, of *Prakriti*," I told her. "The Rajah and I find union in *Purusha*, in all that is beyond matter."

She gave a tight laugh and shook her head. "You think you are a scholar now, Saraswati, but you are naïve beyond my comprehension. May God protect you."

I tried to explain my belief, well, it is Vyasa's, but I believe it too. He says that our bond is not merely a union, but rather a reunion, that we have been in each other's company in the boundaryless, timeless place of love over the course of many lifetimes.

> I do not tell Varani that we sometimes play that I am his amma and he is my child or that we are brothers to each other and even sisters. It is great fun. If she saw us like that, playing and laughing, it would ease her worries. She would know that I am safe, and as my mother, she is protected also.
>
> Vyasa and I sing sacred songs and also silly made-up songs we compose for each other. I have taught him some of the simple steps and we dance together too. It has been a year of great joy. In fact, tonight we will celebrate two years since I came to the palace for the first dance. When we are apart during the day, I think only of the flow, that great river of love that carries us toward each other, in which we nightly drown.

. . .

WENDY SIGHS OUT RELIEF as she sets the manuscript down. She sees that night has fallen, and she's missed dinner. She should have picked up something after evening meditation. Some exercise would be good before she sleeps tonight. There can't be more than forty pages left. Certainly, she can read them tomorrow before the program starts. She's almost afraid to finish—doesn't want to, actually. She loves steeping in this story; wishes there were a volume two, a trilogy.

If the woman on the train is the Saraswati who wrote this, why didn't Vyasa protect her when the devadasis were outlawed? Wouldn't marriage have saved her? She grabs her fleece jacket and takes off, moving as quickly as possible to unhinge her tight joints. The scenes between Saraswati and the Rajah are so tender. She can't get their romance out of her mind. A brisk walk around the ashram grounds and meditation in the empty hall should bring her back to her center, to the truth that she has everything she needs, that nothing is missing. Romance is fleeting, she tells herself.

Tomorrow she will dive back into the contentment that comes most days, even after a meditation full of thoughts.

In the morning, the manuscript is the first thing she turns to, even before her mantra. But she stops herself. Meditation with the community is what she needs to prepare for the end of this story. She's been too much alone this week, too much rumination, too many memories. The shower feels good, and she's sitting on her cushion in the meditation hall for the earliest round. After breakfast, she will read and likely finish.

1946

There are many arguments with Varani now. She is needlessly fearful. When I return this morning, she is entertaining a visiting temple priest. She must have spoken of me to him, because when he comes down, he asks if he can speak and then tells me of the great disruptive force I am inviting into my life and the lives of my family, and perhaps the entire village. "By playing the maharini, you are disturbing the natural laws of the universe."

"But sir," I say. "I *am* like a wife to him."

Varani comes down the stairs, already yelling. "You are not his wife!"

"I am more than his wife," I say. "I am his everything."

"You are his fool! The only way we will be protected is if he makes you his wife. And he will never do that!"

I have no answer. Marriage has never been a question I have entertained. Devadasis do not marry. I move past them both and climb the steps to the sleeping chamber. I do not want to be a breeder of sons and have a life akin to my sister. Poor Lakshmi is again with child, and of course we hope for a son, so that she may remain in the safety of Shankar's home.

Ha! Safety! What is a wife but a breeder and a servant? Moments later, as I remove my dupatta and prepare for a nap, Varani enters. "This fantasy of yours, Saraswati, it will not last."

I am so tired of this. "Varani, it has been nearly two years that I go to the Rajah. He has never stopped loving me."

"The bloom of youth fades, as does love."

I lie down on the bed, close my eyes and pretend to sleep. I hear the rustle of her sari as she makes her way back downstairs.

Would my Rajah marry me? Is it against the laws of man? The laws of karma? If I asked, would he suddenly turn against me? Would he look for a new, young devadasi who dares not question or demand? There is no mother-in-law in his household to order me about. But would he turn to a new temple dancer if I were big with his child? What we have is perfect! I don't want to be an ordinary wife to him. I want to stop these thoughts. These doubts. I want things just the way they have always been.

Today when I visit, Lakshmi looks worried. "Soon, the baby comes, my sister," she says.

"If it is night, send word to the palace, and I shall come." I whisper.

"I shall try to send the neighbor's child," Lakshmi whispers back. "I shall tell them I want her to sleep with me for comfort."

The other women have joined us now, and I cannot ask Lakshmi all the questions I have for her, but I can see that she is well fed. Her skin glows with the radiance of motherhood. Since we cannot talk, I turn to leave.

"I shall return to see the baby," I say to Ranju "Please inform me at the palace. The Rajah may want to send Lakshmi's new baby a gift, especially if it is a girl."

"A girl!"

"Hissss!" says her sister, Bina.

"She dares not have another girl!" Ranju turns and points her finger at Lakshmi's belly. "This is her last chance!"

"If it is a girl, the Rajah will not be displeased," I say.

Ranju spits at my feet. "Do not bring your ugly curses into my house."

For many nights I have lain awake in Vyasa's arms, waiting and worrying about my sister. Suddenly I hear a commotion just outside the room, and I slip out of bed. In the hall, Basha tells me that a young girl has come to fetch me to Shankar's house. I return to the bedroom, and as I wrap the sari around me, my beloved Rajah wakes up.

"Where are you going, my dear?"

"It is my sister's time. I must go to her."

"Has she not many womenfolk to tend the birth?"

"This is true, but she has no one to protect her and her newborn, if it is a girl."

"And what can you do to keep the infant alive?"

"Forgive me, My Prince, but I have said that you will offer a gift, if the baby is a girl."

"This I can do, Saraswati, but I cannot send gifts each day to keep her alive."

"No, darling Vyasa. Just this one gift and a promise of a modest dowry should do."

"Oh, my little one. You drive a hard bargain." He shakes his head with a laugh. "A dowry! You must come give me a kiss for that."

I lean over him, and holding his loving face in my hands, I

kiss his lips. "I am so grateful for your love, Vyasa. You are my life."

He takes my hands and gazes up at me. "It is you, Saraswati, who has given new life to me. I bow at your rose petal feet and offer a gift for the infant who will be born this night.

You have seen the box of gold trinkets on the second shelf of the armoire. There are small pieces to adorn a small body. Choose something suitable."

I fall to my knees and bow my head before him. "Thank you, Vyasa. You are the rain on the dry earth of my sister's life."

He places his hand on my head. "And you are the sunrise in my heart. Now, go to her and help her birth a boy."

"I shall do my best, Your Highness."

"Take my car. Tell Basha to prepare it."

I think of the look of disdain Basha gives me each night as he leads me to my Rajah. I cannot give him orders.

Vyasa looks at me. As if he reads my mind, he says, "I know it's hard for you, Sara, my precious, but you know I have told him to take orders from you." He rings the bell to call Basha, and when he comes in, Vyasa tells him to awaken the driver.

Riding through the dark streets, I am terrified that Lakshmi and her newborn may not survive this night. "Divine Mother," I call, "spread your loving arms around my sister, so that she may bear a healthy boy. One baby boy, dear Goddess."

The house floods the dark street with light, but the front door is bolted shut when I arrive. I knock, but though there is movement within, no one responds. I begin to pound. "Let me see my sister," I cry. "Let me in!"

Shankar opens the door. "The midwife is with her. She doesn't need you."

I hear a scream. "Shankar, do you hate her so much, you would deny her wish? She sent word for me. She wants me with her now."

"Go away, Saraswati. Your presence is a dark wind that brings a chill upon this house."

"I will offer a gift for the healthy infant from the Rajah."

He looks back, and I see Ranju standing behind him. "Let her in," she says.

He steps aside, and I move past him to the sound of my sister in labor.

"Saraswati," she cries, and reaches for my hand. She lies on a low wooden table, drenched in sweat and her lips are parched. The midwife is preparing to deliver the infant. "She is ready. The baby's head is here, but she will not push. She holds the infant back."

Ranju stands in the doorway. "That is just like her. If she kills another grand ..."

"Get me a bowl of water, Ranju, and a cloth," I say.

Ranju says nothing but returns with the bowl. Kneeling beside my sister, I wipe her face and neck and chest. "All will be well," I whisper, then begin singing a chant that Amma loved. She would hold us on her lap and sing to the Goddess. *Bhaja mana ma, ma, ma, ma; bhaja mana ma, ma, ma, ma.* Lakshmi smiles at me through her tears, and between contractions she mouths the words with me. "I am here, dear Lakshmi," I say. "No one will harm you or your new baby. You are safe. It is time to bring your baby into the world."

Lakshmi begins to push, then, and her cries are fierce and loud. She squeezes my hand harder with each push.

"Almost," the midwife says. "One more push and you shall have your new baby."

I can see the head and shoulders, and now Lakshmi bears down hard with a groan, and there is a little wail from the baby.

"You have a son!" The midwife cries, and there is much commotion. We sob together as her baby is brought to her breast. She has one hand on her son, holding him to her, and the other hand she keeps on my head.

Slowly I lift myself up. My sister is the mother of a son. The blame for having born two girls first will be all but forgotten in the jubilation. Tears stream down my face. Lakshmi is safe.

I can return to Vyasa with the news. I rise to go, leaning down to kiss her forehead. When I straighten, Ranju is standing across from me.

"You brought the child a gift?" she says.

"I almost forgot." I take the gold chain from my pouch. "This is from His Highness, the Rajah for your grandson."

"We are honored by his generosity. We shall call the boy Vyasa."

CHAPTER
Twelve

WENDY NEEDS EXERCISE. Her back is stiff and achy as she stands and puts the remaining pages on the bed. She rolls out her yoga mat and begins with simple movements to loosen her tight spine. Then she counts out one hundred sit-ups and thirty leg lifts. She manages fourteen pushups before she lowers her belly onto the mat and breathes her way into cobra pose. The backbend feels good and she moves into bow pose, and then downward facing dog. Soon, she is up and doing sun salutations and then her entire practice, ending with a shoulder stand and fish pose in lotus. She lies on her mat for a few minutes deciding whether to meditate again or return to the manuscript. The manuscript wins.

1946

The driver is asleep on the front seat of the royal limousine, and I shake him. "It is time to return to the palace to welcome the sunrise." It is still dark when we enter the palace gates, and the coach draws up to the doors. As the door opens, I see Basha standing to greet me in his red coat. Has Vyasa asked him to wait up for me? I smile. "Hello, Basha," I say. "My sister ..."

His look is fierce. "Return to your own house," he says.

"But, the Rajah ..."

"The Rajah is ill."

But this is impossible! "He was fine when I left this evening."

"He is not fine now."

"I must see him," I say, trying to push past Basha. "I am sure he wants me with him."

He blocks my way. "Who are you to presume to know what the Rajah wants?"

"Did he not tell you to receive orders from me?"

Basha laughs. "Do I take orders from his favorite horse? His favored peacock? You are an amusement, not a maharini. Who do you think you are?"

I take a deep breath and look Basha in the eye. "I am Saraswati. I am a devadasi favored by His Royal Highness."

"I do not take orders from a devadasi. If the Rajah does not live through the night, in the morning you shall take orders from me. I will be your Maharaja."

"But what is wrong with him? Who attends him?"

"I have already told you all you need to know. It is time you returned to your own house."

"I am sure if he knew I was here, he would ask for me. Please tell him, Basha. I shall wait."

The uncle claps his hands twice and two palace guards appear. "Escort this ... devadasi home."

"I can find my way alone."

"Even a devadasi should not walk the streets at this hour. Wait one moment." He turns to the guards and says something I cannot hear. One of them gives me the kind of look I have known from Chandrakant. The other one smiles in a familiar way, as though we are old friends.

I turn and begin walking quickly toward the gates. "I will go alone," I call over my shoulder. "There is no need for guards." But they are beside me in an instant. Each one takes an arm.

"We are here for your protection," one says.

"And your pleasure," says the other, his mouth on my ear.

I do not know where I am. There is darkness everywhere, and I am stumbling down this rough road. Where is my house? Where is Varani? Where is my beloved? There! I see Vyasa hiding behind that cart. He will surprise me. Out he steps in his white robe, his arms open wide for me, and I run to him. But my sari is loose, and I trip and fall, on my knees, and when I look, he is gone. "Vyasa! Your Highness!" I cry.

"Be quiet!" A voice rises up from the street, where someone sleeps. What street is this? What time is it? It must be time for my Rajah to awaken and take me in his arms. What will he say when he sees me like this, half-dressed and dirty from the street? I must bathe in the holy river. I must take a ritual bath, for today I am to marry the Rajah. But where is the river?

I walk, and I fall, and I get up again. I know my way to the river now. I must purify my body. I must wash away my sins. What will he think of me, I wonder, when he sees me for the first time, and when I dance for him, and sing of love? I sing now so all may hear of my devotion to him.

"Go home to bed!" someone calls.

"Shut up, whore!"

"Who dares insult the Rajah's bride?" I cry. There is laughter and there are curses. Those men will not live long once Vyasa hears of this.

I see the gleam of starlight on the river and move towards the steep slope. Here I shall be cleansed of all darkness. I shall be morning light rising at the feet of my Rajah. I open my arms to fall forward into the cool water, and someone grabs my waist, pulling me back from the edge.

I struggle with my assailant, hitting his face and chest, kicking his legs. "I must bathe for the Rajah!" I cry.

My attacker hits me hard across the face. "Enough, Saraswati! Wake-up."

I cry with the pain of the blow, and my ruined plans. The Rajah must not see me filthy, with a welt across my face from this villain. But all my strength is gone. I fall against the evil one and let him take me where he will.

We are suddenly at Varani's door. "Saraswati!" she screams, holding the lamp over me. "Where was she, Shankar?"

"I found her by the river. She ran past our house screaming. Lakshmi recognized her voice and sent me after her. She was about to jump."

"Set her here on the mat. It looks like she is injured."

I look down at myself and see the blood on my sari. And then I remember the guards, holding my throat, my arms, roughly spreading my legs, stabbing me with their bodies. "The Rajah is dead!" I cry. "They have murdered my beloved. My husband! Oh, my husband! I shall die with you."

"Calm yourself, Saraswati." She turns away and calls for Pushpa to wake up. "Stoke the fire. We need hot water fast!"

I thrash and roll on the mat. "Let me die with my husband! Let me go!"

"Shankar! Help me hold her down."

I feel the weight on my arms and legs. The king's guards are inside me again. "May you shrivel and die! Let me go! The Rajah will have you burned alive."

There is warmth on my forehead. I see Varanima stroking my face with a cloth. I smell the fragrant herbs she has put in the water. I release the struggle and receive her gentle touch. "Today I am to marry the Rajah."

There are tears on Varanima's face.

"Do not cry, Ma. He will pay for the wedding. We need not sell any of our jewelry."

She lowers her head to my chest. "Oh, Saraswati. What has happened to you?"

. . .

WENDY DROPS THE MANUSCRIPT on the floor and leans her head back against the chair. Her arms and legs are heavy. She feels the burden of unshed tears in her chest and the weight of the half-promise she made to the woman on the train. There are still pages to read. And beyond the reading, there is the grip of the woman's eyes, binding her to this book, urging her to see that the story is brought into the light. She already knows that her life will be changed by the telling.

When she stands to stretch, she sees that once again, the noon meditation is starting without her. She puts on a sweater and throws her old shawl around her. Despite the time, she heads to the path through the woods towards the temple, anxious now to lift the weight of this story from her chest, the burden of twenty untold years.

The meditators are putting on their shoes and filing out in silence when she arrives. She passes them with head down, picks up a cushion and climbs the spiral staircase to the sanctuary. Alone beneath the domed ceiling, her gaze travels up the pillar of light to the skylight. She loves the symmetry of the ceiling—the glow of small lights that drape across the vast expanse to form a perfect Star of David around the pillar. There is suffering, she thinks, and there is also this. Already, she feels lighter. She sits down on her cushion and closes her eyes.

She is unaware of how much time has passed when a rustling brings her back. Someone has come in or is leaving. She sits noticing the sound, the air on her skin, slightly cool on her face. She is aware of a rumbling of hunger in her belly. When she opens her eyes, she sees another meditator climbing to his feet. She follows him down the staircase, and they are silent as they put their pillows in the bin. He sits beside her on the bench outside the temple, putting on his sandals as she slips on her clogs. "I'm Peter," he says and gives her a smile.

She nods without volunteering her name. Her meditation was deep, and though her limbs feel lighter, she is still carrying the story inside her like a torn black cloth.

"Are you taking the yoga for depression program this weekend?"

The question pulls her out of rumination, and she nods, rising.

"Might we climb the hill together?"

He's got that look, common at ashrams and Bruce Cockburn concerts—the salt and pepper hair pulled back in a ponytail, the Birkenstocks. It's a look that appeals to her tribal sense of connection. His eyes are something—penetrating, blue, set in folds of sun-aged skin. He's tall and lean but slightly hunched, like he's protecting his heart. He's dressed in grey cargo pants, a white shirt rolled at the sleeves and malas around his wrist. "Yes," she says and decides she means it. She's been nearly silent all week. But there's something else—the little flutter of attraction. Part of her wants to run away from the feeling and the man who has inspired it. "I should warn you," she says, offering a disclaimer to cover her fear. Why is she so scared? "I've been reading something tragic all morning. I won't be good company."

"Would you like to talk about it?"

"I don't know. I'm just saying, I'm not good with the social niceties right now, like asking you where you're from and if you come here often."

He laughs. "Well, that makes two of us. I'm not a fan of cocktail party banter. I attend too many of them."

She doesn't ask him why he attends cocktail parties, and they set off silently, passing the stone elephants and the garden of vibrant zinnias and asters still blooming along the walkway. When they reach the wooded path, she turns to him. "Walking up the hill through the forest is part of my meditation. Is it okay with you if we're silent?"

He smiles at her, nods, and says nothing.

Sensing him behind her, not talking, makes her nervous. She's not sure what to say or do, which could mean she's attracted. It's been so long; she can't even tell! "Gosh," she says, turning to him again. "I'm not very meditative at the moment."

"My mind is busy, too."

"Then I guess it's time to pretend we've had a drink or two at one of your cocktail parties. My name is Wendy. I don't believe we've been formally introduced."

He laughs. "It's hard to make someone laugh on retreat, especially me. Thank you for that. My name is Peter. Did you ever notice that it's easier to share intimate secrets with a total stranger on retreat than laughter?"

"In a setting like this, there can be more tears shared than laughs."

"Ah, suffering, the great leveler. Like the Buddha said, none of us can avoid it." He gives her a smile, but his eyes look sad.

"It's what connects us," she says.

"Look at that. We've already transcended cocktail party talk."

She laughs and turns back to the trail.

They resume walking in silence up the steep part of the path.

"I think ..." she stops, slightly out of breath, "even if there's nothing redeeming about something we've suffered, we do try to seek meaning from it. If we can't, we're doomed to remain disconnected and alone."

"What meaning is there in the Holocaust? Or the families dying in their escape from Syria? Or the crazy school shootings we've been having in this country?"

How much his questions remind her of Becky's. And in those vulnerable moments, her own. "Oh, I don't mean there's a takeaway," she says, "a lesson learned. But research says that most of us can find meaning in our individual suffering. After three months, we can actually be happy, despite trauma and loss."

"That's hard to wrap my mind around," he says. "I know vets who've never been the same since coming home."

"PTSD is treatable, though. Untreated, it only gets worse."

"Are you a therapist?"

"Uh-huh."

"Figures." Peter shakes his head. "I wonder what it takes to say something like, 'It's God's will,' after the loss of a child?"

"I would never say that."

"My mother would, but she was a good Pentecostal Christian, not a psychologist."

She nods. "Religious Jews might say something like that too."

"I've been running away from fundamentalists all my life. My was-wife used to say stuff like that, and she was a yoga teacher. She thinks everything can be fixed with yoga and meditation, even me."

"She thought you needed fixing?"

"Well, she was probably right, but her attempts just fixated me in my depression. She was well-meaning, but not exactly accepting. It's hard to live with me."

"But you're here on retreat. Something of her good intentions for you must have rubbed off."

He nods. "I do have her to thank for being here. When I was going through a rough patch, she gave me the book the presenter wrote about depression and yoga."

"It's not a panacea, but I do think yoga and meditation can help. I've seen clients recover and manage their moods when they began a daily practice. That's why I'm taking this program. I want to be able to help them, not just with therapy but with some simple practices they can do at home."

"Meditation can be a kind of spiritual asbestos, I think. Trouble is, when I'm down, I can't do it. I can't do any of the things I love. That's why I'm here. I've been meditating on and off for forty years, but I need a jump start."

They are standing in front of the dining hall now, and she's not thinking about food. "We all need a reboot now and then. I think you've come to the right place. I've been coming here for over twenty years to reboot."

"Yeah. I flew in a couple days early to adjust to the time change and reinvent my practice."

"You're from the West Coast?"

Peter nods. "Originally from Ohio, but L.A. has been home for over thirty years. I needed a change of scenery though. I've been down. Situational this time. Sony didn't renew my contract." He looks up at the dining hall. "Can we take this conversation inside? The smell of tofu curry is making me hungry."

She laughs. "Of course."

They chat about the overabundance of beans as they make their way down the food line. Once they're seated with trays in front of them, she asks him if he's a musician.

"Television writer," he says.

"I don't watch much TV. What do you write?"

"*Did* I write. I'm currently unemployed. Two seasons of *Grey's Anatomy*, some pilots you've never heard of cuz' they didn't get made, and the first season of *The Blacklist.*"

"Wow! I actually watched the first season. I love James Spader."

"Yeah well we get hired and fired a lot. Not a good recipe for positive mental health."

It's the second or third time he's mentioned his depression. She's been warned. So why does it make him seem even more attractive? She's always been a sucker for those Leonard Cohen types. "I came early too, so I could give myself a personal retreat."

He angles his head toward her. "Why are you reading something tragic on retreat?" She could sink into those eyes. Something in her tightens, and she looks away.

She tells him how she acquired the little red book in India nearly twenty years ago, and gives him a brief synopsis of the story.

"Fascinating," he says. "I'd like to read it."

"I haven't finished it, but I could send you the PDF. I think it was given to me for a reason. I feel a duty to see it made public."

"Sounds visual."

"I think so. Saraswati asked me to paint it, but I gave up art years ago."

"Why?"

"Being an artist wasn't a formula for being a mother. Lots of women can handle it, but I wasn't good enough in either job."

"Maybe that's the silver lining in the tragedy you're reading. You'll paint again."

She sighs. "It's a journey back to canvas and paints."

He nods. "I understand. I start small—give myself short writing assignments during sieges of unemployment so I don't get rusty."

"I get that."

"Do you have a sketchbook?" he asks.

There's that penetrating look again that she feels in her belly. "I bought one recently but haven't done much with it." She stands and picks up her tray. "It's been great talking with you, Peter. I want to finish this manuscript before our program begins."

He stands too. "Let me take your dishes back this time," he says, brushing her hand as he reaches for her tray. "Because I hope there's a next time."

Wendy thinks about Peter as she walks down the path to her room. This decent-looking, single guy seems interested in her. A depressive. Artistic temperament. Successful. Scary. He lives far enough away not to be a threat to her life—her work, her connection to Becky. He's not the sort of guy you have a fling with, though. He's earnest, too serious. If there's going to be someone new, she needs someone who can make her laugh, even on retreat. She feels that excitement, the kind that might keep her from sleeping tonight. He's interested. Something feels awake in her. She smiles as she opens her door. As dark as he is, Peter is like the sun breaking through clouds that have hovered for a long time. Cal has been her sunblock—his face in her mind protecting her. Trouble is, she can't quite conjure it today.

 1947

Varani squats down beside me. "You cannot sit before the altar any longer, Saraswati." She plucks at my sari. "Remove your white shroud. You are no widow." She holds my chin so that I must face her. "It has been a year since you danced in the temple. It is time to resume your duties. The dance master comes this afternoon, and your father is here to see you now." She releases me and stands.

I cannot dance in a place God has abandoned. Varani knows this. I explained it to her when I first came to sit here, but she does not see. She still thinks God resides in the little statues she bathes and dresses each morning at the temple and puts to bed each night. She thinks her devotion will liberate her from worldly suffering. I know my only salvation is to forsake the pleasures of the senses, to forsake all but my absorption in God. I sit, day after day, meditating on the name of God, and my true master comes to me. Shiva no longer dances me about the room or caresses me for His pleasure. He simply sits as I sit. There is no light. No fire. But we are dark and deep together, and I am whole. It is my own true nature I know in knowing God. I do not answer my poor, misguided, Varanima. I have lived in silence, but there is a drone that never ceases, a low tone that vibrates through my heart.

"You are a devadasi, Saraswati, and you are my daughter and the daughter of your father. You have duties to your tradition and to us. You cannot stay here any longer." She turns toward the door. "Pushpa! Come and help me."

Pushpa enters. Together they lift me off the floor and drag me to the bathing tub which is already steaming with hot water. I do not fight as they remove my clothes, but I pray to my divine Lord that I be allowed to continue to serve him in complete devotion with all the gifts He has given me.

After the bath, they wrap me in a new sari. The color is red and very bright. "Look how skinny she is," Pushpa cries. "What happened to her beautiful breasts?"

"She will become full again as she takes on her duties," Varani says while she combs my hair.

When they are finished with me, Varani takes my hand. "It is time to see your father. You must speak, Saraswati." She leads me into the next room, and there is my father. I see his rounded shoulders as he sits on the mat. He looks older, thinner. I wonder if he is ill.

I touch his feet and then sit on the mat across from him.

"How are you, my child?"

I nod and reach my hand towards his. I would like to speak with him, but it has been so long since I have used my voice. It is trapped, like a small, furry animal, in my throat.

He holds my hand in both of his. "This life you have chosen is not your dharma, daughter. You are no ascetic, Saraswati. You are a woman, and your duty to God is as a temple dancer, not as a nun. It is time you gave our Rajah a proper mourning. His revered soul has departed from his body, and your prayers cannot bring him back."

Varani sits down next to my father. "Today the dance master comes to review the dances you have learned," she says. "In three days' time, you resume your duties in the temple. You must eat all that is set before you, for you are promised to a wealthy patron."

"You must do this, my daughter," my father says. "The very survival of our family depends on it. I lost my position at the palace when Basha assumed the throne, and now, in the long drought that has befallen us, I can find no work. Your brother Ganesha goes hungry, my daughter, while you sit in silence."

"Ganesha?" I say. It is the first word I have said in a year, and it sounds almost like a cough. Like my Amma's cough.

"Yes. Ganesha," my father says. "Our life has changed. The wild Goddess Kali dances and stamps her feet through all of India. There is independence from the old order, my child, and Shiva, the great destroyer, is clearing the path for a new day. Since the division of the Punjab, there is much fear among the people."

Varani nods and continues. "They say that in the north stalls are burned and looted every day, and Hindus and Muslims beat and kill each other, right in the street. It is still peaceful here in the South, but no one knows what will happen tomorrow."

"Varani has spared you this horror, as you meditated at your altar. Now it is time for you to take care of your family. We depend on you."

I swallow. The animal claws at my throat. I try to speak.

"Varani, bring her some water," Appa says and waits for her to return.

Varani hands me the cup. "Let this water caress your throat so that you may sing in the temple once again."

I drink all that is in the cup. I look into Appa's eyes and see God there, and know it is time for me to dance in the world once again. I bow to my father. "I will do everything I can to serve you, Appa." My voice is a whisper, unrecognizable, scratching my throat.

Appa touches my head, and I rise. "You are a blessing, Saraswati." His eyes are filled with tears.

"And Lakshmi, has she been spared this catastrophe?" I rasp.

"She is with child again, and her son, Vyasa, grows strong, but Shankar has also lost his position. It does not go well for them."

"Vyasa—my beloved nephew." And suddenly, I know the sound of my own voice again. "May I see him soon? And Lakshmi and the girls?"

"When you have danced in the temple and fulfilled all your duties as a devadasi, it will be arranged. Ranju has left her body and Lakshmi runs the household now."

All at once, there are tears of joy. I have the strength to stand, and I embrace my Appa. I can feel a smile cracking my face.

"Tat tat tem tat tem," the dance master calls above the sound of the drum, and I move my feet and hands in the ways I have been taught, but I do not feel the mood of the poetry, the subtle *bhava* of the music. Those on their way into the temple stop to watch me. This festival performance is like a second debut; for most have forgotten me or have heard such stories that they never expected to see me again.

Now, entering the courtyard from the street is a young man in white with the sign of his devotion painted on his forehead. His chest is bare, and he is tall and slender as my Vyasa. *He is my beloved Rajah returned to see my dance. How can I be anywhere else, when he is here?* I am one with the rhythm now, moving and interpreting, bringing all to the dance. Each moment, each movement, bringing me closer to my Rajah, my

God. He is with me now. I feel his strong hands moving up my legs, across my back, my belly, even as I stamp and whirl and thrust myself toward him. I look again and feel his dark eyes burning the edges of my heart. He turns to enter the temple, and my body thrashes through the dance, moving as the dance master instructed, but there is wildness in me. When the dance is through, I run to the entrance, but I cannot see him in the temple hall, and I am not permitted beyond to the inner sanctuary.

I return to Varani who stands with a little group of devadasis.

"I will do my duty at the temple from now on," I say. "You need not worry about me."

"Your spirit returned to you in that dance, my child. You are very beautiful."

"I am too thin. Pushpa must fatten me up!"

"There is one who wishes to be with you tonight, Saraswati. Are you ready?"

"If he will have me as I am. Has he seen these protruding bones?"

"He has seen you dance, just now. His servant has spoken to me."

"The tall man in the white *dhoti* with *namam* on his forehead?"

"No. It is Kilol, who owns the tobacco factory." Varani points to a man dressed in silk that stretches over a belly as big as that of Nandi, the bull. Tonight, I shall know Shiva through his incarnation as a bull.

Something is pinching my arm. My body rolls from side to side, but I cannot open my eyes. They are sealed in shame.

"Saraswati, you must wake up. You have been sleeping all this day, and your offering of *pushpanjali* is tonight."

"I cannot dance again before God."

"Of course, you can, my child." Varanima says as she runs her fingers through my loosened hair, pulling it away from my face. "Whatever happened with Kilol, God is with you always."

I cover my ears. "Do not talk of that man again."

"But he wishes to see you tomorrow. And he sent two cows yesterday, and a fine silk sari. He treats you very well."

"He does not treat me well, Varanima. I did things you never taught me. You taught me everything about pleasing a lover, and I knew nothing of what he expected."

"Are you harmed? Did he hurt you?"

"He defiled me. I cannot speak of what I was asked to do. He gave me a potion to drink, which caused me to leave my body, but I looked down upon all that happened."

"You were not injured. That is what is important. The rest is like a children's game. It cannot touch your soul."

"Will other patrons require these things of me? Have you had such experiences, Varanima?"

"A few. Most have been kind. Many I have enjoyed."

"Must I return to Kilol tomorrow night?"

"He has much land. He can make you rich, Saraswati."

"I do not need land."

"This house does not belong to us. Land may be more important than you realize."

I sigh and open my eyes. "I want a bath. And I want to see my sister."

. . .

WENDY GETS UP and turns on the hot water spigot in the tub. It's the middle of the afternoon, but she has an urge to cleanse herself of whatever Saraswati endured. She adds a few drops of lavender oil and a cup of Epsom salts, imagining she prepares a bath for the little temple dancer.

After a long soak, she feels relaxed, but she has mixed feelings about picking up the manuscript again. She already knows from the woman on the train what happened to the devadasis after Indian independence. She hopes Peter is right about the silver lining—something redeeming for Saraswati too.

Maybe she should take a walk. Look for Peter. Find romance. She laughs at herself. Loving Cal for so long has kept her clear of such distractions. That's all Peter would be right now. She dries herself off, dresses in comfortable clothes—her old sweats. She's down with the diary for the night.

1947

"Ask him for land tonight," Varani says as she combs my hair, preparing me for my visit to Kilol.

"I do not want land," I say again.

"But you must ask him."

"Why must I?"

"I did not wish to tell you until your strength had returned. But now I see you need to know."

"What, Varanima?"

"There is talk that we will be forbidden to serve in the Temple. There are some who call us whores. They see the dance as something impure. There is talk that there will be no more dedications."

"But the dances are sacred. Devadasis have performed them for over a thousand years."

"There is blood in the streets, Saraswati. Now is not the time to talk of traditions. Old customs will not save us from this rampage. There are those in government and many Brahmins who say we defile the traditions of Hinduism."

"What do they want to do to us?"

"They may pass a law against us. If we cannot dance, we will be no different from the prostitutes in the city."

"But we are most auspicious women, Varani. You are called for every important wedding and ritual in this town. You are consulted for your herbs and potions."

"All that will change. Even the patrons may desert us, if we are brought low. And certainly, if this happens, we shall lose this house and everything else."

"That is why you ask me to return to Kilol?"

She does not answer. "There," she says, and turns me around. "You look better each day. Go now. Do not keep Kilol waiting." She hugs me to her. "Let it be a game," she whispers. "Imagine yourself somewhere else as you play. My love will protect you from harm." She pushes me toward the door.

I walk the dark street, where once I rode in the Rajah's coach. Ahead I see a pack of dogs tearing at their prey. The putrid stench reaches me before I see it is a human corpse.

When I reach Kilol's door, my hand begins to tremble, and I cannot knock. It is a tall house with many windows where lights are burning. I stand frozen. I am about to run from here to the river, when the door cracks. It is Kilol's daughter, Mangala, who peers out.

"What do you want?" she asks.

"Kilol has summoned me."

She opens the door and spits at my feet. "He is upstairs," she hisses. "The farthest door."

I walk slowly, counting the stairs as I climb. I will count each breath I take in this house.

"Enter," he says, when I knock.

The room is dark, and at first all I can see are his naked buttocks rising and falling on the bed.

"Ah, Saraswati," he moans. "Take off your clothes and join us."

I undress as slowly as possible, silently singing a song that Amma sang as she rolled her beedis. I imagine myself with Amma now, rolling beedis beside her, as I walk toward the bed. Underneath Kilol is his second daughter. Her eyes are wide, but I do not think she sees me as I climb on his back. I do not think she sees anything.

And now, I enter our home. It will soon be morning, and I can rest for I have done my duty as a devadasi. I climb into the bed, and Varani rolls over.

"Are you alright? Did he hurt you?"

"No, he did not hurt me. I did all that he asked, Varani, but he did not give me land."

"What did he say?"

"He laughed. Maybe we will receive another cow tomorrow." I roll away from her.

"What is it that you sing, Saraswati?"

"I'm sorry, Varani. I did not know my voice would carry. It is nothing. An old song. Go back to sleep."

CHAPTER Thirteen

THERE'S A KNOCK. Wendy takes off her reading glasses and blinks into the late afternoon light. It's like emerging from a dark cave, holding your breath against the smell of guano. Maybe it's someone knocking next door. Who even knows she's here? There it is again, louder.

"Yes? Who is it?" she asks through the closed door. "It's Peter. I hope I'm not bothering you."

She looks down at her favorite old sweats. There's a hole in the knee. She opens the door a crack.

"I thought we might have dinner together."

There he is, handsome in that old hippie way she likes. Her hair is undone, there's a streak of toothpaste on her Bennington tee shirt. She's not ready for company, especially him. "Hi. Thank you, but I am down for the night. I'm reading."

"I can bring you something back from dinner, if you want."

"I have food here. But, thanks."

He stands there, without speaking, and she's not sure what to do. "That's very kind of you to offer, though," she adds.

He clears his throat. "Would it be okay if I came in for a minute? There's something I want to ask you."

He's already seen her at her worst. He's a distraction, she tells herself, but she opens the door. "Sure," she says with a smile. "I wasn't expecting company, so I'm not really dressed."

"You look great. You have a natural glow."

"Must be the evening light. You look pretty good yourself."

He smiles, and a look passes between them. "Want some kombucha? I have some in the fridge?"

"I could use a cold drink."

She busies herself with pouring their drinks into coffee mugs, trying not to read anything into this surprise visit and her uncertain feelings about it. About him.

Since there's only one chair, they sit on the floor, she in half lotus, he leans against the bed.

"I'm sorry to interrupt. I know you said you wanted to finish reading before our workshop starts, but …"

"No, it's okay. I'm glad you came by. I almost went looking for you earlier."

"Really?"

"But I decided to finish this tonight," she picks up the remaining pages, "if I can."

"I've been thinking about you." There's that look.

This time she glances away.

"Anyway, I was thinking about what you told me, the Temple Dancer's story. You mentioned the PDF. I was wondering if you could send it to me."

"Sure."

"Tonight?"

"Okay."

"It might deserve a treatment."

"A treatment? Like for a film?"

"Maybe." He finishes the little bit left in his cup.

"I wonder what Saraswati would think of that," she says.

"You said she wanted you to paint. The screen can be a huge canvas."

Wendy laughs, shrugs. "I'm not so sure, though. It could be viewed as a form of cultural appropriation. I'm sensitive to that, especially since neither of us is Indian."

"We would get consultants, Indians familiar with classical Indian dance and its roots. I know several Indian writers who I think would be keen to collaborate with us." Peter pushes himself up.

"Well I don't know," she says, rising. "I think Saraswati would appreciate your interest. *I* certainly do."

"Yes, I *am* interested," he says and continues to gaze.

She backs away a little. "If you give me your email address, I'll send the file over in a few minutes."

He reaches in a back pocket and hands her his card.

"Thanks, Peter." She smiles as she opens the door.

He stops with his hand on the door jamb and looks back at her.

"Goodnight," she says. "I'll take a rain check on that dinner."

After he leaves, she feels rattled and elated, all at once. She hopes there's enough internet connection to Google "screen treatment" and also "cultural appropriation." That's what this is about, this unsettled feeling.

1947

I am tired after my night with the coffee merchant Hari, but grateful that I no longer attend Kilol. Though there have been many husbands since his heart gave out during the festival of Diwali five months ago, none have brought me shame, and one or two have brought me pleasure. It is as Varanima said it would be. Pushpa comes into the courtyard, where my thoughts drift along the edge of sleep, as I try to read again the volume of verses Vyasa gave me long ago.

"A young *sannyasin* is here to see you, Saraswati."

"Send him to me here." I place the book beside me on the swing, wondering what his guru would say of this visit to the home of a devadasi. This renunciate is either very brave or very stupid.

Although I have not seen him in nearly a year, I recognize him as the man from the temple, for whom I danced after my one-year absence. But now he is dressed in the saffron robe of a monk. The sign of devotion is on his forehead from this morning's puja. His smile rests peacefully on his face. He is younger than Vyasa was when I first saw him, and yet there is something in his eyes that reminds me of my Beloved. He is not in a hurry. He merely looks at me for a long time with that pleasant smile, and I look back.

"My name is Ramakrishna," he says, bringing his palms together with a slight bow.

"I am Saraswati."

"You are none other." He says it slowly, and then kneels to touch my feet. He rises then and begins to speak. "I have heard that you did not come to the temple after the death of the Rajah. Since the day I watched you dance, I have wanted to ask you about that time. I am told it was a year."

Husbands have praised my beauty and my skills over this year of rumor and worry, when each dance in the temple might have been my last—the last for all of us. But not one husband has come to me with a question about myself. "What is it you wish to know?"

"I do not wish to cause you any pain. Do not answer, if the question makes you sad. I only wish to learn a little about the soul I glimpsed as you danced. I did not see a woman who came from deep mourning, Saraswati. I saw a saint. My question is—what happened to you in that year of silence?"

"I would not answer were it to come from anyone else, but I see you are sincere. You are wrong. I *am* a woman in deep mourning. The death of my beloved Rajah affects me at every level of my existence. I could do nothing. But as I sat before my altar, doing nothing, I found myself listening. Ramakrishna, you might think me a fool, but maybe you will know what I mean." I look into his eyes for a moment. "In the nothing, there is everything."

He smiles. "When we hear the silence itself, we hear the entire universe."

"Yes!" I restrain the impulse to reach for his hand. "You *do* know what I mean. I was not separate from God."

"I saw the state of *moksha* in your dance."

"I danced for you."

He nods. "Saraswati, goddess of wisdom."

"You have come, Ramakrishna, but too late. I have lost the equanimity of that union."

"It is always there, Saraswati. It is yours. You need only return to silence to know that the clutter and impurities of your daily life cannot rob you of your pure awareness, the knowledge of who you really are beneath your dancing costume."

It is only my beloved Vyasa who has spoken to me of this. "Would that I was an ascetic. Are women permitted in the ashram, Ramakrishna?"

"It is said you would be a distraction."

"And yet you come here."

"When I can so clearly see the light of your soul, I am not distracted by the shade."

After Ramakrishna leaves, I cannot return to my book. His presence has shown me how far I have traveled from my happiness. It has been too long since I knew the bliss of pure awareness, of the emptiness so full of sorrow, so full of joy. I no longer know God's bliss in the commerce with a man—not since the embrace of my beloved. Somehow, I must return to the silence.

I hear a man's voice in the hall, and I know that Sudhir, my husband for the afternoon, has come. I rise and move to greet him.

"Look, my dear," he says. "I have brought you bangles and a lovely shawl. Homespun, in honor of independence."

"Thank you," I say, but I do not look at the gifts sitting on the table. "Come." He follows me up the ladder to the bed.

Before he has finished with me, I hear below the sounds of Varani's return from the temple. Her voice is raised and fretful. I do what I can to move Sudhir along, for my concern is to be with Varani in her distress. Finally, he is done, and while he sleeps, I pull my *salwar kameez* over my head and rush down to Varani.

She sits on the floor and Pushpa is beside her, holding her hand. I kneel down close to them. "What is it, dear Varanima? What is wrong?"

"They have done it, Saraswati! Those vicious Brahmin priests and those high-minded English ladies have ruined us. Jealous! All of them are jealous! A thousand years and we are through, just like that!"

"We cannot dance in the temple?"

"The gates were barred to us for this morning's puja. The Madras Council passed a law."

"If the Rajah were alive, he would have stopped this nonsense."

"The Rajahs and Maharajahs have no authority now. Even your beloved Vyasa would not be able to protect us."

"But we have devoted our lives to the dance. Surely this ban cannot last. How can they worship without us? Who will tie the tali and care for the temple deities?"

"I do not know, my child. I do not know what will become of me. You are young and beautiful. You know how to make your way with men. You will be alright. But I am thirty-seven years old. I do not have the patrons I had in my youth. What will become of me?"

"What about Chidanand? He still comes to you."

"Less and less. He has taken another wife. She is very young."

I wrap my arms around Varani. Silence. I want only that. "I will take care of you, Varanima," I say.

The room darkens as bodies fill the doorway. Chandrakant and another priest block the light. A third man, very fat and dressed in fine cloth, stands with them. He is a trustee of the temple.

"Varani Desai," the third man says. "I have come to inform you that you must remove yourself from temple property at once. The Sivadarshan Temple no longer requires your services. This house is for those who serve."

"But we have no place to go. What will we do?"

"God will provide for you," he says.

"But she has given her life to temple service," I say.

"She has had all the compensation and support she needs over the years from her activities. And as for you, Saraswati, who has provided so little to us, you have no right to speak."

"We must gather our belongings and make other arrangements, Sahib," Varani says. "We need at least a week."

"You shall have until nightfall. There are two of you to do the work." The trustee and the other priest turn to leave, but Chandrakant remains in the doorway. His head bobs from side to side, and his hands come into prayer position. "It is karma, Saraswati," he says with a grin. "There is nothing to do. You must accept."

"If this is my karma, then it is yours as well. You will bear the consequences of this act."

Chandrakant laughs. "What harm can come from a woman's curse? You are defiled in the eyes of God." He turns and follows the others out of the house.

All afternoon we sew bundles out of rugs and sturdy cloth and fill them with our belongings. By nightfall there are seven, and none is light enough for us to carry. Pushpa goes in search of a cart to take us I know not where, for since the departure of the temple officials, Varani has not spoken. She has worked hard and fast, and pointed me to certain tasks, but has not said a word.

It is dark by the time Pushpa returns with two men, a cart, and two oxen. I watch as they load our bundles atop the straw. I feel a movement behind me, and suddenly I am grabbed and dragged into the house.

"I will have what is mine, what was promised and taken away."

I scream and Chandrakant slaps my face hard and throws me to the floor. Varani and Pushpa are on his back, screaming and cursing. He throws them off, knocking Varani back against the wall. I rise and kick him hard and run from the house. I cling to the cart where the men are standing. "Help us!" I call, but they look away.

Chandrakant emerges from the house. "I curse you to a whore's funeral!" he shouts as he limps away.

I run back into the house. Pushpa is kneeling over Varani. There is a pool of blood around her head. Her sari is soaked with it. I sink to my knees, tears streaming down my face. "Varani!" I cry. "Do not leave us. I need you, my Amma. Stay with me."

Her breathing is labored, and she speaks slowly. "Go to the city of Hyderabad, my child. That is where we were headed. I will remain here. Go now, before the officers come to drag you away."

I cling to her. I cannot speak.

Two arms clasp my shoulders, pulling me back. "Save yourself, Saraswati," Pushpa says. "Go now."

"But where in the city? What shall I do, Pushpa?"

"You will do what you have learned, only you will receive money for your services," she answers.

"I cannot leave her," I cry, tearing myself away from our beloved servant.

"Take the small pouch from around my neck," Varani says, her voice a hoarse whisper. "There are rupees for your journey, and an address. Asmita is there."

"You will come with me." I grasp her small hand in mine. "I will take you there."

Varani's hand is cold and limp, and I bring it to my lips to warm her. She continues to speak, but her words are barely audible. "Go, go, my child. Go now."

"Asmita will help you," Pushpa says from behind. "She has helped many girls make their way in the city."

Tears blind my eyes. "I love you, Varanima. I cannot leave you. Not now. Not ever."

Varani opens her eyes and looks straight at me. "Clean the blood from your hands," she says, and her voice is strong. "When they find me here you must be gone, or those very men we have given pleasure will blame you for this deed. Go quickly, before they come. You have my blessing, child. Never forget you are a devadasi, a most auspicious woman!"

Her body shudders and a sigh escapes her lips. I put my ear to her chest, but the beat of life is gone. "Varani! Amma! Ma!" I gather her in my arms.

"You must escape!" Pushpa cries. "It is her last wish."

I hold her to me for several moments, struggling to dam the ocean of tears, and Pushpa lifts the pouch over her head. As I bow to lay her down, Pushpa gently lowers the cord around my neck. Slowly I rise, and Pushpa walks me to the cart. "Will she be given a devadasi funeral?" I manage to ask.

"I do not know," Pushpa says, crying into her sari.

"Her body should be laid before the temple God. She has served him well."

"I will talk to the other devadasis and tell them what happened here tonight. We will give her a devadasi funeral, Saraswati."

"Thank you." I reach for her, and she takes me in her arms.

"Be careful, my child," she says, whispering against the crown of my head. "I have heard that there is rioting and killing. Do not travel through the poor sections of the city." She pushes me away, then wipes the blood from my face and hands with the edge of her sari. "Go now. She gave you her blessing. Go, before it is too late."

I hug Pushpa to me again. "Thank you for all you have done for me." For a moment, I think I shall never let her go, but I release her and remove a gold bangle from my wrist. "Remember me with this," I say, and then I climb onto the cart. I feel through the hill of bundles until I find the one I have packed with silver plates and gold ornaments. I rip through the stitches and hand Pushpa a gold plate and a heavy golden bell. "Use this for a funeral that brings honor to a great devadasi."

Climbing higher, I find a soft bundle of saris to lean against.

"Hide yourself, Saraswati," Pushpa calls. "Even here, the streets are no longer safe."

Then the cart lurches forward, wrenching me from this life. I look back but can barely make out Pushpa's figure standing by the door. I turn to stare at the two men on the bench in front of me. I can see nothing beyond their dark backs. There is no moon tonight.

I must have fallen asleep, for all at once I am aware of loud shouts in the street, and the pounding sound of wood and metal. The sudden jolt of the cart rolls me against something hard and sharp. I reach my hand to feel the object and know it to be Amma's lamp. I tear through the bundle to reach inside. As I hold the brass lamp to my chest, I am not afraid. There is the smell of burning, the incense of kerosene. Flames light the sky, but above I see stars, only stars. I say a prayer of honor for my dear Amma and ask for her protection. Rocking the lamp as though it were a baby, I have no fear of God's will. *Om namo bhagavate Vasudevaya*—God's will, oh Lord, not mine. And I repeat Vyasa's words like a mantra—*Tat vam asi*—Thou art that. I am that. No separation. I hear my Amma's voice now, whispering in my ear: "Use the key, my little one, and we shall be united in the silence of the universe." But my mind cannot remember the words she gave me. I try and try, but they do not come.

I do not know what is to become of this life, but Varanima has taught me well the ways of pleasing men, and Kilol has shown me the worst of what I must endure.

There is a cry and then another, and then an ocean of anguish washes over me, until I sink in the single sound of a thousand angry voices. I cannot see the men and women who wail, but only the star above me, shining brighter than all the others. As I gaze on it, the lamp grows warm in my hands, as though a flame were contained within. I feel the heat against my heart, and looking up at the star, I see it begin to grow larger in the sky. Suddenly the night sky explodes in white light, and as the flames of star burst across the sky, I see Vyasa's face. His eyes are soft with loving me, and his lips open slightly for the coming of my kiss. It is his face that surrounds me now like a cloud of smoke, so that I can breathe but lightly. And then his face begins to change. It is the body of my Lord, God Shiva, dancing. His many arms scatter the stars and his feet crush the demon of unknowing. He dances for me, calling me now with his fingertips. And I rise to him. *Om Nama Shivaya*. We move in the dance of love. He holds me with a deep embrace, and I ride him through the flaming sky, free of all that binds me. I am the sky that holds his dance of clouds. I am the earth on which he stamps and leaps. I am the torch that ignites the fire in his hand. I am the ocean into which he sails. All that is, is one. I am. And there again, I see my Vyasa's lips, coming to meet my own.

Again, I feel the lamp burning into my chest. And now I remember the secret name of God. Vyasa's breath is hot now. My whole body burns with it. The universe is on fire. My beloved's breath is a torch, igniting the world. Golden flames leap and spin with the passion of his love. My body jerks as the pouch Varani has given me to wear around my neck is ripped from its cord. There is light all around me now, brilliant white and gold. God is on fire. The flames in Shiva's hands come down to touch me, to raise me up with him, and we burn together in union, his deep flame penetrating mine. And I know no other bliss than this.

CHAPTER Fourteen

WENDY IS TREMBLING as she puts the last page on top of the stack. Did Saraswati die in that fire? Who sat with me on the train? She tries to remember if she saw burn marks on Saraswati's arms. What she remembers clearly is the feel of her hand. Rough. Cold. It's been so long since that train ride. Oh, my God. She can barely remember the woman's face. Beautiful, she recalls, but also something else. What?

She can't move. She sits for a long time, eyes closed, the scene playing out in her mind. Flames. Cries. The cord ripped from Saraswati's neck. The union with Vyasa. The union with Shiva. A trance? A death? If she died, who wrote this last entry? Who wrote the first page, the prologue, if that's what it was?

And then Wendy is up. She throws on a jacket and runs into the cool evening air. The sun has set but enough glow remains to find the path through the woods to the temple, which at this hour will be deserted. She runs, stumbling over roots and rocks, cursing Chandrakant and Basha and the Madras Council, as though they were all still alive. Had they ever been alive? Why is she sobbing, if none of it ever happened?

It is dark by the time she reaches the temple and though the bells are still chiming, the gates are locked. She collapses against them; her tears dry now. She begins the Mahamrityunjaya mantra, singing the healing prayer to all the devadasis—to Saraswati, to Varani, and to the tender soul of Vyasa. This praying, this chanting, this remembering—it is all she can do. Becky's face hovers behind her lids, and she sings the chant for her daughter, wishing her ease and protection and peace and joy. And then she grows quiet inside.

She doesn't know how long the stillness surrounds her, but she becomes aware of a voice she recognizes—the caretaker Jai who lives on the grounds. She opens her eyes and meets the concern in his. She can't make out his dark features against the darker sky, but she whispers his name.

"Can I help you?" His voice is kind, and when he reaches out his hand, she lets him help her to her feet and then into his truck. Five minutes later, he drops her off at the dining hall where lights still burn.

She can't face the hubbub, the clatter of dishes, Peter. Back in her room, she gets ready for bed. As she packs the translation into her backpack, she notices there is a handwritten note on the back of the last page. She almost missed it. His handwriting is small and cramped and she turns on the lamp by the bed.

Translator's Endnote:
As translator for this manuscript, I have my own questions. First and foremost is the question of whether the small red book from which I worked, is indeed a diary. It shows the wear and tear of age that leads me to believe that the book could be a fifty-year-old document. It begins as such but is written from a perceptive and insightful mind that may reach beyond that of a eight-year-old

girl's capability. Of course, there are historical examples of genius flowering early. In Hinduism, Adi Shankaracharya, the Eighth Century philosopher and theologian credited with consolidating Advaita Vedanta comes to mind. As a child, he debated the Samkhya yoga philosophers of his age and was already writing commentaries on the Vedas (sacred Hindu texts) by age twelve. Could it be a memoir rather than a diary? That explanation might account for passages that were written beyond the scope of a diary, as in the burning scenes that begin and end the manuscript. Perhaps its author began it as a young precocious child in diary form and then completed it as a memoir? Or can it be a work in fiction, as it leaves the reader to question the very survival of its author? Whichever it may be, as a Hindu myself, steeped in the tradition and caste of instrumentalists who accompanied the devadasis, I found the voice of the manuscript authentic and the events described, while not verifiable, as recognizable and likely to have occurred. It is now Ms. Rabin's responsibility to convey it to its final destination: publication for academic archive and perhaps a wider audience.—NMK, 6/3/99

The mystery remains, yet in a deeply meditative mind, in the big mind beyond the limits of time and place, Wendy is sure. She is in a deep sleep by seven-thirty.

She lies in bed, as though a heavy hand were pushing on her chest and misses the first morning meditation. You can only go forward, she tells herself. Make hotel arrangements for Sunday, enjoy the yoga program this weekend. She is sitting in the hall by the second meditation at 6:20 am, her shawl draped over her head.

When she puts her cushion away an hour later, her mind is clear, and she notices hunger. The slanted light on the red maple outside the door makes her smile. She stops on the quadrangle of grass between the buildings and does yoga stretches and standing breathing exercises. It's a beautiful day, and she is grateful to notice birdsong and the wisp of breeze on her face. The sun rises. Life goes on.

She thinks of the research she mentioned to Peter—how for most of us happiness returns, despite loss, despite trauma. She notices a pang of disappointment when she sees him at breakfast talking with a young woman. He doesn't look up when she passes, and she sets her bowl down at another table. She's just taken her first spoonful of oatmeal when he sits down across from her.

"May I join you?"

"I would be happy if you did."

"Thank you for sending the PDF. I read almost half of it last night. It's terrific!"

"Here comes a spoiler alert, I finished it."

"Tell me."

She tells him the manuscript ends sadly, that she's not sure the temple dancer survived.

"Then who gave it to you on the train?"

"I don't know."

"That's intriguing. That question could make a treatment even more interesting. How do you feel about the ending?"

"Last night, I gave in to grief. I put myself to bed early."

"I'm about to start work on a new HBO series, but we get hired and fired all the time. I'm always looking for a new project. Maybe we could work on a treatment together."

There's a shimmer of excitement, like stepping up to the high dive—everything she's avoided for twenty years. Those shows he's written are good—multilayered and complex. Peter's dark side could add depth to the characters. But something is holding her back. Maybe it's his dark side. Or maybe it's that they are both white Americans, not Indians. "Let me think about it," she says.

Then the conversation turns to everyday things, personal stories. He tells her about his son in medical school at Stanford, and his parents, living in Arizona now. His father, he says had been a surgeon in the small town in Ohio where he and his four siblings had grown up. But when he left for school, his father had taken a job as a physician in Window Rock at a hospital serving the Navajo Nation. Two of his sisters had followed their parents to the state, and they all lived in Tucson now. All of his siblings had gone into medicine. He was the only outlier. When he started writing for Grey's Anatomy, he finally felt like he was one of them. He'd gotten his neurosurgeon brother a consulting gig on the show. Peter moved on, but his brother is still there.

"Why didn't you join the family business of doctoring?" she asks.

"I caught the theatre bug in high school, performing in plays. I directed "West Side Story" my senior year. I had a theatre teacher in high school who encouraged me to write. Skits at first, then plays, but I loved performing—musicals, drama. I played bass guitar and sang in a band in high school. I still jam with friends when I can. What about you?"

She tells him about art and her MFA. Turns out he has one in dramatic writing from NYU and lived in New York City for three years afterwards, auditioning, writing. Paying his share of the rent with tutoring gigs and freelance editing. Eating cheese and crackers and raw broccoli at art openings. Not making it. She's glad he's spent time on the East Coast. He graduated five years ahead of her, but they grew up with some of the same cultural references, listening to the same bands, watching the same TV shows. So far, there are no red flags.

Throughout the weekend of mudras and mantras and meditation and movement, even as a glimpse of Peter across the room makes her smile, she is calm. She learns practices that the teacher says, "give the mind a bone," creating focus and softening distracting thoughts. But sometimes when the room grows quiet, her own mind gnaws on the bone of the manuscript—maybe she or Peter could write a contemporary frame around it? And she is off, imagining the story—how her character meets a woman on a train in India, just after her divorce is final. She opens her eyes to see how much time has elapsed and sees Peter's eyes open too. There is an instant of connection. Something real passes between them, and then she closes her eyes. She fantasizes the contemporary story ending when the main character meets a television writer at an ashram and moves to Santa Monica. She wonders where he lives. She takes a slow deep breath and draws her mantra in, like reeling in a fish. Soon, the waves of thoughts are calm, and the tide is low, her mantra lapping against the shore.

They sit together at lunch on Saturday, and he asks if she would be willing to fly out to L.A. "I have a guest room in my condo in Marina Del Rey with a partial view of the harbor."

"Let me look at my schedule." She stalls, afraid to say "yes;" afraid not to. "It's hard on my clients when I take too much time off around the holidays. What about your work?"

"I've just been hired on. We're reading treatments now, fleshing out characters, meeting the actors. We don't start writing episodes until the new year."

CHAPTER *Fifteen*

IT'S SUNDAY AND SHE'S excited. She's leaving the ashram with the thrill of something unexpected in her life—a name in her mind like a new mantra, drumming out the old—and she's found a great rate on Hotels.com at the New Yorker in Midtown. If she lands at LaGuardia on time, she'll meet Becky in the lobby at 9:00 tonight.

When she turns on her cell phone on the tarmac, she reads a text from Becky. "Skylight Diner at 34th and 9th at 10? Coming from rehearsal space on 10th Ave. Want you to meet Abhi." Wendy has been keeping ashram hours for a week. If she wants to keep up with Becky, she will need to adjust quickly. The Skylight is one long block from the hotel, so she texts back "K" and then texts again, "Abhi?"

On the shuttle to Penn Station, she gets a text back. "Abhinaya." And there are hearts and flower emoticons following the name. Wendy jolts upright from a sleepy slump. From the translation, she knows that abhinaya is the Sanskrit word for the dancer's ability to express emotion and to … what was it Varani said to Saraswati? ... "Draw anyone who beholds you into your world." Wendy Googles the word on her phone and sees that yes, it means all that, and it's also a girl's name in India. A Hindu name.

Wendy has checked in, unpacked, and is sitting in the Skylight at 10:00 pm, absorbed in a profile of Leonard Cohen in the New Yorker, whose abhinaya has touched her on every level. Yes, abhinaya. She loves the word. The ability to express meaning. Cohen does that in every lyric, riff, and melody. He's 82. She reads that his body suffers from multiple compression fractures in his spine. He's in pain, but his mind is clear. His beloved Marianne has recently died in Norway. They have not been lovers in decades but in the last moments of her life, they have touched each other's hearts. She can't help it. She is humming "So long Marianne," and her eyes are moist when Becky walks in. Becky is with a beautiful girl with striking porpoise eyes; skin the color of aged teak and a gleaming braid of dark hair that falls down her back, nearly reaching her waist.

"Mom, what's wrong?" Becky asks, as Wendy rises from her seat to hug her. How Wendy loves the scent of the dance, mixed with her daughter's lavender shampoo.

"Oh, it's not anything, really. Something I was reading moved me to tears. Sweet tears." She wipes her eyes and holds out her hand. "You must be Abhinaya. Please call me Wendy."

Abhi takes hold of Wendy's hand. "I am so happy to meet you!" She says it with such force, that Wendy believes her.

"And I am happy to meet you, Abhi. Your name is my new favorite word."

Becky's eyebrows draw into question marks.

"Sit. Please. I'll explain."

The two young women sit down across from her in the booth, and Wendy closes her magazine and shoves it into her bag. "I was just reading about Leonard Cohen."

Both women look at her blankly.

"Canadian singer-songwriter? Poet? 'Bird on a Wire'?" No response. Wendy shrugs. "Before your time, I guess. You've heard his 'Hallelujah.' It's been covered by hundreds of artists."

"Oh! Right." Becky nods vigorously so that her blonde and purple curls fall into her face. "Sexy old guy with the gravelly voice and a big backup band. Cool dude."

"Got it!" Abhi says. "Dresses in a suit and a fedora, right?"

"That's him." Becky smiles at her girlfriend.

"I like his lyrics. He's not afraid of the dark," Wendy says.

"Actually, I think he is, Mom. The point is, he addresses his fears."

"That's probably true."

"You can see that, Honey," Abhi says, "because that's what you do in dance." Her eyes give off light, Wendy thinks. Something between awe and love. She's happy for her daughter.

"I don't know."

"What about your dance, 'Dark'?" Abhi continues. "The lights going on and off, dancers moving through spots and floods and flashlights, in and out of darkness. Tell me you weren't dealing with your fear of the dark?"

Becky looks sheepish. "I guess so."

"Do you still sleep with a light on?" Wendy asks gently.

"Not so much. Sometimes in a new place. But, you know, I haven't since the first night with Abhi. Have I, Sweetie?"

"Which is also when 'Dark' premiered." Abhi adds. "I can't take full credit for the cure!"

"Is that when you met?"

"Abhi auditioned about six months ago, and there was amazing chemistry between us. We've been ... uh ... together for about six weeks."

"Seven," Abhi says, "but who's counting?"

"Are you still living with Cassie and the others?

Becky nods. "Yeah. That's fine. Cassie's with someone now. And Abhi lives with her sister in Midtown."

"On 34th just east of 5th. It's a rent-controlled apartment that's been in my family since the 70s."

"Nice!"

"But my sister is getting married next month ..." Abhi gives Becky a look.

"So, I'm planning to move in."

Wendy reaches for her daughter's hand across the table. "I'm happy for you." She looks at Abhi. "And you, too. Blessings to your sister."

"Thank you! The whole family is kveling—over my sister's wedding, I mean."

Wendy laughs. "How do you know Yiddish?"

"You can't navigate this City without it. I grew up here. Actually, my father's Jewish. From an Orthodox family in Borough Park. But he doesn't practice. I inherited the cultural references, not the religion."

"Tell my mom your name, Sweetie." Becky is grinning.

"My name is Abhinaya Gita Goldman."

"Oy!" Wendy laughs, shakes her head. "This is getting complicated!"

"You said you liked her name, Mom."

"I do. It's my new favorite word." Wendy explains how she's

learned the word means expression, but so much more than expression, more like connection—the way any true art evokes an emotional response in the observer.

Abhi gives her a surprised look. "Where did you learn that?"

When she tells them that she's been reading a diary in translation—a record of a young devadasi's life that someone gave her in India twenty years ago, Abhi's face changes.

"What?" Wendy says.

Abhi looks at Becky who gives her an almost imperceptible "no" with a twist of her mouth.

"There's something you're not telling me," Wendy says with an awkward half smile. Had she said something offensive?

"It's just a long story, Mom, and we agreed to give it a rest for a bit. It's sort of all we've talked about this month. Can you wait until you see our rehearsal tomorrow night?

"Sure, honey." Wendy turns back to Abhi. "Do you come from a traditional Indian family on your mother's side? Are you out to them?"

"Both my parents and siblings are cool. I've never met my Brooklyn grandparents. My father died to them when he married my mother."

"What a loss for them and for you."

"I guess. I can't imagine that I'm missing much. They're so closed minded."

Wendy shook her head. "It's a shame though."

"My mother's side were mainly theosophists from Chennai, both Indian and an American who followed Annie Besant to India. They've been intermarrying for a couple of generations. They're pretty progressive, so they're okay with my identity."

"Chennai. That's the old city of Madras, the center of Bharatanatyam, right? Where the famous school for Indian arts and culture is?"

"Kalakshetra, yes. It was originally on the grounds of the Theosophical Society Campus in Madras. That's where my mom grew up. Her mother was a contemporary of Rukmini Devi Arundale, the Indian Theosophist who founded the school in the 30s. My grandmother taught there briefly in the mid-forties, until she disagreed with the school's philosophy."

"Here we go," Becky said. "I didn't think we could get through our eggs without talking about the devadasis." She leaned against Abhi and gave her shoulder a playful nudge.

Wendy felt goose bumps. "This is … well, kind of remarkable. The woman I met on a train in India twenty years ago, the one who gave me the diary that I finally got translated and read last week, she talked about that—how the devadasis lost everything in 1947."

"My great grandmother, Saraswati Devi …"

"Wait!" Wendy interrupted. "That's her name—the woman on the train and in the diary. When did your great grandmother die?"

"Way more than twenty years ago. I'm twenty-seven, and she died before I was born. I think Saraswati may have been a common name among dancers. My great grandmother was a hereditary dancer, a true devadasi from generations of temple dancers. My mother says she was well-known in the thirties and forties. But she couldn't truly dance after the ban. She had a few students from Europe, and she was lucky, because one of her wealthy patrons actually married her."

"And so … your name?"

Abhi nods. "To honor the lineage. My mother gave it to me, even though she didn't follow in the matrilineal footsteps. She's a gynecologist."

Wendy laughs. "Here in Manhattan?"

Abhi nods again. "My dad's a psychiatrist."

"So, in a way, you are stepping back into the female lineage."

"In a way. I studied ballet and modern dance at Sarah Lawrence and danced in small companies for a few years. Then three years ago, I went back to Chennai where we still have relatives. Despite the feud about the way the school changed the dance form, my mother was happy when I went to Kalakshetra to study Bharatanatyam. Really, it's the best place to learn Indian classical dance, the cleaned-up version of what our ancestors danced in the temples. Rukmini Devi hired the dance masters and my mother believes, that in her ambition to raise temple dance to a high art, she cleansed it of its passion, its ..." she laughs, "its abhinaya."

"That's pretty much what Saraswati told me on the train twenty years ago."

"Abhi can get really fired up about it," Becky adds.

Abhi leans in, her eyes bright despite the hour. "My great-grandmother's cousin, Balasaraswati had an international reputation before the ban, so she continued to dance but as a performer. She couldn't do what she loved, what she was trained to do."

"In the temple, you mean?"

Abhi nods. "Or in religious festivals. She was a true devadasi, not one of those Brahmin-born daughters who kept the form alive but drained it of its spirit. They say it might not have survived without Kalakshetra, but the school wouldn't hire the hereditary dancers. The most famous devadasi who ever lived, Mylapore

Gowri, died in poverty in Madras, without enough rupees to be properly buried." She leans against the back of the booth and sighs. "I'm sorry. I get on a soapbox about this sometimes."

"I am totally with you, Abhi," Wendy says. "You have no idea how ... I was going to say fortuitous, but that seems too weak, how providential, this is. Just sitting here, listening to you. I think we've come full circle. Or not us, exactly ... it's not just us sitting in this booth at the Skylight Diner. It's as though there are generations of women sitting with us."

Becky rolls her eyes. "I told you my mom was uber spiritual."

Abhi laughs. "In your heart of hearts, Ms. Becky, you are too."

"Who, me?" she says, and she gives a little wiggle.

"What about your new dance? Are you telling me that's not spiritual?"

"That's not spiritual. Wait 'til you see our dance, Mom. Abhi and I choreographed a piece that includes Indian dance—eye gestures, hand movements, everything. I wanted you to see it first, before we started talking about temple dancers."

"But it's not really temple dance," Abhi says. "Just references throughout. It's got more in common with the Becky Rabin Resilience style than it does with Bharatanatyam. Becky made it. I added some spice."

Becky reaches her arm around Abhi and gives her a squeeze. "But it's not woo-woo." She nuzzles Abhi's neck.

"I can't wait to see it, spiritual or not."

"Rehearsal starts at eight. We can go over together."

Wendy turns to her daughter's girlfriend. "You know, you don't fit the Rabin Resilience bio, Abhi. It doesn't sound like you just got out of rehab."

Abhi laughs.

"I hold general auditions now," Becky breaks in. "I changed that about a year ago. Resilience has more than one meaning. I loved Abhi's story about her great-grandmother—she was resilient." She kissed Abhi on the cheek. "So is Abhi!"

Wendy reaches for her daughter's hand across the table. "So are you, Sweetheart."

After their eggs and her tea, it is past midnight. Wendy has to get to bed, she tells them. "So, honey, can you stay with me tonight?"

"Sure, Mom. That was the plan. To spend a little time together. Abhi understands."

"Absolutely. I know you both want to talk. Besides, my day job starts in," she looks at her phone, "nine hours, and I need to sleep at least seven of those hours!"

"You're a lot closer to a bed at my hotel than to yours across town. Would you like to stay with us? There are two beds."

"That's okay. My day job is around the corner from my apartment. Thank you for the offer, though."

Wendy rolls off her yoga mat to look at time on her cell phone. The sun has been up for nearly an hour and she's been awake and practicing long before that. There's a soft glow of sunlight on the pillow where Becky sleeps, her face in profile and fanned by her halo of golden ringlets and dark purple curls. Wendy has to capture this. She unplugs her phone from the wall outlet and takes several photographs before Becky's eyes flutter open. "Mom," she whispers, "what are you doing?"

"I won't put them on Facebook without your approval. You look beautiful. I can't help it. I'm addicted to capturing beauty, especially yours."

Becky wraps the pillow over her head. "What time is it?" Her voice is a moan.

"Almost 8:30. Want a massage?"

"Sure!" She rolls onto her belly.

Wendy loves this part of the morning, sending love through her fingertips, her palms, her knuckles, as she kneads and presses Becky's back. Her hands speak better than words. Give them enough time, and words will come between them, sometimes with a crash, and sometimes with a quiet burn. But there is none of that now, and as she massages her daughter's shoulders, her neck, her back, she feels deeply relaxed, as though she's receiving the touch.

She finishes with a flourish of rapid taps, little chops with the side of her hands, up and down Becky's spine.

Becky rolls over with a sigh. "Thanks, Mom. That was great. You're the best!"

"It's a pleasure!" Wendy is sitting on the bed and now she tries to stretch out beside her daughter. "Scoot over."

Becky makes room for her. "What did you think of Abhi?"

"Oh, I like her a lot."

"God, me too!"

"As God is your witness?" Wendy teases.

"Uh. Let's leave Her out of it."

Wendy laughs. "I have a feeling She is drawing nearer. You don't think Abhi believes in God?"

Becky rolls her eyes. "She does. Both her parents were around when she needed them most, which must be the foundation for faith in a benevolent God."

Wendy feels her breath catch. There's a tightness in her throat. She takes little sips of breath, before she lets out a long sigh, and then she can breathe again. In the silence between them, she feels her daughter reaching for her hand.

"I'm sorry. I shouldn't have said that. It wasn't your fault that you weren't there."

"It's okay, honey. If I hadn't wanted the divorce ..."

"Yeah, but you had needs. I get that."

Wendy sits up. "I couldn't have prevented what happened at camp, even if I had stayed married to your father, but not being there afterwards ..." She shakes her head. "I've forgiven myself. But those six days of trying to get back to you were hell."

"You wouldn't have gotten that devadasi's diary if you had been in town."

"True ..." Wendy pauses. "Maybe you and Abhi would like to read it?"

"Abhi will jump at the chance."

"You know, she may not have been molested, but we've all had our hearts broken. Every one of us has been wounded, betrayed, abandoned in one form or another. I think our woundedness can be a pathway to God."

"Why do you keep bringing God into the conversation?"

"You were blaming your lack of faith on what happened to you. I'm just saying we've all had bad things happen—maybe not as bad as what you went through, but we've all been broken. It's through those broken places that some of us find our faith."

"It's not that I don't believe. I just don't know. No one can know if God exists. I do know one thing, though."

"What?"

"If there's something beyond our physical existence, we can't approach it directly. I don't believe anyone has a direct link to God. You have to approach God or whatever is there sideways, at an angle. Through dance or art or, okay, yoga, or breathing practices—something that opens the doorways of the senses, makes you accessible, because God isn't accessible. You are."

"'God isn't accessible. You are.' I love that. What about prayer?"

"Sideways prayer, yeah. Prayer that's sung, chanted, danced, painted, wept. You know, felt from a place of total absorption in the song or the chant or the dance or the painting. But not like kneeling and talking to God and expecting an outcome. God is not accessible!"

Wendy pauses. Nods. "I get it. We make ourselves accessible to the divine, as we each know the divine, through our practice, be it art or yoga or, for some, I think it can be prayer. True prayer from the heart. Like, I'm thinking about saints and shamans—characters like Teresa of Avilla or John of the Cross?"

"They had an intermediary. They didn't go direct."

"Okay, so Jesus."

"Yes, and all those Hindu Gods and Goddesses—they give believers an angle in sideways. Nobody gets direct access."

"How about Rumi?"

"He had Shams," Becky asserts.

"True," Wendy acknowledges. "But Jews pray directly. Our prayers don't require an intermediary."

"And how did that work for us in Europe in the last century?"

Wendy sighs. "Becky Rabin, sometimes I think you're too smart for your own good."

"Actually, Mom, the Chassids dance and chant their prayers, and the Kabbalists have mystical meditation practices."

Wendy nods. "I can relate. Connection to the divine eclipses form, no matter the religion. So, we find expressive ways to clear the space, to, as you say, make ourselves accessible to that connection."

"I love you, Mom." Just then there's a buzzing. "Is that your phone?"

Wendy looks, smiles. It's a text from Peter, saying he's landed and has finished the manuscript. He's been thinking about it and thinking about her. She looks at her daughter. "I met someone," she says.

"I want to hear every detail!"

"That shouldn't take too long. I just met him last week."

Twelve hours later, Wendy is sitting on the floor, leaning against a wall in the rehearsal room.

Becky is going back and forth on the tabla soundtrack, cuing up the second section again. "This would be easier if Manish, our tabla player were here."

Wendy is feeling a kind of cosmic smile throughout her body. There is almost nothing better than watching Becky and her dancers perform. The dance feels perfect to her, but of course, Becky is making adjustments to the choreography, simplifying the call and response of movement. Abhi's eyes flash and roll just the way Wendy imagines Varani's eyes must have moved. Her feet drum the wooden floor as she dips and flows around the room. In the first section, she's a fairy, temptress, damsel in distress, flitting in and amongst the other dancers who go about their business, dancing out their daily chores and concerns in duets, small ensembles and solos. Abhi is invisible to them.

But in the second section, the dancers are beginning to sense her, turning suddenly to catch a glimpse and failing, or as though to brush off a mosquito, but only the audience can see her. In her movements, there is more and more the expression of the yearning to connect. As the longing grows, conveyed in gestures and dashes in and around the dancers, sometimes even knocking them down, some grow frightened and withdrawn, clearly feeling her presence through some sixth sense that the five senses can't comprehend. Some of the dancers grow frustrated, then angry, and others, led by Becky, begin to pursue her, longingly, aimlessly around the floor, grasping at air, even as Abhi pursues them, pines for them. The second section ends with the ensemble seemingly at battle with each other as some defend themselves against the unknown energy that is charging toward them and some long for her in a myriad of expressions. It's nearly eleven and they haven't danced the final section yet. Wendy both wants to see it and is afraid she'll fall asleep if they don't quit soon.

"Okay, Lovelies," Becky says. "You've been wonderful tonight. Thank you all for coming. I can tell my Mom loves it."

"I do! I'm enthralled. I've never seen anything like it."

"It'll get better," Cassie says. She is dancing the role of the leader of those who seek to rid themselves of Abhi's elusive presence. "We're still working it through."

"Will you rehearse the final section tomorrow night?

Becky laughs. "We don't know what it is yet. What do you think should happen?"

"Well it's dark, but I have an idea." Wendy looks from Becky to Cassie to Abhi. "I think Abhi's character dies. No one sees her, hears her, acknowledges her, so she doesn't exist. She wilts."

Cassie lights up. "Like those babies, the orphans, after World War II," she says, "who weren't held or cuddled, because the medical thinking was to keep them sanitary in a germ-free environment, safe from infection."

Wendy nods. "They didn't gain weight and many of them died. Failure to thrive, they called it."

"Right!" Abhi says. "Which is exactly what happened to the devadasis."

"Maybe," Wendy adds, "you could call it 'Failure to Thrive.'"

"I like it!" Becky says. "Come hug my mother, everyone."

The group hug of eleven sweaty females nearly knocks Wendy off her feet. She falls into an embrace that goes on for nearly half a minute.

"Now, that's what I call a hug," she says, when they let her go.

"Look at her," Cassie says, smiling at Wendy. "She looks younger, doesn't she?"

"She's thriving in our love," someone says, she's not sure who.

"Okay, Darlings," Becky claps her hands. "Tomorrow night!"

"I can't wait," Abhi says. "I get to die of abandonment."

Becky puts her arms around her girlfriend and pulls her close. "You will wilt; you will dissolve; you will disappear before our eyes. It's a great role. I would love to play it." She drops her arms, hangs her head, and puts on a pout. "Instead, I have to pine for you and go on without you. How dull life will be. We'll play out the same actions as in the first section, but without hope, with dread, with oppression. The movements will be sluggish and boring, even when the dancers move quickly."

"Yeah," adds Cassie. "Everyone, even those who wanted to destroy you, will be diminished without your presence."

"Oh, this is going to be so cool," someone says.

"A metaphor for the divine feminine!" another woman adds.

"It actually happened to the devadasis," Abhi says.

"It's what's happening right now," another dancer says.

Wendy shakes her head. "Maybe not if Hillary wins."

"Oh, my Goddess, but if she doesn't!" Cassie says.

"How can she not?" Becky says, gathering her things, and moving toward the door. "Let's go everyone, or the rehearsal hall will charge us for another hour. It's eleven o'clock."

As they head down the stairs, Becky whispers in Wendy's ear that Abhi has the day off tomorrow.

When they get to the street, Wendy extends the invitation for a sleepover at the hotel again and this time Abhi accepts.

"Slumber par-teee!" Becky chants, as she waves her fist in the air, and Abhi and Wendy join the chant.

Both women are sound asleep and spooning, when Wendy rises from her meditation cushion. She refrains from pulling out her phone to capture this beauty. She rolls out her mat by the south-facing window, where dawn is streaking the high-rises in mauve-tinted brilliance.

When she finishes her practice, she sees that Becky is blinking her eyes open and smiling at her, and she sits down on the edge of her own bed, facing the younger women.

"Good morning." Her voice is a whisper.

Becky responds with a whisper, and Abhi stirs behind her. Abhi's eyes open. "I'm awake," she says.

Becky turns on the pillow with a kiss that lands on Abhi's forehead. Then she turns back to Wendy. "You are so disciplined, Mom."

"Not really. Not about most things. My practice makes me happy. Like dance does for you. You're disciplined about that."

"But I think meditation would help me. I just can't get myself to do it. Abhi meditates."

"Well, maybe the two of you can come with me to the ashram sometime. It could get a practice in gear."

"I'd love that!" Abhi says, sitting up, eyes bright and unclouded by sleep.

Becky sits up too. "I don't know. Sometimes, when I've tried to meditate, I get to a place that scares me."

"What do you mean?" Abhi places her hand over Becky's.

"It's like I'm dangling in a harness over an abyss."

"Maybe you're suspended over bliss, honey," Abhi says, "and you just have to let go."

"No way."

Wendy puts a hand on Becky's knee. "Going on retreat with us might allow you to trust whatever you're hovering over."

Becky pauses, looks from her mother to her lover, then shakes her head. "I envy you, but I think my harness is too tight."

"Hey, Baby," Abhi says. "Maybe it's there to help you fly. You know, like the original Peter Pan."

Becky leans back against Abhi's chest with a sigh.

"I bet you can make a dance out of it," Abhi says.

"I was already thinking that, actually. Maybe we can collaborate with Joanna's company and try some aerial choreography."

"Lean forward, Sweetie." Abhi pushes Becky away from her. "Let me give you a little massage. Your neck and shoulders are so tight."

"Only if mom gets up in the bed with us, so I can rub her shoulders, too. Come here, Mom. It's your turn."

Later, as they nurse their lattes at Stumptown, Wendy unzips the backpack beside her on the couch and pulls out the translation.

She hands it to Abhi. "This is your legacy. I think it belongs to all three of us."

Abhi's eyes glisten. "The diary?"

Wendy nods. "Or whatever it is. We need to get it published. It came to me for a reason. Partly that reason might be you, Abhi. As a direct descendant of devadasis, you may be the one to publish it. Or dance it. Peter, the guy I met at the ashram is a television writer. He thinks it could be a film."

Abhi holds the manuscript to her chest. "We're on!"

Becky leans back, her legs jutting out. The look on her face, Wendy thinks, is 'what about me?'

Abhi puts the translation on the table. "As long as there's a part for a flying girl in a harness."

As she unpacks, she wonders what might happen if she goes to California. She doesn't trust happy endings, not in novels and not in life. She remembers act three in "Failure to Thrive." No redemption there. She empties the plastic bag of laundry into the washing machine and starts the delicate cycle. On her way through the kitchen, she considers opening the cabinet, taking out a nice merlot and pouring herself a glass. One glass, not a running away from how scared she is of this possibility with Peter. Not a numbing out. It will put her to sleep, she reasons. Yes, and then it will wake her up in the middle of the night with a headache. She turns out the light in the kitchen and continues to the bedroom to finish unpacking.

As she puts her jewelry back in the vanity drawer by the sink, she sees the gold bracelet with the tiny diamonds that Cal gave her years ago. A tennis bracelet, she thinks it's called. So not her. She doesn't dress up to see clients and she never did. There had been better gifts—woolen shawls and capes and footed pajamas. They were practical, wearable, lovable. They wrapped around her, kept her warm, feeling loved, shopped for, cared about. The bracelet came during his seven days of separation from Denise. Some part of Wendy must have known it was a pass me down gift, rejected by his wife, and she'd never worn it.

Now and then, her cell phone lights up with the flash of his name. There are birthday greetings, anniversaries of un-kept promises, and now and then messages come without reason, but when did reason ever guide their relationship? "Knowing you are reading this, keeps me going," he says. Sometimes she writes back, to keep him going, she tells herself, saying what she would say to any old friend—nice to hear from you. Or glad to know you're well.

She hasn't seen him in what? Ten years? He's still running, she thinks, but down from marathons to 5Ks, coming in first or second in his age group. Not too much competition over 65, he says. She knows this because once and a while there's a call. She doesn't pick up, and his voice hangs around on voice mail until she's ready to delete his name.

She is more herself now than she ever was. Losing Cal, letting him go, has peeled her down to what is real, the raw bones of her life. She wonders if others can see that. She feels transparent, revealed—like Shiva, dancing in his incarnation as Nataraja, in the ring of fire, burning away the clouds of unknowing, the fog she lived in for all those years of loving Cal.

With stents in his heart valves and a vigilant wife, he's not likely to come back into her life. She would walk the other way if he did. She used to think that, like the Velveteen Rabbit in Becky's favorite children's story, he would be even more lovable for the wear and tear of time. But those days have passed. The pining is gone, or out of sight, moved to the periphery. The steady drone of longing has slipped like the sun beneath waves on a moonless night. One day, he will be gone. If somebody comes looking for him, they might find him inside her, right beside Norma. And then one day Wendy will be gone too. As she puts her suitcase in the closet, she thinks about how they couldn't get her fingerprints when she applied for Global Entry last year. She will fulfill her duty to Saraswati before she melts away, one fingerprint at a time.

AUTHOR'S NOTE

ON THE DAY I stood in C. S. Lakshmi's office in Mumbai, looking at a calendar created by "Reaching Out," a group of Indian feminists, my eyes locked on the eyes of a little girl who gazed into the camera. *Rohini stood holding her mother's hand. She was six. She had knotted hair. Her mother said that she was going to be dedicated the coming year. Rohini stood silently.* Stunned and momentarily breathless, tears welled with the knowledge of what "dedicated" meant, of what this beautiful child was destined to become.

This moment occurred while traveling in India in 1994. I was visiting the award-winning author Ambai (the pen name for C. S. Lakshmi, academic and feminist). I had contacted her after falling in love with her novella, *A Purple Sea*, on a trip to India the previous year. Lakshmi showed me the calendar she and her colleagues created in 1982, to raise awareness of the plight of poor female *beedi* rollers in the Indian state of Karnataka. Because of their exposure to tobacco in unventilated spaces, the beedi rollers often developed lung diseases, including tuberculosis.

Many of these women were dedicated to the Goddess Yellamma, the patron saint of poor women, often of a lower caste. What this meant in 1982, and continues to mean, was that the young girls' families were committing them to a life of prostitution, often to help the family survive. Temple dancers have been outlawed since 1947 and dedications to Yellamma have been banned since 1934, so those dedicated since then, are not dancers. They often become sex workers. Accompanying another picture in the calendar is this: *Sangeetha here is 12 years old. When the first knot in her hair was cut off, she became sick. Her father died. Then it was decided to dedicate her. "I will be happy," Sangeetha said smiling, not knowing the implications of dedication.* Thousands of young girls are taken to the Yellamma Temple in Saundatti, a village in Karnataka, to be dedicated to her every year.

A month earlier, on that same trip, before I had ever heard of a *devadasi*, I was wandering the dusty village streets of Kayavarohan, in the state of Gujarat, where I was studying for the second year in a row a Kripalu-sponsored yoga program at the Lakulish Institute of Yoga. I stumbled into an open-air temple that may have once been a sacred site but was derelict and unkept. Rising from the earth were iconic stone *lingams*, Hindu symbols representing the god Shiva, half-buried in sand. A skinny cow wandered through. Dancing in the corner, was a woman wrapped in a saffron *sari*. Her gray hair was down and tangled around her shoulders. There was *vibhuti* ash on her forehead. Strangely, her wrists were wrapped in white bandages. I joined her, following her movements and her *mudras*. After a time, we bowed and smiled.

These two moments, the one in Lakshmi's office and the one in the derelict temple, stayed with me. I didn't intend to write about them, or to write a temple dancer's story. But when I returned to New England, the impact of meeting six-year-old Rohini's gaze stayed with me. Several weeks after my return, the voice of Saraswati began to pour through me. I had been writing fiction before, contemporary stories about love and work, but I have never had an experience like this one before or since. It was as if her voice found me and used me as a vehicle to tell the story of the devadasis.

Once she was finished speaking, I researched devadasi culture. I learned that for approximately 1200 years, temple dancers, or devadasis, were once auspicious women responsible for maintaining community life cycle rituals, like tying the sacred gold thread, the *tali*, around the bride's neck, and leading religious processions. Devotees, they often lived on the temple grounds and bathed and dressed the temple deities. They studied for many years, learning the intricate dances, the sacred mudras and the accompanying Sanskrit songs. They were honored, yet unchaste. When they reached puberty, they were ceremoniously dedicated and then often taken as the mistress to a wealthy patron or sometimes the Brahmin temple priest or the region's *maharaja*. This secondary duty could bestow power. Their wealthy patrons might provide gold and land and cows for their services. Some devadasis accumulated assets of their own, unheard of for women in mid-twentieth century India, and they were better educated than most women.

I spent time at Wesleyan University in Middletown, Connecticut, which has one of the largest world music libraries in the United States. There, I read several dissertations on devadasi culture. I also met Kay Poursine, a contemporary master of Indian classical dance, who had studied with Balasaraswati and other famous devadasis. I attended her performance of Bharatanatyam and, over the years, other classical Indian dance recitals. The research didn't change Saraswati's story. Rather, the research validated her story and provided details to enhance the rituals, ceremonies, and depiction of her long years of study.

Although I am not Indian, Saraswati's story and the research I embarked on to explore the history and rituals that comprised a vital aspect of her world, compelled me to write her story, fully aware that I am from a completely different time, space, and culture. In 1994, I felt I had been given a gift, as her character spoke, and I wrote. Like Wendy, the artist turned social worker who was entrusted with Saraswati's diary, the gift carried with it a responsibility to share it with a larger audience, despite possible criticism of cultural appropriation I might encounter as a white Western woman. After Saraswati's portion of the novel was complete, I asked several Indian readers and a Bharatanatyam performer to review the manuscript and offer their thoughts. In 2019, I asked another master performer and Indian teacher of Bharatanatyam to review the manuscript. Theirs was a warm embrace of the story I had written.

I wrote *Temple Dancer* as an homage to the devadasi tradition of temple service and devotion to sacred temple dance. I stand in awe of this 1200-year-old institution and the lineage of women who devoted their lives to its practice, and as an outsider, can never fully understand it. However, I researched devadasi culture with the intention of shedding light on a nearly forgotten, once auspicious, and later profaned society of women. I wanted to honor devadasis whose lives were dedicated to learning and who had more freedom and power than ordinary Indian women. Most women in mid-twentieth-century India belonged to their fathers until they were virtually sold to their husbands' family through the dowry system. After the arranged marriage, the new wife, often still a young teen, could become a servant in her mother-in-law's home. If we want to talk about sexual slavery in relation to temple dancers, we need to talk about it in the larger scope of every day Indian life, as a wife was often subservient to her mother-in-law and considered her husband's property. If she proved unsatisfactory as a wife, not bearing a son, for example, or if her family couldn't meet an ever-increasing dowry demand, a bride burning could be the result. In fact, there continue to be an estimated 5,000–8,000 such bride burnings every year. On the other hand, the devadasis belonged to none but God, to whom they were ritually married; they were educated, and some became wealthy from the gifts of their patrons. It could be argued that they "belonged" to these patrons, however they had more freedom than most other Indian women, which may have contributed to their downfall. I was appalled to learn from my research that the lives of the devadasi were disrupted by the 1947 ban against temple dancing, one of the first acts of the Madras Council after Indian independence. After more than 1200 years of temple service and devotion to the dance, the women were devalued as unchaste. In the effort to preserve the dance as a cultural icon, male dance masters, rather than the devadasis themselves, were hired by the colleges to preserve a sanitized version that we see as Bharatanatyam, or classical Indian dance. The devadasis were evicted from their homes, which were often on the temple grounds. Without homes or means of support, many turned to prostitution. Some, like the famous Balasaraswati, already had international reputations and could continue to perform in secular settings and to teach privately.

Beyond the emotional moments described earlier when my eyes locked onto six-year-old Rohini's in C. S. Lakshmi's office and I danced with the mysterious woman in the derelict temple, there may have been another seed to the character's emerging voice, even more esoteric in nature. By the time I sat down to write after my return from India in 1994, I had, unbeknownst to me, been meditating with the Goddess Saraswati's *mantra* for more than twenty years. I didn't know of my mantra's association with the goddess, because I was warned by my Transcendental Meditation teacher against speaking the sound out loud. I was told that the mantra had no meaning. I didn't realize until I read Russill Paul's book *The Yoga of Sound* (New World Library, 2004) that the mantra I had silently chanted for years belonged to Saraswati. Nor did I know of my mantra's association with the goddess, when the young Indian girl spoke through me, identifying herself as Saraswati, named by her mother after the Goddess of music and wisdom. Unlike any other writing experience, I felt as though I were taking dictation. I listened closely, lovingly, and with great respect. For me, it felt egoless.

Whether imagined or received, I was compelled to write Saraswati's story. For twenty-five years her story lived only on paper and in the hearts and minds of a few trusted readers. Like Wendy, the painter and clinical social worker who is the American protagonist in this novel and who received the "diary" on a train in 1997, I have felt a duty to let Saraswati speak. Saraswati has languished too long in my heart and mind and deserves her own hearing from you. I have written a contemporary story to surround the original tale that begins before the end of the Raj in India. In some ways, Wendy's story of love and loss and shame mirrors Saraswati's. Their sense of the divine cannot be separated from their sexuality. They both have lived alone in my imagination. May they flourish and be nourished by yours.

ABOUT THE AUTHOR

Amy Weintraub is the recipient of the Allen Tate Memorial Award for the Short Story. She is the author of *Yoga for Depression* (Broadway Books), *Yoga Skills for Therapists* (W.W. Norton), and numerous articles and book chapters. As a television documentary producer in the 1980s, Amy won numerous national and regional awards, including the Broadcast Media Award from the National Association of Broadcasters and was a one of two finalists for a national Emmy. She is a yoga therapist, the founder of the LifeForce Yoga® Healing Institute and is a pioneer in the field of yoga and mental health. Amy has a Master of Fine Arts degree in Literary Fiction from Bennington College and lives in Tucson, AZ. Visit her at amyweintraub.com.

Made in the USA
Monee, IL
08 July 2022